Problems at the Lakeside Hotel

MELINDA HUBER

Problems at the Lakeside Hotel

All rights reserved.

Copyright © 2023 Linda Huber

The right of Linda Huber to be identified as the Author of this Work has been asserted by her in accordance with the Copyright Designs and Patents Act 1988.

Apart from any use permitted under UK copyright law, this publication may only be reproduced, stored or transmitted, in any form, or by any means, with the prior permission in writing of the author.

All characters appearing in this work are fictitious. Any resemblance to real persons, living or dead, is purely coincidental.

Cover image by Go On Write

Also by Melinda Huber

Saving the Lakeside Hotel
Return to the Lakeside Hotel
Christmas at the Lakeside Hotel
Wedding Bells at the Lakeside Hotel

Chapter One

Saturday, 5th May

Alex Berger grasped the box of groceries in the boot of his car and manhandled it onto the pavement. Yikes – good job he went to the fitness centre regularly, because Ma's shopping weighed a ton this week. Judging by the amount of sugar and flour on the list, though, not to mention birthday cake candles, she was going to be baking – which was a good thing. Making cakes for other people's happy events kept her mind off her own problems, and it meant she was in contact with the outside world, too. Whistling, Alex heaved the box into his arms, strode up the steps of his mother's apartment building in north-east Switzerland, and jabbed the button for the lift with his elbow.

His phone buzzed as the lift arrived, and he fumbled it out with one hand while his stomach somersaulted in anticipation. Was this the message he'd been waiting for – and dreading, in case it contained bad news – ever since his interview for the receptionist job at the Lakeside Hotel last Monday? They'd said he'd hear by the weekend, one way or the other. He had no idea if this would be by text or an email, but please, please let it be good news. He flipped his phone case open and – ah. A warning from his pollen app; the grass pollen season had started. Alex stuffed his phone back into his pocket. Panic over.

Denise Berger was waiting at the door of her first floor flat, and Alex put the box down for their usual hug.

'Hey, Ma. Did you see me coming?' She'd have been standing at the window for the past half hour; he was late today.

She snorted. 'No one could miss you. I'm sure you drive the only bright yellow car in Rorschach!'

Alex took her shopping through to the kitchen and shoved the ice cream into the freezer. Ma got most of her stuff online, of course, but he did an extra shop for her at the weekend when he could. She followed, and unpacked the rest while Alex put the kettle on for their usual Saturday morning mug of English Breakfast. She seemed more down than usual today – maybe she hadn't had any visitors yesterday. Alex grimaced. Agoraphobia was the pits, and she'd had it for as long as he could remember, though it wasn't always so overwhelming that it confined her to the flat. The past three or four weeks had been bad, though. She'd always been nervous – his father used to say it was post-traumatic stress due to the time she'd spent in Sarajevo between the start of the war there and her escape home in 1994, but as Ma refused to go anywhere near a doctor and Dad had given up and left her to it when Alex was barely ten, there was no official diagnosis. Hopefully, she'd soon get back to going out for the odd trip around her home town here in Rorschach.

The kettle boiled, and Alex took his tea out to the balcony. The flat was near the top of a steep hill, so the view was terrific. It was fortunate Ma had bought this place when she and Dad split up, because she'd never be able to afford it nowadays. She barely scraped a living making alterations to clothes, curtains, etcetera, for people, and baking cakes. Alex leaned on the railing. It was horrible when someone you loved had problems and you were powerless to help them. A view was no use when it was people you needed.

He stared into the distance, the wide sweep of Lake Constance spreading out in front of him while the roofs of Rorschach peppered the foreground below. The other side of the lake was Germany, and the mountains of Austria towered in the distance to his right. Further along the Swiss bank you could see the various little towns and villages – Horn, Grimsbach, Steinach, all the way along to Romanshorn, where the car ferry to Friedreichshafen over in Germany was pulling out of the bay. Alex shaded his eyes. The Lakeside Hotel was in Grimsbach. If he had binoculars, he might even be able to make it out from here. He slid his phone out. Nothing. 'By the weekend' – that was today, wasn't it? Or tomorrow?

Denise joined him on the balcony, and to Alex's dismay she sat down right by the French door. Hell – she was having a bad go of it this time if she couldn't make it over to the railing.

She sounded bright enough, though. 'What are you and Zoe up to today?'

'Markus and Selina have asked us over for pizza tonight, but Zoe isn't feeling great this morning, so here's hoping.'

'Not the flu, I hope? They were saying on the radio yesterday there's still a lot of it about. Late this year.'

'Dunno. Don't think so.'

Alex tapped his fingers on the balcony railing. Flu had nothing to do with it. Zoe was in a blue funk because she wanted to move to Zurich, and that was impossible, unless of course she decided to leave him. No way could he abandon his mother – and living on the banks of the most international lake in Switzerland was pretty special too, wasn't it? The only downside to the place was he didn't have a job at the moment; he'd been temping ever since his old company closed down last year. Otherwise, lakeside life had a lot going for it, but Zoe was more of a bright lights girl. He could understand that as a musician she'd have better job opportunities in the city, but–

Alex's phone buzzed again, and he pulled it out. Oh... Sweat broke out on his brow, and the phone shook in his hand. Lakeside Hotel was right there on the screen; this was either a 'yes, you have the job' or 'sorry, we don't want you' kind of call. His heart thumping, Alex swiped to connect.

The voice in his ear spoke English. 'Hello, Alex, this is Stacy Townsend at the Lakeside Hotel in Grimsbach. I'm calling to offer you the receptionist's job you interviewed for this week.'

Alex punched the air, then gathered his best English to reply to her. 'Thank you – that's fantastic. I'm really pleased. When would you like me to start?'

'Are you still available right away? The fourteenth would be ideal for us, then Karen, who you're replacing, can be there on your first day to show you everything. Her grandchild's come early, so she's keen to leave as soon as possible.'

'That sounds excellent.' They arranged a few details about signing contracts and times, then Stacy rang off and Alex grabbed his mother in a bear hug, waltzing her round the balcony and back into the living room.

'I've got the job at Lakeside! That's the hotel I told you about, with the spa and the lovely terrace. Maybe I'll be able to get special staff rates for you at the hairdresser – or the beautician!'

Denise was laughing, and Alex's day brightened even more. She hadn't minded that dance across the balcony – that was a good sign, wasn't it? They'd soon have her out and about again. She reached up and cupped his face in both hands, then brushed his hair back from his brow.

'Well done, Alex – I'm proud of you, son! But you'll need to get that mop cut if you're going to work in a hotel!'

He kissed her. 'Thanks, Ma. Things are looking up, eh? We'll get you out for a visit to Lakeside before the summer's over, okay?'

'You're the boss. Off you go and give that girl of yours the good news.'

Alex ran down to the ground floor, then turned at the car to wave. His mother was standing on the balcony – not quite at the edge, but definitely on the balcony. It was a start. And he had a fresh start too.

Ten minutes later, he was running up the stairs to the flat he and Zoe shared on the other side of town. It wasn't as posh as Ma's building, in fact it wasn't posh at all, but the rent was reasonable and it had suited them for the past few months. You couldn't afford to be choosy when one of you was job hunting and the other was your typical penniless musician. Zoe played the violin in the Bridge Theatre Orchestra in St Gallen, around ten kilometres away. She didn't earn a fortune, and he'd had to dip into his savings to pay his way recently. That would change when he started at Lakeside.

Alex turned his key in the lock. 'Anyone home?'

'Here! And you'll never guess!'

Zoe whirled into the hallway, clutching the briefcase she kept her music in. Gone was this morning's misery; just two hours later, Zoe looked as though she'd swallowed the sun. She deposited her briefcase by the coat stand and flung her arms around Alex. Wow. By the look of things, he wasn't the only one with good news.

He spoke into her hair. 'I never will – tell me!'

'Poor Phillip jammed a finger in the boot of his car last night, so he's off work for a couple for weeks and oh, I know it's awful for him, but they've given me his solo while he's off!'

She danced back into the living room and seized her violin, and the haunting opening notes from *Fiddler on the Roof* filled the flat. Alex watched, captivated. Zoe was a different creature when she played; her whole body was fluid, moving with the music, part of a different world. For a few seconds, the air in the flat sang, then she laid the violin back in its case and beamed at Alex.

'We're rehearsing this afternoon, so I'll have to leave soon. I'll go straight to Markus and Selina's later. Oh, Alex, this could be my big chance!'

Alex had to force a smile. Another kind of fear was churning in his gut now, and he hated himself for it. Ever since he'd known her over a year ago, Zoe's ambition had been to move up the ladder in the music world. A solo in *Fiddler on the Roof* was a dream come true. The production was attracting an audience from all over Switzerland as well as nearby Germany and Austria, and some of them were big music people, too. Being noticed was everything, and Zoe, with her long dark hair and moving, passionate face when she was immersed in her music, stood out in a crowd.

Was this really the best time to tell her he'd just accepted a job that would tie him indefinitely to this area, far away from the Zurich crowds and bustle that Zoe was longing to get back to?

Chapter Two

Monday, 14th May

Eyes tightly closed against the early morning sunlight shimmering through the curtains, Stacy Townsend stretched a hand across the bed, only to find a dent in the pillow where Rico's head should have been. Ah, well. She lay still for a moment, then stretched luxuriously. No Rico, but she had five whole days off work in front of her, and after weeks of wall-to-wall rain, today looked like being gloriously different. Time to get up and remind the love of her life that they were, technically, on holiday. The trouble was, live-in spa hotel managers were on call 24/7, and Rico was the dedicated sort.

The silence in their flat at the top of the Lakeside Hotel told her she was home alone. Stacy had a quick shower, then headed straight for the kitchen. The day was always more manageable after a shot of caffeine. She pushed a strand of blonde hair away from her face and flipped the radio on while her coffee burbled through the machine, then took her mug out to the long wooden balcony off the living room.

At long last, a sunny day. Across the lake, Germany was even visible today, after being shrouded in rain for so long. Four floors below on the terrace, a few guests were having an early breakfast outside, something that hadn't happened this season yet. Stacy beamed at the waterlogged geraniums in their terracotta window boxes lining the balcony. At long last, the hotel was going strong, and how odd it was to think it was a year almost to the day since she and her friend Emily had breakfasted down there as guests, on the terrace of a failing hotel. Little had she known back then that she'd return to work at Lakeside. Not to mention finding the man she was going to marry here – and come to that, where was he?

She was heading inside in search of her phone to call him when the flat door banged open before slamming shut again. Rico's lanky form appeared in the hallway, and Stacy jerked upright at the sight of his face. He hadn't looked this uptight since he'd had to wait for the results – fortunately good – of his chest scan in January. He flung himself down at the kitchen table, and she grabbed his hand.

'For heaven's sake, what's wrong?'

'We're going to have a problem, Stace. A huge one. The lake.'

'What about it?'

He shot her a hunted look. 'I went to give *Lakeside Lady* a polish – Dad'll go bananas if she's still all rain-splashed and wet when he arrives this afternoon – and I noticed the water level had risen. A lot.'

Lakeside Lady was the family cabin cruiser, and the apple of Ralph's eye. Stacy could well imagine what he would say if the boat was anything other than pristine when he arrived.

'Water in the boat? I guess some got under the tarpaulin? We should have put her in the boathouse during all that rain.'

He was gripping her hand so hard it hurt. 'It wasn't water in the boat. It's the lake, Stace. It's way higher than it was a few days ago. I'm really scared we're going to get flooding.'

Stacy gasped. The hotel was only a handful of metres from the lake bank, hence the name Lakeside. And after their extensive renovations last winter to add the spa facilities, a flood was the last thing they needed. On the other hand, Rico was the kind of person who worried about things that were never going to happen.

'I'm sure it'll be okay, Rico. I heard the forecast this morning and it's all about hot sunshine for the rest of the month.'

He glared at her. 'And what happens in May when we get hot sunshine?'

Stacy opened her mouth to snap back, then changed her mind as the penny dropped. 'Oh. The snow in the mountains will melt and come down–'

'–into a lake that's already way higher than it should be. Come and see.'

He grabbed her hand and pulled her out of the flat and down the wooden staircase into the hotel. Stacy followed him across the front hallway, busy with guests going to and from breakfast on the terrace or en route for the spa rooms. 'Good morning' came from all directions and in several languages as Stacy and Rico moved through the crowd. At the reception desk Karen was at the computer with Alex, the new bloke. He was looking pretty hot and bothered, fine sandy hair standing on end where he'd pushed a hand through it. Stacy gave him a smile, and left them to it. She would check in with Alex later. He'd be a good addition to the team, and after the unpleasantness caused by Karen's jealousy last year, a change of face at reception could only be a good thing.

Lakeside Lady was moored at the tiny hotel jetty, and

heavens, yes, she was higher in the water than she usually was. Stacy's heart sank. Lake Constance was huge – however much water would you need to raise it – what? Thirty centimetres? More, she decided, peering down between the cabin cruiser and the jetty.

Rico strode ahead into the boathouse, a grey stone building open to the lake at one end with water channelling into the middle section. He walked along the narrow platform that ran around the other three sides of the boathouse, then crouched down beside the mooring post furthest from the entrance.

'Here. Back in 1999, the lake flooded badly. I was just a kid, but I remember biking through water all along the lake path. And we had pumps in for weeks to keep the cellar dry. Dad marked the water levels on this post every Saturday. Then in 2016, there was a bit of flooding again, and we added that year's levels and freshened up the old marks. Look.'

Stacy leaned over and peered. The 2016 marks were nowhere to be seen, but the lake today was nearly as high as it had been in mid-May 1999. Standing straight again, Rico pointed to a mark over a metre higher than the lake was now, and Stacy's mouth went dry.

'Tell me the water didn't get that high.'

Rico stood up. 'I'm afraid it did. And the situation in ninety-nine was similar to this year's in every way. Massive snowfalls the previous winter, followed by a very wet spring. This could all go pear-shaped any day. I'm worried, Stace.'

Stacy was worried now too. How cruel it would be if half their lovely new renovations ended up underwater. The sauna was in the cellar, not to mention the brand-new fitness room with all the machines. She stood straight and gazed across the lake. All that water, and more on the way... and there was no way to control it.

She took Rico's arm on the way back to the hotel. 'We'll hope for the best, Rico, love.'

He sniffed. 'And we'll prepare for the worst while we're doing it.'

She couldn't argue with that.

Back inside, most of the guests had moved on into the spa areas or gone out for the day, and the new receptionist was alone at the desk.

Stacy let go of Rico's arm. 'I'll have a quick chat with Alex.'

'See you upstairs. I think I'll phone the water insurance people and check we're insured for everything that might happen.'

Rico loped upstairs, and Stacy stared after him. No point saying it was too late to get insurance for something that could happen as early as tomorrow. She swung round and went over to the reception desk.

'How's it going? The first day anywhere's pretty intensive, isn't it?'

He grinned. 'Karen showed me the booking systems and the spa lists, etcetera. I hope I remember everything.'

'Give me a shout if you have any problems. Is Karen…?'

'She's gone for a quick break. No problems so far. I'm really pleased to be here, and it's quite different to my last job. That was ninety per cent telephone work. This is much better.'

'Receptions are different everywhere, I guess. We chose you for this job because your English is so good – you even have a bit of an English accent. Plus, you're local to the area, which is important when guests want information.'

'Thanks. My mother and I sometimes speak English for fun, and she speaks it like a native. She has a hotel background too – she and Dad met in Sarajevo in the eighties when they were working in a hotel there. They left in the nineties when the war got going, though.'

Stacy stood still. Sarajevo, wow. 'That must have been a hard time for them. Do they live locally?'

'Ma's in Rorschach, but she and Dad are divorced. He runs a hotel in Goa now.'

'So you're carrying on a long family tradition of hotel work. You should bring your mum here and show her around, Alex. If she'd be interested, that is.'

His face clouded over. 'I'm sure she would, but–'

'Problem?' Karen bustled back, frowning.

Stacy moved away. She didn't want to stamp on Karen's toes on the woman's last day at work.

'Not at all, I was just saying hello. I'll see you both later!' She moved away, stepped into the lift as it was standing there with its doors so invitingly open, and jabbed the button for the fourth floor. It would be interesting to meet Alex's mother and hear about the hotel she'd worked in. Stacy did sums in her head as the lift jerked upwards. Alex wouldn't have been born until several years after his parents' return from ex-Yugoslavia. It must have been a traumatic time for the couple – and the marriage hadn't survived, too.

In the flat, she joined Rico on the balcony. 'Full house, but Alex seems to be taking it all in his stride. Bit different to this time last year, isn't it?' She sat down on a deckchair and stretched out her legs. Sun tan, here she came… and this week, she could relax with an easy conscience.

Rico poured her a glass of iced tea. 'A lot of it's down to you. All I hope is we don't have to start handing out wellies as well as room keys when the guests arrive!'

His voice was strained in spite of the little joke, and

Stacy's heart melted. Rico cared so much about Lakeside – for him, the hotel was his mother's legacy, and he was desperate for it to be successful. Business was picking up nicely after the long sticky patch after Edie's death a couple of years ago. More than nicely, actually.

She sipped her iced tea. 'Try not to worry. Your dad'll be here this afternoon, and he'll know if it's time to start issuing the guests with extra towels and wellies.'

Ralph, Rico's dad, was ex-manager at Lakeside, though he now lived in Lugano in the Ticino, the southern, Italian-speaking part of Switzerland where he'd grown up. It would be lovely to see him again, and this time he was bringing his brother Guido and sister-in-law Julia. The plan was to have a big party for Ralph's birthday on Friday, and Stacy was looking forward to it – and to showing Ralph how well the hotel was doing. In spite of this latest worry, it was a lovely feeling that she was part of the new Lakeside, with its smart spa rooms and all the etceteras, and while her position as head nurse and assistant to Rico wasn't quite what she'd envisaged at the start of her nursing training back in England, it was interesting and fun and – best job ever, in fact. Surely a mere lake wouldn't spoil that.

Their visitors arrived shortly after two o'clock. Stacy was tidying round the flat when voices on the landing had her running to open the door.

'Ralph Weber – you can't be here already!'

He hugged her tightly, and Stacy hugged back. She had a lot of time for Ralph. He hadn't had an easy life since Rico's mum died, but he was always cheerful and generous – he'd given Rico the chance to prove he could get the hotel back into profit. Come to that, he'd given Rico the hotel.

He winked at her. 'Yup. Lugano to Grimsbach in two and a half hours. Not bad.'

'Bet you were speeding.' Rico took Stacy's place hugging his father, while Stacy went on to be given the usual Swiss right-cheek, left-cheek, right-cheek kisses by Julia and Guido.

'Are we in with you, or have you put us in the bikers' flat?' said Ralph, indicating the second flat on the top floor landing. It was fitted up as basic accommodation for cycling tourists, who generally moved on after one night.

'In with us,' said Stacy. 'If that's okay?'

Ralph lifted his case. 'Lead the way.'

Stacy grinned, listening to the banter flying around in both German and Italian as her guests unpacked. They'd have a fun two weeks with the Swiss family, then she and Rico would have plenty of time to get the place straight again before Mum and Dad arrived. And oh dear, that might not be such a light-hearted visit. Mum had been unexpectedly despondent last time they'd phoned. Stacy's happy mood evaporated as she thought back to what Janie had said. *'Of course, we'd originally planned to come later in the summer and bring you home at the end of your year, darling. I suppose that won't happen now?'*

Stacy waggled her left hand with the diamond and emerald engagement ring. 'Bringing her home' definitely wasn't going to happen, and it was hard to know why her mother had even asked. A roar of laughter came from one of the bedrooms, and Stacy cheered up again. When Mum saw the place, she would love it as much as they did.

'Right – I'm ready to try the famous tubs!' Julia came out of her bedroom and looked expectantly at Stacy.

'You're on. Anyone else feel like a soak?'

The men opted for a beer on the balcony, and Stacy showed Julia round the large spa room where the tubs were, and the small spa which held the manicure and hairdressing rooms, with the massage therapist just across the hallway. And how brilliant was this? Today, she could behave like a guest in her own hotel. Well, in Rico's hotel. Stacy joined Julia in the tub, leaning back as the warm water and soft music relaxed muscles she hadn't realised were tight. Oh yes, she could get used to this.

The feeling of being on holiday continued that evening, when they all went for dinner in the hotel restaurant. Stacy took her place beside Rico at a window table and sighed happily. This was fab – having a trained chef on hand when you had guests was one of the boons of living in a hotel. They'd reached the coffee stage when Stacy's phone rang in her bag and she scrabbled for it. Heavens, it was her mother. Mum didn't usually phone this late – was anything wrong? Better take this somewhere more private. She hurried out to the deserted entrance hallway, swiping to connect as she went.

'Oh, Stacy, love, thank goodness. We've had a problem here and I hope I've found the right solution, but...' A huge sigh came down the phone.

'Is everyone okay?' Stacy sank down on the leather sofa at the side of the front door.

'Yes, but Sue's been given a date for her new hip. You know she's been on the waiting list for ages. It's on the 5th of June, and of course that's the middle of our stay with you. Your dad wants to be here for Sue, so I've changed our flights – we're coming on Wednesday. That's all right, love, isn't it?'

'Wednesday?'

Her mother inhaled sharply, and Stacy gripped her mobile, trying to sound more hospitable. 'No problem. What time's your flight?' Phone clutched to her ear, she went over to reception for pen and paper. She could understand John Townsend not wanting to be out of the country while his sister was having major surgery. But, oh dear… Stacy wrote down the new flight details, her brain racing. This meant Mum and Dad would be here at the same time as Ralph, Guido and Julia. The upside was her parents would meet the Swiss family and be here for Ralph's birthday party; the downside was they couldn't all stay in the flat.

'I'm sorry it's such short notice, but I couldn't bear not to see you for months, darling.'

Help, Mum was nearly in tears. Stacy leapt in before the deluge started. 'It's great, Mum. Even better, in fact, because you'll meet Rico's family. We're having a birthday do for Ralph on Friday.'

They chatted for a few more minutes, then Stacy went into the reception computer to look at guest numbers and vacant rooms that week. They'd need to do some reshuffling, but it would be possible. They would manage.

She went back to the others, who were speaking Swiss German now. Rico raised his eyebrows at her.

'Mum and Dad are coming on Wednesday,' she said, also in Swiss German, and Ralph patted her shoulder.

'Good for you! We'll make a Swiss citizen of you yet.'

Stacy joined in the laughter, but uneasiness was growing in her middle. Rico's family were so different to hers. And if Mum wasn't happy about Stacy's decision to make her home here in Switzerland, the next couple of weeks might not be easy.

Chapter Three

Tuesday 15th May

Alex turned in the hotel gates, and pulled up in a free space at the far end. The car park was almost full, but then, it was still early. Not many guests would be out and about before half seven in the morning, even though it was another glorious day. He sat for a minute gathering his thoughts – and his courage – for his first day alone at the helm of the Lakeside reception. It was a complicated job as he not only had to book in guests and hand out information, but also take spa bookings for the tubs, the sauna and the fitness room, and then there were all the dozen or so other things that kept hotel receptionists busy all day. He was on until five tonight, with an hour's break at lunchtime. And now he should get started. Go, Alex.

Inside, he organised the reception desk to suit his way of working, with the computer screen to one side instead of in the middle where it obliterated his view of the front door when he was sitting behind it, and checked the bookings for today. Only three new guests were arriving, and none were leaving, good. The spa was busy, though Karen had told him that returning visitors went straight in without queueing up here, so that should be relatively uncomplicated too. What he couldn't prepare for, of course, were all the questions and problems the guests could fling at him. At this point in time, they knew more about daily life in the hotel than he did, but that would change, and after growing up in the area, he should know enough to make a good stab at most tourist-info questions. Alex took a deep breath to settle his butterflies, but the arrival of one of the bosses made him jerk to attention. Rico Weber was one of the tallest people he'd met.

'Morning, Alex! Stacy reminded me it's your first day alone. Do you have both our phone numbers for emergencies?'

'Yes – but I'll try not to use them. Karen said you were actually on holiday this week.'

'Call it a working holiday. We have family visiting, but we can still be on call. Stacy did a bit of room reshuffling last night as her parents are arriving early, but it's all in the computer.' He grinned at Alex. 'I don't suppose Karen told you to help yourself to coffee in the terrace bar when you want a cup, but you can!'

'Great, thanks. I see we're pretty full this week – you've really pulled the place up, haven't you?'

He wished the words back as soon as they were out. Was it too familiar, reminding his boss that the hotel hadn't been doing well for the past couple of years?

But Rico was grinning. 'Good to hear we have someone with local knowledge on board. We're happy with how it's going now, though I hope the lake isn't going to be a problem.'

'It's high, isn't it?' The arrival of a pair of guests put an end to his conversation with Rico, and Alex pulled out a map of the area to show the couple the most scenic route to St Gallen. No sooner had they departed, the phone rang, and he took a booking for dinner for four on the terrace that evening, and by the time that was finished, a middle-aged couple was standing at the desk, a teenage girl of about sixteen slouched behind them scowling at her phone. Judging by the suitcases, the new guests had arrived – didn't they know they couldn't check in until two? His heart sinking, Alex turned to the trio. This might be his first real problem in his new job.

'Roberts. We're early, but that's not a problem, is it?' The man was English. He smiled stiffly as his wife stood beaming beside him and his daughter rolled her eyes.

'Happy to see you any time, Mr Roberts. Let me check when your rooms will be ready.' Alex tapped on the keyboard. The Roberts family were from north London, so they'd either flown over at the crack of dawn, or more likely, they'd been holidaying somewhere else in the area until today. As he'd feared, their rooms were still waiting for the green light that meant they were ready for occupation. He lifted the phone and made a quick call to housekeeping before turning back to the family.

'Your rooms will be ready in half an hour,' he said. 'Would you like to leave your luggage with me in the meantime, and have a look round the village – or a coffee in the terrace bar?'

Mr Roberts was scowling almost as hard as his daughter now, but his wife pulled at his sleeve. 'A drink of something would be lovely, Andrew. Wouldn't it, Timea?'

'Whatever.' The teenager rolled her eyes again. She was wearing the most ripped jeans Alex had ever seen, and he hid a smile. Timea was evidently making a statement.

Alex leapt into action. He wasn't about to leave them feeling hard-done-by or in the mood to complain. The family were here for two weeks, so it would be best to start out well, at least.

'Excellent idea. I'll put your luggage back here where it's

safe.' He seized the two larger cases and took them into the office behind reception, relieved when the girl followed with her own case. She might be a scowler, but she was a helpful one.

He treated the family to his best receptionist smile. 'If you come this way, I'll show you the terrace.'

A word to the bar staff outside, and Alex was striding back to reception, feeling as if he'd run an entire marathon in the past ten minutes. He slid behind the desk again, almost falling over the large white cat sprawled comfortably in a patch of sunlight by the key cupboard. It miaowed at him plaintively, and Alex laughed.

'Hello, you.' He scratched around the cat's ears, and it purred. He was kept busy for the next hour with a mixture of calls and guest queries, including the Roberts family when their rooms were ready. The cat disappeared at some point, and Alex was surprised to see it was twelve o'clock already when Stacy arrived to remind him about putting the buzzer on the desk when he was at lunch.

'It rings through to Flavia, our springer. She'll cover the desk while you're on a break.'

Alex pulled out the buzzer and plugged it in. 'Good system. I met your cat, by the way.'

Stacy looked blank. 'We haven't got a cat.'

'No? There was one here, oh, about an hour ago, looking pretty much at home. White, longish fur. Friendly. Likes ear scratches and snoozing in patches of sun.'

Her lips twitched. 'I guess it popped in to check us out! Scoot it straight back outside if it reappears, Alex – we don't want it to get used to snoozing in the front hall.'

She moved on into the restaurant, and Alex grabbed his lunchtime sandwiches and went down to the lake path. Half an hour away from the hotel would do him good. He found a shady bench by the water and flipped his phone open. Oh – a message from Zoe. She didn't usually message during the day… The orchestra was rehearsing today for the last three performances of *Fiddler on the Roof* tomorrow, Saturday and Sunday. Phillip wouldn't be back for another two weeks at least, so Zoe was still soloist.

He tapped to open the message. *You. Will. Never. Guess – Daniel Marino's coming to tomorrow night's concert!!!*

Right… This was where you were glad of the internet. Daniel Marino was a famous name in the music world, but who was he? Alex opened a search engine and discovered that Daniel Marino was the conductor and head of the world-famous Zurich Alhambra Orchestra.

He tapped. *Wow – is he just in the area or–?* The answer came in seconds. *Don't know – but he'll see me play!! This could be my chance!!!*

Alex's heart sank. He couldn't wish she didn't have her chance, but if Zoe ended up working in Zurich, she'd want to live there too, or at least move a lot nearer. Musicians worked odd hours and late ones, too. No way would she want over an hour's drive between her workplace and her home. But where would that leave them as a couple?

Suddenly, Alex wasn't hungry any more. He fed the rest of his sandwiches to the ducks, then trailed back inside. The desk was quiet when he arrived at reception, and he spent an hour familiarising himself with everything in the computer system. It was all very up-to-date, but of course Rico Weber was in IT as well as hotels, wasn't he? Shortly after two, the lift doors pinged open and Alex looked up to see Timea Roberts, now dressed in a yellow mini skirt instead of her ripped jeans.

She gave him a hopeful smile that transformed her face. 'Can I get onto the lake path from the terrace bar?'

'Yes, you can. The path's behind a hedge, but there's a gate on the left side of the lawn.'

Another bright smile, and she vanished out to the terrace. Alex went back to his computer. Wouldn't it be great if all the queries he had were as easily dealt with?

Half an hour later, Timea's mother was standing at the desk. 'Have you seen my daughter? She's not in her room.'

'Yes, she went down to the lake path.'

'Oh dear – she shouldn't have gone out alone. She's delicate, you know. She had pneumonia last winter, and on top of her asthma, well, it's so worrying. She *will* keep doing too much.' She bustled off to the terrace.

Alex frowned. Timea hadn't struck him as delicate, but then you couldn't tell by looking, could you? He tapped into the reservations folder. The girl was seventeen, older than she looked, and she didn't appear to be what you'd call amenable to her parents' ideas about what she should and shouldn't do. Ah well – not his problem. Alex went on with his examination of the computer system until Mrs Roberts' voice approaching at speed had him ducking into the office.

'…told you before, Timea, you must always let me know whenever you go anywhere – in fact, in a strange place you shouldn't be going out alone at all. You have to be careful–' The lift doors closed, and Alex re-emerged. Well. It didn't sound as if the Roberts' family holiday was going to be a peaceful one, did it? He glanced at his watch. Almost three, so two hours until home time, three before he could reasonably expect Zoe to be back. His stomach lurched. If Zoe had her way, their own peaceful life could soon be over, too. And there was nothing he could do about it.

Chapter Four

Tuesday, 15th May

Rico's heart thudded to his boots as Ralph whistled through his teeth before straightening up, rubbing his back and scowling. 'You were right. It's rising fast.'

They were in the boathouse, checking the water level on the post for the second time that day. How deceptive the lake was. Looking across to Germany, all you saw was deep blue water in harmless late-afternoon sunshine. Rico tried to quash the panic surging inside him. Lake Constance had flooded many times over the centuries, but why now, in his lovely newly furbished hotel?

Stacy was beside him. 'I still can't imagine the water rising so high it reaches the building.'

Rico rubbed his cheeks as despair engulfed him. 'It doesn't have to. When the water level rises, so does the water table – that's the level of saturation in the ground. If that's high enough, you get water pushing up through the drains, and in odd places nowhere near the lake. Add to that the swollen rivers bursting their banks… You get the picture.'

His father's face was grim. 'Back in ninety-nine, we had pumps running in the cellar twenty-four hours a day for weeks, and the garden was so soggy no one could walk in it.'

Stacy was silent, then she braced her shoulders, looking from Ralph to Rico. 'So we need to plan how we'll cope when and if it happens. A phone call to the builders to ask how the new drains for the tubs would be affected might be a good start.'

Shame flashed through Rico. He should man up; she was doing this better than he was. 'I'll do that,' he said, turning back to the hotel. 'The sooner the better.'

'I'll get onto the authorities at the town hall for you,' said Ralph. 'We'll have time to get sorted, otherwise they'd have been in touch about flood preparations already. Guido and I can get sandbags organised for you. Good thing we're here.'

It *was* good; Dad's experience would make planning easier. Rico trailed behind Ralph and Stacy as they walked across the still un-soggy garden to the hotel. Nothing would stop the water rising, but it was sickening that damage limitation was the only way forward. Back inside, Rico shut himself into the office behind reception to call Andi Schmidt, who had project-managed the spa renovation and knew the drains like the back of his hand.

The other man sounded harassed. 'You're right to be worried, Rico, and you're not alone. I'll come round tomorrow and we can go over the plans. The cellar's going to be a problem. If the drains go you won't avoid water in the sauna.'

Rico grimaced. The sauna was only half the problem in the cellar; the brand-new fitness room was full of expensive equipment, some of which was electrical and most of which was heavy. Not the kind of stuff you could tuck under your arm and shift at a moment's notice. He arranged a time the following day with Andi, and had put the phone down before he remembered Stacy's parents were arriving tomorrow. But this was more important.

Stacy was talking to a couple of guests in the doorway of the large spa, but she came over as soon as he appeared in reception. 'Did you get Andi?'

'We're having a builders' meeting tomorrow at four. How does that fit in with your mum and dad arriving?'

'It doesn't, but you don't need me at the meeting, do you? I'll pick them up by myself.'

Rico wanted to hug her, but they'd agreed from the start that the manager and his assistant wouldn't get physical in front of the guests. 'I'll make it up to you,' he whispered, and she gave him a smile that said *you bet you will*, and returned to the spa rooms. Cheered, Rico looked round for his father, and eventually found him outside in the terrace bar, an espresso in front of him and deep in conversation on his phone. He waved Rico over as his call came to an end.

'We're joining forces with the Alpstein to get sandbags.'

The Alpstein Hotel was a few hundred metres further up the lake. Rico pulled a chair out and signalled the waiter for a coffee. 'Great.' He filled Ralph in about the next day's meeting.

'Good work, son. The better prepared we are, the better we'll cope. I mean, you'll cope.'

In spite of his fears, Rico laughed. 'Oh, Lakeside will always be your baby too, I know that. Let's hope hard we'll be preparing for nothing.'

Ralph pulled a face, and Rico took a sip of his coffee. They'd survive, no matter what. But… hell, this was tough. It had all been going so well, and secretly, he'd been hoping that come the autumn, he'd be able to take time off and start his master's degree, even if it was part time to begin with. If the flooding was going to cost them too much hard cash, he wouldn't be able to do that. He glanced up at the hotel – *his* hotel – sitting there as welcoming and as peaceful as anyone could wish for, a real holiday haven. But maybe that was an illusion.

Stacy wandered up the driveway from the family's private part of the garden, where she'd spent the past hour on a lounger. Julia had gone shopping in St Gallen, and the men had adjourned to the bar and were most likely still mulling over water tables and sandbags. Surely it wouldn't be that bad... It was a scary thought. Stacy greeted two guests heading for the car park, and was about to go inside when a white flash moving under the shrubs to her left caught her eye. Was that the cat Alex had seen this morning?

The shrubs were well over head height, a mixture of lilac, now past the blooming season, some gorgeous yellow forsythia that was still hanging on to its flowers, and a blueish one she didn't know the name of. Stacy walked along the row, making 'puss-puss' noises as invitingly as she could – and there it was again, a moving, brighter patch in the depths of the bushes. Stacy parted a few branches and was treated to a loud hiss, followed by a streak of white as the cat exited the garden at speed. Friendly, Alex had said? There'd been no chance of scratching its ears this time, anyway. Grinning, she went on inside.

'Your cat doesn't like me,' she informed Alex, who was tidying the desk ready to hand over to Maria, the evening receptionist.

'No?'

Stacy explained, and he laughed.

'She was lovely with me. She must be a guy's cat.'

'Hm. Help, look at the time – I have to cook tonight. Well done on your first solo day, Alex. See you tomorrow.'

Stacy ran upstairs – at least she ran the first two flights before slowing to a more sedate shuffle for the second two. Living on the fourth floor was as good as going for a daily jog.

In her room, she laid navy capri trousers on the bed and held her new pale blue top against her front. Rico liked her in blue; he said it went with her eyes. She beamed at her reflection – unruly hair and a couple of tiny freckles notwithstanding, she felt good. It was so great to be living with the guy of your dreams, knowing you were the woman of his dreams too.

The sound of the church clock in the village chiming floated through the window, and Stacy jumped. She'd need to get tonight's mushroom lasagne into the oven pronto. Then she'd have a lovely soak and make herself look more like the woman of somebody's dreams and less like the woman who'd been melting all over the garden for the past three hours. The five of them were eating up here, which would give them the chance to discuss the lake situation without ear-flapping hotel guests around to overhear and worry.

Chopping mushrooms wasn't the most fascinating job, and Stacy clicked the radio on and hummed along to an old Sting hit. This led into the news at the top of the hour, and Stacy scowled at the radio. She understood a lot, but it was still frustrating the way people spoke so quickly. The announcer was talking about their own Lake Constance, Bodensee in German, but much of what he was saying wasn't in her vocabulary – or at least, not at that speed.

Frustrated, she switched the radio off and went through to the TV, restarting the news bulletin on catch-up. It was easier to understand stuff when you had pictures to look at, and you could switch on subtitles on the news – in German, but it all helped. The first item was about the water levels of a couple of lakes. Lake Lucerne was high too, and so were some of the smaller ones. Some footage was shown of the 1999 floods, and Stacy's heart leapt into her throat. Holy cow. There was no mention of Grimsbach, but the old DIY store outside nearby Arbon was like a little island sticking up in the middle of blue water. And there was water right over the railway line going into Rorschach, where the main street had turned into a canal; they'd put up board sidewalks for people to walk along. A moment later she was laughing. The main street shops, the same ones she'd been in and out of so many times, had held an outdoor fashion show along one of the sidewalks while the public stood clapping on the opposite one – talk about seizing the moment. Stacy went back to the mushrooms feeling slightly more cheerful. They should think about what they could do here to seize the moment. Water gymnastics on the lawn? Please, no… Make people sit on the garden wall with their feet in the water before a half-price foot massage? Glory… she was whistling in the dark now.

Chapter Five

Wednesday, 16th May

Stacy pulled into a space near the lift in the short-stay Parkhaus at Zurich Airport, and checked the clock on the dashboard. Good timing, she had quarter of an hour to get to the arrivals hall. Hopefully Mum and Dad's flight would be on time, and they'd be able to start back home before the evening rush hour started. Motorway driving wasn't her favourite way to get around, and Zurich traffic was dire.

The Manchester flight was marked 'landed' when she stepped off the escalator in arrivals. Stacy gazed through the glass panels separating the hall from baggage reclaim, but there was no sign of her parents. She stood by the sliding doors, jerking expectantly every time they whooshed open as travellers emerged, and – there they were!

'Stacy, sweetheart, it's been far too long – come here!'

Janie Townsend stumbled towards her, arms outstretched, and Stacy hugged back, inhaling the usual flowery scent of her mother's perfume. Help. Mum was shaking.

'Welcome to Switzerland! How was your flight?' Eventually she was allowed to hug her father too, then Stacy grasped their luggage trolley, where two cases and two large bags were sitting. 'Golly, you two are as bad as Emily – you've brought your entire wardrobe!'

'Wardrobe nothing. We've brought lots of home comforts for my girl,' said Janie, cuddling Stacy's arm. She looked around. 'Let Daddy take the trolley, darling. Where's Rico?'

'He had to stay at home for a meeting – we have a bit of a situation going on. The lake might flood.'

Janie's mouth drooped. 'Oh. I thought you said his father was there this week too?'

Stacy hesitated at the querulous tone in her mother's voice. What was this about? 'He is, but Rico's the manager. Ralph's on holiday too, though of course he's helping out with the flood preparations as well.' She grinned at Janie, then helped her father manhandle the trolley on and off the escalator – thank goodness you could do that here – then into the lift to the Parkhaus.

'I'm impressed you've learned to cope with the traffic,' said John Townsend, as they drove up the slip road onto the motorway.

'Ralph gave me some lessons when Rico was out of action last winter. It's no problem, once you get used to driving on the other side.' Stacy heaved a sigh of relief – traffic was light. This stretch could be murder at going-home time. She relaxed into her seat. 'Tell me all the news. How are Gareth and Jo – pregnancy going well? And the shop?'

Her mother immediately rushed to tell her about the expected grandchild's latest scan pics, and the difference Stacy's brother and his wife had made to the shop.

'We'll need to get someone in to cover when Jo takes her maternity leave,' said Janie. 'Stacy, darling, I don't suppose…?'

Stacy laughed. 'You don't suppose right. I have a full-time job right here! Nice try, Mum!'

She glanced into the rear-view mirror. Janie's shoulders slumped in the back seat before she joined in the laughter, and Stacy was aware of a tension in the older woman that hadn't been there before. Well, they had plenty of time to get to the bottom of it. A word with her father might be a good idea, too, and come to think of it, he was very quiet today. Stacy squinted across to the passenger seat, the uneasy feeling back in her gut. Dad looked tired, and – had he lost weight? He was always skinny, like Rico, but his cheeks were even more hollow than she remembered. Yikes… something else she'd need to get to the bottom of before she was too much older.

They pulled up in front of the hotel at five to five, and Stacy listened proudly as her mother oohed and aahed over the old wooden chalet. Seeing Lakeside for the first time was always special. Having survived the umpteen downpours of the past few weeks, the geraniums were blooming beautifully in true Swiss style and contrasting nicely with the dark wood of the building. May was a good month to visit, before the more intense heat of summer. Stacy helped her father inside with the cases, then collected their room key from Alex, who was halfway through handing reception over to Maria. This next part might be tricky…

'We've put you directly under our flat,' she said cheerfully, pressing the button for the third floor. 'Rico's family are in our spare rooms, but this way's better – it's a bigger room, you get your own balcony and loo and you can be up the side stairs in less than thirty seconds any time you want to come. Julia's organising dinner tonight – she's a fab cook.'

'That sounds perfect,' said John, but Janie was silent, her lips tight, and Stacy stifled a sigh. Had Mum expected her to turf Guido and Julia out of a room they'd already settled into? She opened the door and led the way into the spacious hotel bedroom.

'Here you go. The en suite's through there, and I had them leave you the spa visitors' kit too, look.' She opened the wardrobe and pointed to two wire baskets, each containing two towels, a bathrobe and a pair of flip flops. 'We'll have a go in the tubs tomorrow, shall we? I'll give you half an hour to get unpacked, then I'll come and take you upstairs and show you everything.'

'Lovely,' said John, and Janie nodded stiffly.

Stacy escaped – it really did feel like that – and took the stairs two at a time, her fingers crossed hard that Rico would be through with his meeting. She could use some moral support.

Rico said goodbye to Andi and his apprentice at the hotel door, then turned and trotted up the four flights to the flat. The meeting had been more positive than he'd expected. Andi had come up with some good ideas – all of which would involve a bit of reorganisation in the cellar, but that was a small price to pay for minimising the damage a flood would cause.

He strode into the flat, panting slightly. 'Anyone home?'

Stacy came out of the kitchen, looking as glum as he'd ever seen her. 'Only me. I left Mum and Dad unpacking. Where are the others?'

'Guido and Julia went to Rorschach. They said they'd pick up some raclette cheese on the way home – Julia thought it would be nice to have something Swiss on your parents' first evening. And Dad's gone to check *Lakeside Lady*.'

Stacy wrapped both arms round his waist, leaning in for a

long hug, and he rubbed her shoulders.

'Stace? You look a bit down.'

'It's Mum and Dad. I might be imagining it, but–'

Rico listened while she told him about John's drawn face and Janie's remark about helping in the shop.

'And she seems so – not insulted, exactly, but she's upset about something. I don't know, Rico. I don't think she's happy about me making my home here.'

Rico thought back. They'd spent a long weekend in Elton Abbey in March, to introduce him to Janie and John and show off Stacy's engagement ring. Janie had seemed perfectly happy about having a Swiss son-in-law then. Surely that hadn't changed?

'Your dad's probably just tired, and as for Janie, could it be that the reality of how far away you are is hitting home after the flight? We'll soon reassure her that Grimsbach isn't the far side of the moon.'

Stacy sniffed. 'I'll talk to Dad, but three weeks is a long time if Mum's going to be awkward about everything.'

'She won't be. She'll be won round the second she steps into a hot tub, don't worry.'

'How was the meeting? Oh – wait. I'd better fetch them up. I said half an hour.'

Stacy pulled away and dashed off. Rico checked the Pinot Grigio was in the fridge, then organised sherry glasses on the coffee table and shook nuts into a bowl. This would be the first time the two families had been together in one room; it was an occasion. A couple of toasts before dinner would soon have everyone in a festive mood.

He was less sure five minutes later. Janie followed Stacy into the living room, gave him a quick hug, then looked around.

'Oh, my goodness – very comfortable. Not much like your flat with Emily, is it, darling?'

'Heavens, Mum, that was a student flat. Rico and I bought the furniture here when we got engaged. It was fun, getting everything the way we want it.'

'It's lovely. I hadn't expected you to be so... settled, that's all.'

'It looks great, Stace,' said John. He wandered over to the open door out to the balcony. 'And the views are tremendous.'

Rico joined him. He could see what Stacy meant; John didn't look well. He pointed to the east. 'Those mountains are in Austria. I'll take you out on the lake one day, and show you the view with our own Alpstein range.'

He stepped back into the room and poured sherry all round. 'Let's toast your arrival. We'll have dinner in an hour or so when the others are back, then we'll show you around the place this evening when the spa rooms have closed for the day.'

Stacy gave him a 'thank you' glance, and Rico handed round glasses. They clinked, and Stacy perched on the arm of the sofa beside her mother. 'Tell us about the meeting, Rico. What did Andi come up with?'

Rico relaxed into an armchair. 'Well, for a start, he says the lake is higher than it was at this time in ninety-nine, but we've set up a strategy to deal with the worst-case scenario. He reckons we'll need pumps for a couple of weeks at least, but they can lead up from the cellar at the side, so hopefully the noise won't disturb anyone's sleep. We won't be able to use the sauna, and he suggests moving the machines out of the fitness room for the duration.'

'Sounds reasonable,' said Stacy. She turned to her parents. 'It's as well you've come early, you two – you'll see the place while we're still pump-free and fully-functioning!'

Rico passed the nuts to Janie, who was sitting with a bright smile that was going nowhere near her eyes. He exchanged a quick glance with Stacy. Janie wasn't happy about something, that was clear, but what could have changed since their visit to Elton Abbey? Leaning back in his chair, Rico took a sip of sherry. Those few days they'd spent with Stacy's parents… now he was thinking about it, they'd talked a lot about his ambition to do a master's degree in IT, and not much about the hotel. It had been all 'English is the language to have an IT career in'. Had Janie imagined he and Stacy would come and live in England?

Home time… Alex turned left out of the hotel car park, the sun behind him as he drove through Grimsbach. If Zoe had been on her way home too, they could have collected their swimming gear and spent the evening by the lake, dipping in and out of the water and chatting about their day. But Zoe would be in St Gallen for hours still. Tonight was the performance that Daniel Marino was attending, and she would be immersed in her music and her last-minute preparation and rehearsing. He couldn't even send a 'good luck' message; her phone would be switched off and abandoned in her locker by this time. He should have called at lunchtime. Come to that, he should have gone to the performance, given that it was such a special one for Zoe. But he'd seen *Fiddler on the Roof* twice already, and after a long day at work, he wanted to spend the evening outside. Did that make him selfish?

He slowed down and stopped as the queue of traffic heading into Rorschach was held up at the level crossing just outside the town. Alex sat tapping his fingers on the wheel. At least the job was going well. One couple had checked out and another in today, both at the correct times, thankfully. The Roberts family had left on an excursion arguing loudly, and returned five hours later still arguing. He'd lost the employees spreadsheet, but found it again before he needed to contact any of them, and the white cat had reappeared in reception, whereupon he'd shooed it straight back into the garden. A typical day at Lakeside? It was too soon to tell.

A goods train clanked over the road, and the gates lifted to let the traffic pass. On an impulse, Alex turned into his mother's street. Mum would appreciate a visit and some face-to-face chat about his job. He pulled into the side and tapped on his phone. What she didn't appreciate was surprise visits, which may or may not have something to do with the agoraphobia, he didn't know. She needed to see a doctor about that, but it was a taboo subject.

'Hey, Ma. Fancy a dinnertime visitor?'

'Lovely – what would you like?'

'How about I bring something from the Thai restaurant?'

Half an hour later, he was sitting opposite her eating Wonton and chicken with cashew nuts. His permanent niggle of worry about her increased as he scrutinised her while trying to appear not to. She was pale, and in spite of the warm day they were eating at the dining table, the balcony door closed tight behind him.

'I hope you haven't been stewing over a hot sewing machine all afternoon? Or an oven?'

Denise Berger smiled faintly. 'No. Pia Lang came round with the pattern and material for her daughter's bridesmaid's dress, but I haven't started it yet. Tell me more about the hotel.'

At least she'd had company. Alex filled her in about his third day at work. She laughed about the Roberts family and the cat, and frowned about the lake, but all the time she seemed… distracted. Yes, that was the word.

'Okay, Ma. What's up? And don't say "nothing", because I can see there's something.'

Another faint smile. 'You'll think I'm silly, but – is Zoe all right? I realised this morning that it's nearly four weeks since I've seen her.'

This was her way of saying, 'you are still together, aren't you?'. At least he could reassure her about that.

'She's very busy with the orchestra. You know it's *Fiddler on the Roof*, and now she has a solo. The last concert of this run's on Sunday, so things'll improve then. She can bring her violin sometime and play you her solo, huh?' Alex gripped his fork. 'Ma – how about we try to get you out a bit again? Not to a concert until you're ready, but afternoon tea at Lakeside would be nice. I'd love to show you round, and Stacy was saying she'd like to hear more about your job in Sarajevo.'

Her face closed immediately. 'We'll wait until Zoe is less busy and then we can all go. Coffee?'

Alex watched as she busied around the kitchen, not catching his eye. Should he be pushing her more about this; insisting she went to a doctor? She wasn't old enough to fade into loneliness and isolation, shit, no one was, ever. Maybe he should go and speak to the doctor about it, get some advice. He should have done that before now. He wasn't being much of a son to her, was he?

Alex sipped his coffee. He wasn't making a success of his relationship with Zoe either, hell. He should be up in St Gallen, supporting her, because right now, she'd be poised with her violin, ready to start the performance that could change her life. If it did, he could end up home alone and lonely. Just like Ma.

Stacy handed round espresso cups after dinner. The meal had gone okay, in spite of her fears. Ralph was at the end of the table with Janie and John to his right and left, and he had kept the conversation going in the way only an experienced hotelier could. It was the first time Mum and Dad had tried Raclette, special Swiss cheese melted in individual pans under a table grill and eaten with boiled potatoes and pickles. Both were cheese freaks so no problems there, but... somehow, they were all behaving like strangers making conversation with their dinner companions on holiday. But it would take more than a couple of hours for them to shake down together as a family, and Julia's heavily accented, ungrammatical English combined with Mum and Dad's non-existent German and Italian didn't help.

'Us old Webers will do the clearing up,' said Ralph, when they had finished their coffee. 'Take your parents round the hotel, Stacy, and show Lakeside off. Rico–?'

'I'll put a jacket on and have a managerial stroll round the restaurant before I join Stacy,' said Rico. 'Thanks, Dad.'

Stacy was only too glad to have her parents to herself for a little while. Maybe now she'd get to the bottom of what was going on with them. The three of them piled into the lift, then she led the way across reception to the small spa.

'Is that receptionist still here – the one who was so rude to you last year?' Janie linked arms as they went into the spa.

'Karen? No, she's taken early retirement. Her first grandchild was born recently, so she's busy babysitting. Like you'll be in July! Bet Jo and Gareth can't wait to be parents!'

Janie brightened. 'I'm looking forward to it. What's in here?'

Stacy showed them round the deserted hairdressing and manicure rooms, then continued through to the tub room. 'I hope you brought your cossies?'

Her father laughed self-consciously. 'It's many a long year since I've been inside a pair of swimming trunks, but your mum insisted I bought some.'

'Good. Come and see my medical room.'

'My goodness – it looks so high-tech.' Janie stared blankly round the little room, which was gleaming with chrome and glass.

Stacy swung the cupboards open to show her parents the supplies they had there. 'That's the idea. This is a good alternative for me, you know. I wasn't made to be a blood-and-guts kind of nurse.'

'As long as you're happy. I must say, it's all very impressive.'

Stacy grabbed her courage with both hands. 'I'm happy – are you? I thought earlier you were both looking a bit tense.'

'I'm fine, darling. Just tired after the long journey.'

'Dad?'

He laughed again. 'Oh, nothing wrong with me apart from the usual terrible summer weather at home. I'll enjoy getting some heat while I'm here.'

Stacy treated him to her best cynical look. She wasn't going to let him get away with that… But a quiet word when Mum wasn't around might be best.

Janie caught hold of Stacy's left hand with the engagement ring. 'Don't worry, darling – your dad and I'll have plenty of energy for making wedding plans, and we'll have all the time in the world to get stuck right into that while we're here. I've brought lots of brochures to show you. Now, how about showing us the rest of the hotel? I'd like to see the bar where Emily and Alan met, and the garden too while it's still light. It gets dark earlier here, doesn't it?'

Stacy smiled uneasily, and led the way. Wedding plans? That was something she'd have to talk through with Rico before Mum got too fixed on anything. 'Sometime this century' was as far as they'd got with their own plans. But tomorrow was another day.

Chapter Six

Thursday, 17th May

The click of the flat door closing quietly jerked Alex out of the doze he'd been dropping in and out of since the late news finished on TV. He wiped his face on his sleeve. Falling asleep in an armchair was a pretty pathetic look, wasn't it? What time…? Jeez, it was after one in the morning – Thursday already.

'Zoe? How did it go?' He staggered out to the hallway, where she was shrugging out of her jacket, and one bleary glance was enough for him to see that she was thrilled with how it had gone. And why wouldn't it go well, the way Zoe played?

She stepped into his arms and whispered, her voice awed, 'Oh, Alex. It was amazing. Just knowing Daniel Marino was listening to me – it made all the difference. And –' She leaned back to see him. 'He noticed me. He came backstage, afterwards. Alex, he asked me to audition in Zurich. I can't believe it.' Huge eyes in a pale face were fixed on him.

Alex pulled her close again. 'I'm so pleased for you, baby. You deserve it. I was wishing all evening I'd gone to watch you.'

Zoe slid out of his arms, smiling a dreamy, isn't-life-wonderful kind of smile. 'Daniel Marino, Alex. And he noticed me.' She floated off into the bathroom.

Alex went to make tea, still with that horrible feeling of being dragged forcibly from a deep slumber. Shit... He started work in six hours; he'd be half dead in the morning. But the feeling that his relationship – and with it his life – was spiralling out of control wasn't conducive to sleep.

'Alex! Alex – what are you doing? Are you all right?'

Oh no, it was Stacy, and she was frowning at him from the other side of the hallway. Alex lurched upright at the reception desk, where he'd been leaning on his forearms while he checked off items on his Thursday to-do list. He hadn't done many of them yet.

'Sorry – I'm fine.'

Stacy tapped across the hall and leaned over the desk, hissing at him while Alex's heart plummeted. A raging boss wasn't what you wanted when you were feeling rough.

'You looked as if you were asleep on the job! That's not the impression we want to give the guests. Are you sure you're all right?'

'I didn't sleep much, that's all. I'll be fine.'

'Go and have some coffee. And...' She sniffed. 'Has that cat been in here again?'

Alex flinched. It had, but he'd scooted it back out as soon as he noticed it. And a cat coming in was hardly his fault, was it? Everyone knew you couldn't train cats.

'I put it out straightaway.'

'That's not what it smells like. I'll bring you a scented candle for the desk. Some of our guests and spa visitors have medical conditions. We can't have stray cats wandering around as they please.'

She stomped off to the lift while misery engulfed Alex. It had been well after three before sleep found him after Zoe's return. She, of course, had dropped into bed and fallen asleep in seconds, as she always did, while visions of a future with Zoe in Zurich while he was here by the lake swirled through Alex's head, painting an ever-darker picture of his life. If Daniel Marino called, Zoe would follow. Which would leave him – where? Impossible to up sticks and leave Mum, never mind his job. And if Daniel Marino didn't call, Zoe would be gutted. Whatever happened, it wouldn't end well.

He was dealing with two first-time spa visitors a few minutes later when Stacy returned, plonked an orange candle in a glass on the desk, lit it, and vanished again without a word. Alex took the couple through and handed them over to Margrit in the tub room, then came back and sniffed at the candle. The smell of sandalwood and orange was wafting over the desk now, but hell, he'd never seen Stacy like that before. Maybe she hadn't slept well either. Or maybe she was worried that she wouldn't have time for her parents, with the lake rising like this. Or maybe… Alex stared miserably out to the driveway, where the white cat was having a wash bang in front of the main door. Maybe she was just being a good hotelier who didn't like her staff lounging around half-asleep on the job. Put like that, it didn't sound unreasonable.

Rico read the email for the second time, then tossed his phone onto the bed. A friend from his bachelor course was planning a master's degree in St Gallen, starting that autumn. Envy of Stefan's freedom burning in his throat, Rico pulled a T-shirt from the fitted wardrobe shelf.

'Rico, I'm taking Mum and Dad to have breakfast on the terrace.'

Stacy came in from the hallway, and Rico went to hug her. Her usual perfume filled his nose, and he breathed in appreciatively. 'Good plan. Dad singing in the shower and Guido wandering around in his pjs aren't what you want to confront your mum and dad with on their first morning. Everything okay downstairs?'

'Pretty quiet, but that cat's been in again. I had to put a scented candle on the desk. Are you coming for breakfast with us?'

'Nah. I'll join you in a bit for coffee.' He flopped down on the bed.

She spun round in the doorway. 'Hey, why so glum? Is it the lake?'

'I haven't checked it this morning yet.' Rico pointed to his phone. 'I had an email from Stefan – he wants to know if I'll be starting my master's this year too.'

And how he wished he could. But if he gave up even half his work at the hotel, they'd have to find someone to take over his job. And although Lakeside was in profit now, the uncertainty about how the coming flood would affect business made it difficult to plan too far ahead.

Stacy came back and sat down beside him. 'If we can manage it, I think you should. Can we talk about it later? Mum and Dad will be waiting for me. And oh – Mum wants to start planning the wedding. Let's grab an hour to ourselves this afternoon and work out what we want too, broadly speaking – half four-ish?'

Rico blinked unhappily. Their talk might flag up more problems than answers. Secretly, he was hoping Stacy would want the wedding here, but he knew it was traditional in the UK for couples to marry in the bride's old home, and Janie was nothing if not traditional. Then there was the whole 'church or registry office' thing. In Switzerland, you had to have a civil ceremony too, even if you were having a church wedding, but it was different in the UK. If he and Stacy were married in England, then they couldn't have any official ceremony here. And it would be so great to marry here, somewhere by the lake, then have a big party in the hotel. He and Stacy would have to talk, but a squeezed-in half-hour at the end of a busy day was unlikely to be enough to have a proper discussion. Why on earth was Janie trying to rush them, anyway?

For the life of him, he couldn't keep the impatience out of his voice. 'Fine. Let's hope we manage it. But, Stace – wedding plans aren't – we don't have time to worry about them now, that's all.'

She gaped at him. 'We don't need to go into details. A broad outline will be enough to let Mum get started. She loves all the thinking and planning that goes with a wedding. It'll be fun.'

The thought of Janie planning his wedding sent Rico's stress levels hurtling skywards. This was his wedding, and Stacy's – you'd think they should do the planning. Or were weddings always organised like this in England? Stacy certainly sounded happy enough about it.

'It's–' His phone buzzed as a call came in. Ah. Andi, and this would be more info about the drains. 'Stace, I need to get this. I think your mum should leave all planning until we've sorted out what we want, huh? It's our wedding.' He tapped to connect to Andi.

Stacy's face fell a mile and a half. She left without saying more, and the flat door banged shut behind her. Rico could have kicked himself. Now he'd upset Stacy, and God knew how he'd manage to keep his cool with her parents for the duration of their stay. Janie was going around with a permanent 'this isn't quite what I imagined' expression. It was hard not to feel rejected.

He dealt with Andi's problem, then joined his side of the family in the kitchen. Julia was making coffee and Ralph, still in his bathrobe, was slapping butter on a croissant.

Rico grabbed one too and bit the end off. 'What's happening with the sandbags, Dad?'

'Guido and I are doing that this morning. What's on your list for today?'

Back to saving the hotel. Rico fetched a coffee. 'I'll get onto the firm who supplied the fitness room equipment first. It's too heavy to manhandle up from the cellar ourselves. I'll have to get them to collect and store it for the duration. That won't be cheap, but there's no other way.'

Ralph leaned back in his chair. 'You should think about relocating the gym to the ground floor.'

Rico slumped. Ground floor space was at a premium; he couldn't think where they could fit in the eight large machines and two stationary bikes. 'I know. I'll have a mull over the plans with Andi. I wish we'd considered having a gym from the start.'

'You'll work something out. Ha – see what I did there?' Ralph slapped the table top. 'Where do you want the sandbags, when we bring them back?'

Rico tried to smile, but the depression surging through his head was unstoppable. 'Put them in the boathouse. Nice and handy for the flood.'

Ralph got up and clapped Rico's shoulder. 'Chin up, son. We'll cope.'

The waitress reached their table with the thermos jugs, and poured coffee refills all round. Stacy sipped gratefully. Thank heavens for caffeine. She needed it as much as Alex did this morning. Oh dear – she'd been pretty uptight with him, and it wasn't his fault she was worried Mum and Dad weren't going to fit in with the Weber family. Not that she wanted her employees poured over the reception desk, but she could have been less snippy about it. The guy was tired and he'd done a good job until now. She'd have a word again later.

John Townsend leaned back while his cup was being filled. 'It's a nice change, having breakfast outside. Not often we get the weather for it in Elton Abbey, is it, love?'

Janie smiled wryly. 'I'm glad we don't have heat like this at home!' She flapped a hand in front of her face, and Stacy rose to put up the sunshade behind their table.

'Better? It's pretty intensive, isn't it? I couldn't believe the heat when I was here last year.'

And here they were again, talking about the weather in true British fashion. But at least Mum seemed more relaxed than she'd been last night. No sooner had the thought gone through Stacy's mind than Janie frowned, peering round the terrace.

'I thought Rico was joining us?'

'He has a lot to organise. He's worried about the effects a flood would have on the business.' Stacy bit her lip. Planning their wedding had to take second place to the hotel in the current circumstances; she got that, especially as they weren't even reckoning on getting married this year, but… Rico had never been so offhand with her before. What did it mean?

Her mother was frowning too. 'Oh, Stacy, I don't like to see things so insecure for you. Could you get a proper nursing job here, if the hotel doesn't work out? Wouldn't it be better if you both came home to England? Rico's English is good enough for him to study there, isn't it?'

'Mum, for heaven's sake, you're being a worrywart. Hotel-keeping's always a seasonal, chancy business, but Rico's family have been doing it for decades. We'll be fine.' Stacy touched her mother's hand to soften the words. Like mother, like daughter. And like Rico too. Worrywarts, the lot of them.

Janie gave her an uncertain smile and vanished behind her coffee cup. To Stacy's relief, Rico came jogging across the terrace and pulled out the chair beside her. He was smiling, but it was more of a 'being polite to guests' kind of smile than a 'straight from the heart' one.

He sat back. 'Morning. How was your first night in Switzerland?'

'Very comfortable.'

Unusually, it was her father who answered while Janie smiled but said nothing. The little worm of apprehension in Stacy's middle twisted. Dad was still looking strained, and Rico wasn't meeting her eyes. This wasn't the place to start a complicated conversation, though. She opened her mouth to ask her mother if she'd had any thoughts about what she'd like to do today, then closed it again as Julia appeared, fresh from the lake, a towel wrapped round her swimsuit.

'Can I join you? A coffee would be lovely – that water's cold!' She beamed round the table but spoke in Swiss German, and Janie looked away.

Rico fetched a chair from another table. 'The floods have brought a lot of driftwood into the lake,' he said, speaking slowly in English. 'You should be careful, swimming among that.'

'I saw it. I'll stick to your tubs from now on.' Julia changed into her accented English and spoke to Janie. 'You have tried the spa yet?'

Janie shook her head. 'We can do that later. Seems a pity to waste this sunshine. What's on the programme, Stacy?'

Stacy stifled a sigh. It was up to her, then. A heart-to-heart about wedding plans, not to mention her and Rico's worries about flooding and what Mum was really thinking about it all would have been top of the agenda if things had felt normal, but with Mum being sniffy and Rico sending out strong 'I do not want to talk about anything deep' signals, that wasn't going to happen round this table, anyway. Okay, they would play tourists first. She would show her parents something of the area this morning, and Mum could tell her what she had in mind for the wedding over lunch. That way, she'd be prepared for her talk with Rico that afternoon. He hadn't sounded too bothered about what kind of wedding they had. Stacy smiled at her mother. Heavens, you'd think they were playing at being Cheshire cats, smiles all over the place. But being awkward wasn't like Mum; they would soon get her back to her usual good-natured self.

'I thought we'd visit a couple of the towns along the lake bank and have lunch in one of them, then I'll leave you for a soak in the tubs when we get home in the afternoon. Julia, why don't you join us? I can have the car, can't I, Rico?'

He nodded, but his mind was obviously elsewhere as he gazed to the east, and Stacy sighed. It was the perfect view, the mountains in Austria cutting into the skyline and the German bank a green slick above the water, gorgeously blue today and shimmering as far as the eye could see. Two guests were crossing the garden en route for a swim, and heck, they should warn people about the driftwood. Gorgeous the lake may be, but it was dangerous, too. She'd tell Alex to make sure everyone was aware of it. And now they should start this not-quite-a-holiday kind of day.

Stacy rose to her feet. 'All those coming on the lakeside tour should meet in reception in twenty minutes.'

Julia grabbed her cup and departed with it. 'See you then!'

Chapter Seven

Thursday, 17th May

Stacy leaned back in her chair and stretched out her legs. They'd spent the morning walking round the lake park and the old town in Arbon, including an hour in the medieval castle, which at least was pleasantly cool. Now they were sipping iced tea in the shade of a chestnut tree and waiting for their lunchtime chicken salad at one of the lakeside restaurants, and for the third time at least she'd tried to start a conversation about the wedding, but Janie had blocked her with, 'We can discuss that when I show you the reception venue brochures we have back at the hotel, darling'. Okay, but that didn't mean they couldn't even mention the wedding, did it? Well, yes – apparently it did. Janie was giving all her attention to two sparrows fighting over a stray chip.

'How does the temperature here compare to Lugano?' John asked Julia, and frustration welled up inside Stacy. They'd chatted about Switzerland, the weather, the family stationery shop, films, the royal family, holidays – and now they were back to Switzerland again. An unexpected and unwelcome thought slid into Stacy's head. Was all this superficial chit chat because Mum didn't want to talk about anything to do with the wedding while Julia was with them? Come to that, talking about anything in the future seemed to be off the agenda. Julia's query about British wedding traditions had been skated over, and when Stacy started talking about what she and Rico were planning for their autumn hotel guests, Mum had immediately turned the conversation to the family's October holiday in Cornwall years ago – the last 'whole family together' holiday. What was going on?

The salad arrived, and for the duration of the meal the conversation was about food. On the way back to the car, Julia pulled Stacy to the side.

'You can drop me off at Lakeside on your way to Rorschach,' she murmured. 'I think your mother would like to be alone with you for a while, yes?'

Embarrassment flushed through Stacy, and she squeezed Julia's arm. It wasn't like Mum to be so standoffish. They would have to sit down before Ralph's birthday tomorrow and thrash out whatever was wrong.

The afternoon trip to Rorschach was postponed, however. Janie declared it was much too hot to do more walking around, and they pulled up in the Lakeside car park twenty minutes later.

'Okay – an hour for a siesta, then I'll meet you at the entrance to the spa,' said Stacy, forcing a happy tone into her voice. 'You can have a lovely refreshing soak in the least-hot tub.'

'Sounds like a plan,' said Janie, and Stacy felt like screaming. If she heard one more cliché today, she would go mad.

Rico was nowhere to be found, and Ralph and Guido must still be on their sandbag mission. Stacy went to make sure everything was ready for Ralph's birthday dinner the following evening, and spent a pleasant half hour in the kitchens trying out Rob the chef's new lemon cheesecake. It was amazing how much brighter everything looked when you had a chunk of cheesecake inside you. She marched back through to the hallway, where Kim, the part-time beautician and Stacy's best friend in the village, was on her way in with five-year-old Elijah and three-year-old Ben.

Ben ran to greet her, and Stacy swung him into her arms, speaking in her still rather shaky Swiss German. 'Hello, monster! Come for an ice cream?'

'We've come to see Mama's work,' said Elijah, beaming up at her.

Stacy ruffled his hair. A normal chat like this was what she needed, in the middle of all the flood and parent stress. Kim and family had burst into her life last summer when she'd saved Elijah from drowning, and now he was one of her biggest advantages when it came to learning Swiss German.

'Are you having a manicure?' she teased.

'No–o – but I'm getting gold on my thumbs!' He held them up.

'They're going to be my golden boys,' said Kim, as Stacy put Ben down again. 'I'm glad we bumped into you. I have something that might be interesting for the hotel. One of my clients is about to finish her training as a beautician, and she's looking for a place she could start up and do facials, make-up, etcetera. Could she rent some room-hours from you too, when Viola leaves?'

'That sounds promising,' said Stacy immediately. Kim only worked a few hours a week, with Viola, the other beautician, taking on about sixty per cent. Make-up and facials were popular with the guests, so they were going to need someone else when Viola left in autumn. 'I'll speak to

Rico and if he agrees, we could have her in for an interview.'

'Lovely. I'll tell her. Come on, you two.' She grasped Ben's hand again. 'You don't mind me bringing them here, do you, Stacy? They were supposed to be going to a party, but the birthday boy is down with summer flu. We'll take our golden nails out to the terrace afterwards and have big ice creams to swell your profits, won't we, kids?'

Stacy beamed. It was always a real feeling of achievement that she understood Swiss German so well, and could even talk to the boys.

'You should try Chef's lemon cheesecake,' she said, then laughed with Kim at Elijah's horrified expression.

'Chocolate ice cream with lots of chocolate sauce!' he said, pulling his mother towards the manicure room.

The trio vanished, and Stacy turned to see her parents standing by the lift clutching their wire baskets with towels.

'Ready? You've just missed my friend Kim, but you'll meet her tomorrow at Ralph's party.' Stacy led the way into the large spa, which was about half full. 'Okay, blood pressure check first, then we'll get you into a tub.'

'We heard you talking,' said Janie. 'You're very fluent, aren't you?'

Stacy waved them into her medical room at the back of the spa. 'Well, I've been here eight months, and I still go to classes every week.' She took her mother's blood pressure, then removed the cuff. 'Perfect. Your turn, Dad.'

Janie rose to let John sit down. 'It feels odd, hearing you talking to your friends, and not understanding a word.' Her head drooped.

There was a definite edge to her mother's voice. Stacy watched the machine bleep down, then gave her father a thumbs-up. 'Almost perfect. You are free to soak.'

Her mind was racing as she spoke. So that was the problem. Mum wanted to be part of Stacy's new world, but not only was the distance too great to allow them to meet regularly, there was the language barrier too. Except – there was no reason why Mum needed to know everything she said to her friends. Maybe it was even Mum's contrariness that was making Dad so unlike himself? That wasn't impossible, but it was something she'd need to ask him about when her mother wasn't around. Getting him alone might not be easy; he and Mum were practically joined at the hip, and oh, how she wished there was time for a good long talk about all this with Rico.

Stacy fixed on her best smile, showed her parents where to leave their baskets in the changing rooms, then settled them into the least-hot tub. She would stay with Mum and Dad for half an hour, then they could look after themselves while she had some quality time with Rico. If he was back from wherever he'd gone to.

Alex coming in with the post reminded her of that morning. His mouth was drooping. Oh, heck – she hadn't handled the cat situation well, had she? She was going to have to put that right.

Rico biked along the lake path, a warm breeze ruffling through his hair and his shirt sticking to his back within minutes. Even so, the few minutes outside made a refreshing change from the stuffiness in Grimsbach land registry office, where he'd spent the last hour staring at maps and details about land height and rivers. It was impossible to predict where the flooding would hit hardest. He bounced over a rut where a tree root was close to the surface, and slowed down. The path was narrow here, with a slim belt of reeds to his right, and the gardens belonging to a row of expensive bungalows on the left. Biking along the path was a longer way home than taking the main road, which he'd done on the way there, but here he was riding along in the shade of tall trees and bushes. It was good to be surrounded by nature. He slowed down at the place where the pathway swung round a large and ancient tree, then skidded to a halt, his feet leaving the pedals and landing over his ankles in water. *Shit*, shit. The next twenty metres or so of the path were a path no longer, they were part of the lake. The flooding had started. Sick at heart, Rico pushed off again, and three minutes later he was shoving his bike into the boathouse where it was kept.

He squelched round to the front door, then removed his trainers and socks. Alex was behind the desk, and Rico parked his wet things there too. The scented candle Stacy had mentioned was still burning aromatically – maybe even too aromatically, but at least it would hide any stray pong emanating from his wet trainers.

'Is Stacy back yet?'

Alex pointed. 'She's in the spa.'

Rico wheeled round and went in. Hopefully Stacy didn't have her parents in tow. He would have to put things right with her; it was horrible, this feeling that she was upset with him. They didn't agree all the time, of course, but he'd never felt so uneasy about it before. Rico pressed his lips together. It was a pity Janie and John had come now, when they were so stretched with the prospect of a flood. What was going on with them, anyway? When you compared them to the couple he'd met in England – well, there was no comparison. Janie especially was like a different person.

Stacy was alone in her medical room, tidying the cupboard

above the sink. She stared when he went in. 'Why the bare feet?'

He filled her in, and her face fell. 'Oh no. But if it was only a small section of the path... maybe it won't get much worse.'

'It will. I bet there are a whole lot of spots like that, all the way along the path, wherever it's nearest the lake.'

'Why aren't they sandbagging it?'

'No point. The water will cover it even with sandbags. It would be further up they'd want to protect. Oh, Stace. I wish this wasn't happening.'

She grimaced. 'We'll cope, because we have to. Rico, are we okay?'

He hugged her, resting his forehead in her hair, and here he was again, breathing in the scent of her perfume, this time mixed with the more medical smell of the spa.

'We will be, love. I wish we had more time together.'

She nodded, but pulled away almost immediately, and he could see the shadow in her eyes.

'Not much chance of that for the next few days. Remember it's your dad's birthday tomorrow. Rico, I'm sorry, but we don't have time to make wedding plans now. I need to have a word with Alex before he leaves, and Mum and Dad will be heading up to the flat in five minutes – can you go with them and keep the peace between them and Julia? We'll talk about us another time.' She gave him a quick hug and almost pushed him back out through the spa.

Rico stomped past the desk and jabbed the button for the lift with a stiff, resentful finger. It was true, this wasn't the time to worry about the wedding, and his master's degree and ambition to start his own IT business were dreams for a different day too. And none of it felt right.

Alex grabbed his things from the office and scurried to the front door. At last, at last, it was time to go home. Hopefully Zoe would be there, all ready to give him a hug because boy, did he need one. A hug, a nice meal and about ten hours sleep would set him right again. Surely some of that would be possible.

'Alex! Hang on a sec!'

Hell, it was Stacy. Another telling off wasn't how he wanted to end the most stressful day he'd had here so far. Stacy strode past Maria at the desk, blowing the candle out as she passed, and joined him at the front door.

'Did you get through the day all right? Alex, do you often have trouble sleeping?'

Alex shook his head. At least she wasn't mad with him any more. She was still checking he was up to the job, mind you.

'It's not that. My girlfriend's a musician, so she often works late hours, and last night was an important concert. It all got a bit later than it was supposed to, but it was a one-off.'

To his relief, she brightened straightaway. 'A professional musician – wow! What – and where – does she play?'

'Violin, in the Bridge Theatre Orchestra.'

'Oh, we went to see *Fiddler on the Roof* a few weeks ago – it was perfect! Alex, I don't suppose you have time for a quick coffee and a chat? We didn't have a good morning, did we, and I'm going to be rushed off my feet tomorrow, with the birthday party.'

'Sure – I'd like that.'

What else could he say? Zoe wouldn't notice if he was half an hour late, and he had to keep in with his boss. They walked round to the terrace bar, and Stacy ordered two coffees. Alex leaned back in his chair. It was restful, sitting here with the breeze from the lake wafting over him. The bar was in his line of vision, and he grinned. Timea Roberts was sitting on a bar stool drinking cola and making eyes at Alonso the barman, who was chatting her up like a pro. She seemed to be giving him the right answers, though; his laugh sounded genuine.

Stacy turned round to see what he was looking at. 'Oh... how old is Timea, do you know?'

'Seventeen. Not far off eighteen, if I'm remembering right. Old enough to drink cola without her mum, anyway.'

Stacy gave him a look. 'Mrs Roberts cornered me for a chat about Timea's health yesterday. She does seem a little over-protective, but–' She tapped his arm. 'Polite and professional, huh?'

'Got it.'

'You're off this weekend, aren't you? You should bring your mum to see the place.'

That was the impossible dream. Tired tears welled up in Alex's eyes, and of course Stacy noticed, and somehow, he found himself telling her all about the agoraphobia and how Ma hadn't left her flat for weeks this time and wouldn't even talk about getting help of some kind.

Stacy listened, frowning. 'That's tough for you both. Alex, let me have a think about it. There must be help available, something she wouldn't need a doctor's referral for. Shall I ask – without giving her name – at the community nursing service, and get back to you about it?'

'That would be great. Thanks.'

Stacy stood up and lifted their empty cups. 'Good. I'll let you get off home. See you tomorrow.'

Alex wandered back to the car park, passing Mrs Roberts on her way to the terrace. Oops. By the look of her mother's chin, Timea's chat with Alonzo the barman was about to come to an abrupt end.

'Let's all walk to Rorschach,' suggested Rico, when dinner was over. No one had wanted a big meal, so they'd ordered some snacks and eaten in the terrace bar, which was filling up with locals wanting to enjoy a coffee or a drink overlooking the lake. Conversation wasn't what you'd call flowing, though, and they couldn't sit looking at each other for the next several hours until bedtime. A walk in the coolness of the evening would give them something to do, and they could chat about the scenery en route.

'Good idea,' said Ralph immediately. 'It isn't far – less than half an hour,' he added to Janie and John. 'We can walk there and decide later if anyone wants to come home on the train.'

Julia and Guido cried off in favour of a trip to Arbon and the outdoor pool there, but the rest of them set out ten minutes later. Rico led the way along the path, going sideways most of the time to chat to Janie and Stacy behind, with Ralph and John bringing up the rear. The path wasn't wide enough to walk three abreast. The evening air was clear, making the view across the water to southern Germany and Austria even more spectacular than usual, and Rico was turning to point out the island of Lindau, just off the opposite bank, when Janie tucked Stacy's arm through hers and spoke in a low murmur, obviously intended for her daughter alone.

'Let's you and me start planning this wedding, lovey. We can't begin too early. When did you have in mind?'

Stacy's eyes met Rico's. 'No date in mind yet, Mum, but it won't be for a while, so we don't have to rush – do we, Rico?'

Rico opened his mouth to reply, but Janie got there first.

'Oh darling – we should reserve the church, and organise somewhere for the reception, and you'll need to book flights, of course, and the honeymoon.'

The horror in Janie's voice would have been comical if she'd been talking about anyone else's wedding. Rico swivelled round to help Stacy, walking more or less backwards and trying hard to sound calm and supportive.

'How about if Stacy and I make some preliminary plans as soon as possible, and we can take it from there? There's plenty of time.'

Janie ignored this. 'Stacy, darling, think about what *you* want. We'll have another chat later.' She pouted at Rico.

The blood rushed to Rico's cheeks. It sounded as if Janie thought he'd been refusing to let Stacy plan her own wedding. Had Stace and her mother already spoken about it? But Stacy would have told him – wouldn't she?

'Mum, Rico's right, and we'll make plans another time when he doesn't have to walk like a crab to join in. Are we nearly at the flooded part, Rico?'

Her voice was stiff, so hopefully that meant she was on his side. Janie was being impossible, and very rude, too.

Rico cleared his throat. 'It's round here. We'll need to walk up in the rough grass for a few metres.'

They skirted three swamped areas before arriving on the much wider path outside Rorschach. They were walking directly beside the lake now – and it was within a few centimetres of the path.

'If there's a Föhn storm this week that's going to wash

right over,' said Ralph, and Rico had to agree. Worse flooding was imminent.

'What's Föhn?' asked Stacy's father.

'It's a warm southerly wind from the Alps,' said Ralph. 'It usually brings a day or two of lovely weather, followed by rain. According to the forecast, we'll get Föhn tomorrow, but judging by those clear views, it's here already. Cross your fingers it doesn't bring a storm with it.'

Stacy tucked her arm through Ralph's as they walked on. 'Föhn means you'll have a good-weather birthday. Let's enjoy that first.'

Tears came into Rico's eyes and he brushed them away impatiently. How lovely Stacy was. Janie's remarks still stung, and oh, how he hoped that Stacy's heart wasn't set on a wedding with all the trimmings back in England. That was the problem, actually; he didn't know what she wanted. Somehow, the two of them had stopped communicating with each other over the wedding, and what with visitors and floods and a hotel to run, they didn't have time to put it right.

Chapter Eight

Friday, 18th May

Her phone shrilling into the bedroom woke Stacy from a comfortable doze. Hello, Friday, Ralph's birthday and a special, family day, and hopefully the rising lake wasn't going to impact tonight's party. Stacy fought with the duvet and plonked her feet on the floor, wincing as visions of a waterlogged cellar chased through her head. Rico had got up early to see what the lake was doing, and he hadn't reappeared yet. Poor Rico. His shoulders were permanently up to his ears these days, what with planning Ralph's party and Mum trying to talk about weddings when Rico was worried sick about the hotel. They'd agreed last night that sitting down just the two of them to discuss the wedding would take priority at the weekend, but it might be hard to find a time when neither of them was exhausted and the lake and the hotel and all the parents were behaving. Stacy hesitated. Rico knew she didn't care when or where the wedding was or if it was a big affair or a tiny one. Didn't he? He was still acting… strangely about it. A cold chill pierced through her. It couldn't be he was regretting their engagement, could it? That could be the reason for his grumpiness, though, and Mum playing mother-in-law from hell all the time wouldn't be helping. Maybe Rico would prefer to go on living together, like they were now.

Her phone, charging on the chest of drawers, stopped ringing before she got to it then immediately started again. Who on earth was trying to call her at this time in the morning when she was on holiday?

Stacy grabbed her mobile. Lord, it was Alex on reception – something must be wrong. She tapped connect.

'Stacy, I'm really sorry but there's a problem with some people who want to check into the bikers' flat.' Unusually, Alex spoke to her in Swiss German, and Stacy plopped down on the bed. People didn't normally start arriving at this time of day.

'They're checking *in*?'

He lowered his voice. 'They were camping near the lake last night and woke up to find everything waterlogged. It's a family with two young kids and they want two biker rooms for two nights.'

Stacy stared into space. If he'd dragged her away from a lovely lie-in to ask if that was okay, she would kill him. The bikers' rooms were normally only full at weekends, so where was the problem?

'We have two rooms available for them, don't we?'

'Yes, but…' Alex's voice dropped even further, then she heard a door close. 'I'm in the office. Stacy, I think one of the kids has *Kopfläuse*.'

It was a word Stacy hadn't encountered before. 'What's that in English?'

'I don't know. Hang on.' Tapping sounds came over the phone, then Alex was back. 'Lice? In her hair?'

'What?' Head reeling and phone still clutched to her ear, Stacy stumbled into the en suite and stopped in front of the

mirror. She looked exactly as if she'd just got out of bed; no way could she go downstairs and talk to guests like this.

Alex was still talking. 'I didn't want to turn them away. The kids are little more than babies.'

Stacy thought swiftly. 'Okay. Tell them we're checking if there are rooms available both nights, and sit them on the leather sofa and bring them coffee or whatever they want. I'll be down in ten.' She banged her phone down on the bed. Now for the quickest shower ever.

It was a sorry little family she found in reception, sitting in a row on the sofa by the door, a toddler in the mother's arms and a small girl of about three huddled between her parents. All were wearing damp jeans and T-shirts, and the parents were obviously exhausted. A pile of sodden rucksacks and cycling helmets lay under the coffee table. Stacy smiled at them, then went into the office with Alex.

'They're Italian,' he said, clasping his hands under his chin. 'They speak better English than German. The little girl was wearing a helmet when she came in, and when she took it off I saw something move across her forehead. A neighbour's kid caught head lice at kindergarten last year, and this looked pretty much like what he had.'

He blinked uncertainly at Stacy, and she put a hand on his arm.

'You did the right thing calling me, and of course we have to help them. Lice don't need to be a problem and anyone can get them, but we have to act, and they have to agree to treatment, otherwise they can't stay.'

Alex went back to the desk, where two guests were waiting to check out, and Stacy approached the four on the sofa. 'Hello. Alex says you prefer English?'

'Yes!' Both parents spoke at once, looking relieved. The

father went on, 'I'm sorry we are here so early. Do you have rooms for us?'

Stacy peered closely at the little girl, and yes, Alex was right. The child had thick, dark-brown hair touching her shoulders, and tiny specks like dandruff were plain to see all over her head, and – a live louse was there at her hairline, too. Stacy glanced behind her. The two guests were still at reception with Alex, but as she watched they moved away to the door, smiling goodbyes in all directions. Nice to see happy guests, though the guys here on the sofa might not come into that category when they heard her news.

Stacy sat down on the coffee table to be more on their level, and spoke in a low voice. 'I'm head nurse here and assistant to the manager. We do have rooms, but there's a problem. Did you know your little girl has head lice?'

Trying to look professionally sympathetic, she pointed to the child's head. The mother stared at her daughter for several seconds before her eyes widened and she burst into tears, muttering something in Italian to her husband.

A blush spread over his cheeks, visible even under the suntan. 'We – my wife thought it was…' He paused, searching for the word, then mimed brushing a speck from his shoulder.

'Dandruff?' said Stacy. 'It's an easy mistake to make, and please don't worry – it's not a disaster. But it means you'll all have to be shampooed and combed, and all your clothes and things should be washed, if you want to stay here.'

This wouldn't be a problem as the bikers' flat had its own washing machine, but it would mean no bikers could stay all weekend. Stacy grimaced. Oh, well. Charity begins at home.

'Anything,' said the mother, wiping her eyes.

'Okay. I'll go to the chemist and get whatever's needed.

You stay here, and Alex will check you in.'

She reported all this to Alex back at the desk. 'Where's Rico, by the way?'

'Down at the jetty.' Alex indicated the waiting family. 'Won't we need to fumigate, or something?'

'Heavens, no. Lice don't live long away from the host. We'll leave the rooms empty for a couple of days after they leave; that should do it, along with a good clean. Charge them for two rooms without spa access, and we'll leave it at that.'

Stacy went back upstairs for her purse, connecting to Rico's mobile as she went.

'You're in charge of the medical side,' he said, after listening to her explanation.

'How's the lake?'

'Higher. I'm about to lengthen *Lakeside Lady's* moorings. I'll see you in a bit.' He rang off, and Stacy grimaced. He'd sounded almost tearful there.

Upstairs, Ralph, Julia and Guido were having breakfast on the balcony. Stacy stepped out and kissed Ralph. 'Happy birthday! You'll need to wait for your present, though – we have a mini-emergency on downstairs.'

'Need help?'

'No – in fact the fewer people we have involved, the better. I'm off to the chemist. Won't be long.' Stacy grabbed her car key.

Outside, she jogged past two bikes parked by the front door, one with a child trailer attached. That would have to be cleaned too. Stacy flung herself into the car and turned left into the village. Two minutes' drive, and she was at the chemist's. A quick purchase and – *hell* – Mum and Dad! Stacy grabbed her phone to see the time. She was supposed to meet her parents for breakfast on the terrace at nine, and it was now ten past. They'd be thinking all sorts, the mood Mum was in these days. Stacy tapped on her phone.

'Sorry, Mum, I've been delayed. I'm helping a family who've booked in with a little problem. Start your breakfast, and I'll see you on the terrace soon.'

It was almost half an hour later before she was able to leave the Italian family in the bikers' flat with a supply of anti-lice shampoo and combs. Stacy gave Alex instructions not to let anyone sit on the sofa until it had been vacuum-cleaned and wiped, and ran out to the terrace feeling as though she'd done a full day's work already. Mum would be sending out a search party for her… but thank goodness, Rico was there with her parents.

Rico looked round for the waitress to bring Janie and John more coffee. Janie was more than a little huffy that Stacy had left them in the lurch to order their own breakfast, and Rico's reminder that all the staff spoke pretty good English hadn't gone down well. Ordering breakfast wasn't the problem, Stacy abandoning them was. But thank God, here she was. They had to build some kind of bridge between their two families, but so far, they hadn't had much success. Breakfast in their separate groups had become the norm; they weren't gelling together the way he and Stacy had wanted them to. *Had* wanted? Please, please Stacy must still want that…

Stacy plumped down in the remaining chair and heaved a sigh. 'Sorry, guys – it took a bit longer than I thought, but problem solved.'

Rico squeezed her arm. Bless Stacy, going the extra mile to help people. His mother would have done exactly the same.

Janie covered Stacy's hand on the table with her own. 'You deserve your breakfast, darling – what would you like?'

She signalled to the waitress a mini-second before Rico, and gave him an odd look. Rico nearly rolled his eyes, but stopped himself in time. Clearly, he wasn't looking after Janie's daughter, was he?

Stacy fanned herself with the drinks menu. 'Just coffee and a croissant. Oh, and the chemist said there was no need to leave the flat empty for days to make sure the lice have gone, Rico – an extra-good clean will do. Those head lice are exiting the hotel as we speak, and I'll go in myself with the vacuum cleaner on Sunday morning when the Morettis have gone.'

She bit into her croissant and sat chewing, and Rico leaned back, reassured. Nearly everything they talked about nowadays was one of their various problems, but Stacy's manner was the same as usual, so she wasn't miffed about the wedding convo they hadn't had yet. On the other hand, said convo was important, and they weren't going to have time for it today, either. So maybe it wasn't so important to Stacy. The brief flare of hope faded again.

Janie had followed their talk like someone watching tennis with their mouth hanging open.

'Head lice! By the looks of things, living and working in a hotel is no different to living and working in your own shop – you never know what's going to come through the door, you never get time off unless you leave the premises, and you have to turn your hand to every job in the place. I hope it's not too much for you, Stacy. And on your week off, too.'

An indescribable expression flitted over Stacy's face

before she smiled at her mother.

'Got it in one, Mum, but as you say, it's what we do. My week off was to spend time with Ralph, and the way things have turned out with him doing so much flood preparation, I've barely seen him – so let's all try to make today a happy birthday for him, huh?'

'Agreed,' said John. He reached across the table and took Janie's hand.

Yet more hope speared into Rico's gut, diluting the fear. Wanting to spend time with Ralph… that didn't sound as if Stacy didn't want to get married. But the other important question was still unanswered. *Where* did Stacy want to get married? If she did want to… but please, she must, and oh, how he was hoping it was Switzerland. But that was a discussion for him and Stacy alone. Rico rubbed his hands together, feeling like a caricature of a magnanimous host as he spoke.

'Tell you what. We'll grab a bottle of fizz and go up and toast the birthday boy. Champagne for breakfast will be a great start to the celebrations.'

Chapter Nine

Friday, 18th May

Alex tidied some brochures a guest had left on the desk into a small bundle and slid it into a drawer. Come to think of it, the hotel didn't have a stand for brochures here at reception. The idea might have been discarded for some reason, but it was something he could ask Stacy or Rico about. Most hotels displayed the local tourist attractions in the hallway, or on the coffee table or something. He glanced over to the sofa where the Moretti family had sat. It was dry now, and thankfully before he'd had to stop anyone sitting on it.

He glanced at his watch; half past ten, and the hallway was empty. Four days had taught Alex there was usually a lull around this time. Guests had left for the day or were relaxing in the spa or the garden, and it was too early for people to be thinking about coming in for lunch. His phone buzzed in his pocket as a message came in. Ah – Zoe. He'd left her asleep in bed this morning. Hotel receptionists didn't have five-day, eight-to-five jobs, and neither did musicians, and this week anyway, their days off didn't match. He took his phone into the office and perched on the edge of a chair, his finger hovering over the message. Zoe only messaged him at work when something momentous had happened, so ten to one this was her audition date in Zurich.

It was. *Audition Fri June 1st 15.00. Any chance you're free?* Alex's throat closed. She wanted him to go with her. Did that mean she saw a future for them afterwards, even if she was working in Zurich and he was still here by the lake? They hadn't talked about what would happen if she got the job. Zoe was one of those people who lived today; planning for 'what if' wasn't a concept for her. Alex tapped: *I'll see what I can do*. He added two kisses and pressed 'send'. Three purple hearts came back in reply, and he touched them with one finger. That was Zoe.

The lift doors pinging open had him striding efficiently back to the desk – and just as well, because Stacy was heading his way.

'Hi, Alex. The Morettis are sorted, shampooing as we speak, and I have a number for a woman who works in services for people in housebound situations. Margrit – you know, the other spa nurse – gave me her name. Your mum isn't over sixty, is she? That seems to be the age where adult services turn into senior services.'

Alex twiddled with a pen. 'No, Ma's fifty-eight. It would be good to hear what your contact thinks, but you won't give her Ma's name, will you? I think there's a real danger she'd block off everything if we try to push her. She'd hate people talking about her.' And maybe this whole idea was a mistake. He squinted at Stacy.

'I won't name her, I promise. We'll find out first what's available and what's possible, then we can sit down together and decide what you want to do, if anything. Okay?'

'Okay. Thanks, Stacy. I appreciate you taking the trouble.'

'It's a phone call. I imagine she'll direct me somewhere

else to make enquiries, so I'll get back to you about it at the beginning of the week. This weekend's going to be manic!'

She shot him a smile and vanished into the restaurant. Alex doodled on the pad beside the phone. Whatever they did about his mother would need to be planned carefully, or Ma would simply go on strike. She had her life well organised for staying at home, and it would take a pretty big shove to get her out and about again when she didn't want to.

He spent the next few minutes helping a couple of guests who'd been having coffee on the terrace and somehow managed to mislay their room key between there and the third floor. It was a pity Lakeside didn't have the key card system for locking doors – cards were easily replaced, and those clunky metal keys on wooden hangers must have been around since the place was built. Eventually, one of the bar staff found the key under the breakfast buffet, and the couple departed upstairs. Alex went into the office for a swig from his water bottle and came out again to find Timea Roberts approaching the desk, and wow... She could have been on her way to a photoshoot for a fashion mag. Her shiny dark hair was piled on top of her head, and her dress – white with enormous red poppies – hugged her figure in all the right places. It wasn't an outfit everyone could have carried off, but Timea was rocking it.

She gave him a beaming smile, eyelashes fluttering all over the place.

'Hi, um, Alex – can you do me the most massive favour?'

Faint alarm bells sounded. Alex put on his best smiley-receptionist expression. 'Let's have some details, then.'

More eyelashes. 'There's a train to Rorschach Harbour at twenty to, isn't there?'

Alex didn't need a timetable to answer that. There were

only four departures an hour from Grimsbach and he knew the times by heart.

'Yes, that's right.' That wasn't the massive favour, though, was it? She could have looked that up on her phone.

'Alonzo and I are going, um, into town. He's working tonight, so we'll be back by five. If Mum and Dad ask, you can tell them I've gone shopping in Rorschach, can't you? Thanks so much!'

She plonked down her room key and ran outside before Alex had a chance to reply. He scratched his head, trying not to laugh. She'd played that well. Now he could truthfully say she'd asked about trains to Rorschach, but if that was where Timea and Alonzo were off to, he would eat every key in the hotel… 'Into town' would mean St Gallen at least, and Alonzo's flashy sports car could have them in Zurich in no time, too.

The lift pinged open not two minutes later, and Alex braced himself for the rest of the Roberts family, but it was Rico and Stacy with her parents. They gave him a wave on their way out, and Alex relaxed again. Being on reception was interesting; the world and his wife passed by while you watched…

He had to wait another half hour before the Roberts caught up with the fact that their daughter was no longer in the building. They barged out of the lift and headed straight for the terrace, and judging by the tone of voice and uptight body language it was Mr Roberts who was more upset. Alex straightened his shoulders. Deep breath and brace… they'd soon be back. And here they were.

'Does my daughter have a spa appointment this morning?'

Mr Roberts spoke before he was halfway across the hall, and annoyance flared in Alex. You didn't expect, 'Excuse me, could you possibly tell me…' with every query, but a 'hello' or at least a smile was still the norm, wasn't it? Timea's father sounded like a parody of a sergeant major on an off day.

'I'll check that for you.' Alex took his time staring at the computer screen, then turned back to the couple. Mr Roberts was scowling and tapping his fingers on the desk, while his wife was wringing her hands together, her chin wobbling.

'No, she doesn't. Come to think of it, she asked me about trains to Rorschach a while ago. I guess she's gone shopping?'

Mr Roberts flinched. 'Was she alone?'

Alex managed to look surprised. 'She was alone, yes.'

Mrs Roberts pulled at her husband's arm. 'Come along, dear – we'll drive along to Rorschach. It's not a big place, we have a good chance of finding her.'

Mr Roberts strode off without a word, and the couple exited the hotel, leaving Alex with guilty apprehension churning around in his stomach. He'd done his best for Timea, but maybe he shouldn't have…

Chapter Ten

Friday, 18th May

The weatherman had got it right – this was the hottest day yet. Rico drifted along the shopping mall, not looking at anything in particular – it was enough that he was inside out of the stifling afternoon heat. Air-conditioning rocked. The shopping centre was a mile or two outside St Gallen, and as far as he could see, Janie and John were enjoying their afternoon looking at what Janie called 'proper Swiss shops' and oohing over the prices. He hadn't heard a word about weddings all afternoon, and Stacy was looking more relaxed, too.

They stopped at a stationery shop for Janie and John to dissect the window display before going in for a browse. Rico grinned. Everyone enjoyed a touch of busman's holiday, didn't they? Stacy was hovering by a stand of cards near the door, and he went to join her.

'I think Dad's had a word to Mum about being more positive,' she said. 'He's looking happier, too – I guess he did just need a holiday.'

Rico nodded. She didn't sound convinced about her dad, but she was right about Janie. Thankfully.

'Well, whatever he's said has worked,' he said. 'I'm glad

– it would be awful if there was an atmosphere on Dad's birthday.'

And much as he hated to admit it, this 'families all together' thing was a lot trickier than he'd ever dreamt it would be. The two sets of parents appeared to be dead set on *not* being together. Ralph had gone with Julia and Guido to visit some elderly cousins who lived a few miles up the Rhine valley and weren't able to come to tonight's party, so this was yet another afternoon of no contact between the Webers and the Townsends. The way things were looking, his father and Stacy's people were never going to be bosom buddies. Did that matter? Rico wasn't sure.

'I'll speak to Mum again tomorrow or Sunday,' said Stacy. 'I'd hate to think she's been making herself miserable about something we could fix by having a quick chat. Let's make a point of taking time to ourselves tomorrow to talk about the wedding, then I'll pass on whatever we decide to Mum. She's not going to be truly happy until she can start planning. Mother of the bride, and all that.'

A little smile was pulling at her mouth, and Rico hugged her, unable to stop the shadow falling over his day. She wanted to get married, but that had sounded as if Janie would be planning a big wedding in England. Rico swallowed. A Swiss party without a wedding would be possible, and yes, it would be fun – but it wouldn't be the same, would it?

'My goodness – doesn't Germany look close today?'

Janie sat straight in the back of Rico's car as he drove back down the motorway. It was busy today; he needed all his concentration to manoeuvre around the three lanes.

Stacy twisted round in the passenger seat. 'That's the

Föhn effect. I don't think I've ever seen it look as close as this, though.'

John was staring too. 'I thought the Föhn was a wind? It isn't windy.'

'It's more the air pressure conditions that lead to wind,' said Rico, overtaking a coach. 'The storm'll probably hit us later tonight, so let's hope it isn't until after the party, or we'll all have to grab our plates and run inside.' A glance in the rear-view mirror showed him John and Janie exchanging dubious glances, and okay, stormy weather didn't seem likely when you looked at this perfect sky. But deceptive was the word that came to mind when Föhn was around. Rico crossed his fingers.

Back at the hotel, they walked through the front door straight into a loud and acrimonious discussion in the front hall. Alex was on the front side of the desk with a brick-red face, flapping his hands, while the entire Roberts family and Alonzo, one of the bar staff, stood shouting at each other. Several other guests were hovering in the background.

'…and I won't have it!' Mr Roberts grabbed Timea's arm, and she wrenched it free.

'Let go! I'm not a child and you can't treat me like one!'

Alonzo stepped forward, and Mr Roberts raised a hand as if to push him back.

Rico, frozen to the spot for a second, marched up. 'Stop this immediately! Mr Roberts, Alonzo, please calm down. Can everyone who isn't involved here please leave.' Shit, he'd never had to yell at people in the hotel before. A few guests shuffled off, and Rico turned to the group that was left. Some super-fast thinking was called for here. How could seemingly normal, decent people behave like this? A punch-up between a guest and one of the staff was the last thing they needed.

Out of the corner of his eye he saw Stacy ushering her parents into the lift then coming back to deal with a guest wanting something at reception. Timea was sniffing into a tissue while her father and Alonzo glared murderously at each other and Mrs Roberts was wringing her hands as if she was warming up to strangle someone. The best thing would be to get these people right out of reception.

Rico spun round. 'We'll take this into the office. This way. You too, please, Alex.' He led the Roberts family and Alonzo into the office, which was pretty full by the time Alex squeezed in at the back.

Rico stood struggling to find the right words, and it wasn't easy finding the right tone of voice, either. He was too young to be fatherly, and although he was seething about the scene he'd just witnessed – how long had they been yelling at each other like that? – anger wasn't the right response. He opted for calmly neutral. 'What's the problem? Timea? Are you all right?'

She was scowling, rubbing her arm where her father had grabbed it. 'Alonzo and I went shopping this afternoon. My father thinks he can forbid me to go out alone.'

Rico gaped at Alonzo. He'd been here since the start of the summer season, and he seemed like a perfectly normal, reasonable guy. The guests liked him, and hell, this was awkward. He couldn't dictate what his staff did in their free time, could he? He'd taken Stacy and Emily on outings when they were here as guests last year.

Alonzo's mouth was a thin slash. 'Timea and I went to St Gallen, and then we came back. I don't think we did anything wrong.'

'And you didn't know where Timea was?' Rico turned to

the Roberts, who were standing there with pursed lips, though Mrs Roberts had gone a bit red, too. A guilty conscience?

Mr Roberts cleared his throat. 'No. The receptionist thought she'd gone to Rorschach. We went looking for her there.'

Rico went back to Timea. 'Why didn't you tell your parents where you were going?'

This was beginning to feel like an episode of something on TV that you never got to the end of.

'Because they'd have stopped me. But the minute I'm eighteen, I can do what I want, you know. Alonzo, I'm sorry you were dragged into this. And I'm sorry we made such a noise in the hall. I'm going to my room.' Timea grabbed the shopping bags she'd dropped on the floor, and left.

Rico jerked his head at Alonzo, who followed her out. Alex's face was tripping him, and Rico went over to stand beside him.

'It sounds as if it was a misunderstanding,' he said, mentally crossing his fingers. 'Mr and Mrs Roberts, perhaps you can organise something with Timea that gives her enough freedom and leaves you knowing where she is? I know it isn't easy with teenagers, but as she says, she's almost an adult.'

Mr Roberts inclined his head. 'I apologise for my daughter. There will be no such scenes in future.'

'That's all we want.' Rico walked with them to the lift. 'I'm sure you'll come to an agreement with Timea. She's a nice girl.'

The lift departed, and Rico turned back to Alex, who was behind the desk again. Stacy was nowhere to be seen. 'What made you think she was in Rorschach?'

Alex wiped his forehead on his sleeve. 'She asked about

the train times before she left. Alonzo wasn't with her then.' He was still red.

Rico gave up. Interrogating Alex wouldn't solve anything. 'Okay – you can get off now, and I'll mind the desk until Maria arrives. Go and have a cold drink before you go home. Your first week ended with a bang, didn't it? But well done, at least you stopped it getting physical.' He clapped Alex on the shoulder, and the younger man shot off towards the terrace.

Rico went into the computer and opened the Roberts' registration file. Hm. Timea Roberts was eighteen… next Monday. There could be stormy times ahead for the little family. And as they were staying here until the weekend after the birthday, there could be stormy times ahead for Lakeside, too.

Stacy was out of the shower and trying to decide between a blue and a yellow top when Rico arrived back in the flat. He came into the bedroom and flopped down on the bed, his expression more resigned than flustered or angry. By the look of him, you'd never guess he was on holiday…

She blew him a kiss. 'Holidays at home are the best, aren't they? You can really switch off and forget all the day-to-day, running a hotel stuff. Seriously, did you manage to prevent murder and sudden death down there?'

He grabbed her hand and pulled her down beside him. 'Only just. I can understand the Roberts were worried, but they seem to be trying to keep Timea on an extremely tight rein and she's not letting them.'

Stacy leaned against him. 'I know. I spoke to her and Alonzo when they came out, and she said she won't sneak off again. She's eighteen next week – I was wondering if we should do something? A birthday breakfast, maybe? I think I'll have a word with her mother tomorrow when they've all calmed down, ask about the birthday and smooth things over a bit more. Timea said her mum's still worried about her health – the poor kid had complications after pneumonia last year, but she was given the all-clear months ago.'

Rico heaved himself up. 'Do that. Tomorrow. But for now, get your glad rags on, woman. We have a party to go to.' He vanished into the shower.

Stacy pulled the blue top over her head and reached for her perfume. It was lovely to get all dressed up – tonight was going to be brilliant. This was the best kind of party, not huge, but all the people Ralph cared most about were coming. Intimate, that was the word. They'd sectioned off part of the terrace bar for the twenty guests, who were arriving after six for a meal at seven. And how lucky were they with the weather? Föhn or not, it was wall-to-wall hot sunshine, ideal for an evening meal outside.

By quarter to seven, the guests had all arrived and were mingling on the wooden decking of the bar. Stacy jumped as Rico nudged her, nodding at the place beyond the terrace where the garden merged into a stony beach and then the lake. Her heart thumped. What the–? It was hard to believe what her eyes were telling her – a good two metres of beach had disappeared below innocuous blue water since yesterday. Stacy shivered. Not good, Lake Constance, not good at all…

A warm breeze was blowing over the terrace as the guests took their places at the long table, with Rico and Stacy and her parents at one end, Guido and Julia at the other, and Ralph in the middle with everyone else in between.

'Goodness!' said Janie, lifting her face to the wind. 'This

isn't just a warm wind, it's hot! How funny.'

'That's Föhn for you,' said Rico. 'It'll get worse, too, I'm afraid.'

Stacy looked up at a perfect sky. White clouds were forming on the horizon, and they weren't your harmless powder-puff ones, either. These guys meant business.

She turned to Rico. 'Do you think the weather'll hold for the party?' How awful if it didn't.

He held up crossed fingers.

Ralph got to his feet to say a few words, and Stacy relaxed again. It was lovely to have Ralph at Lakeside, surrounded by friends in the hotel where he and Rico's mum had been so happy. Beside her, Rico was blinking hard as his father talked about their years of managing the hotel, and Stacy moved her leg to touch Rico's under the table.

'She's with us in spirit,' she whispered. It was true, too. If Edie was anywhere in spirit, it would be Lakeside. A lump rose in Stacy's throat – how she wished she'd known Rico's mum. And thank heavens, Ralph had moved on to a couple of funny stories about retirement in Lugano, and Rico was smiling again.

The waiters brought out the starter, mushroom and cheese crostini with a salad garnish, and Stacy smiled at her father as he made a start on his. Dad did enjoy his food, and the chef here made even something simple like this taste divine. And once they had this party safely behind them, she was going to make a point of snaffling Dad for a father-daughter chat. Just because he was looking better didn't mean the problem, whatever it was, had gone. Holidays had a habit of letting you ignore what was going on in your everyday life. But by the look of things, whatever was up with Dad wasn't anything physical, which was a huge relief.

Most of the guests knew each other, and chatted and kidded away briskly, with Ralph beaming in the middle. After the starter plates had been cleared away, he announced that he wanted to speak to all his guests during the meal, and everyone except him, Rico, Stacy, Guido and Julia should rotate five places after each course.

'Take your glasses!' he said, and the guests shuffled round good-naturedly.

Stacy's new neighbours were a hotel-keeping couple from Rorschach, and Karen, the ex-head receptionist and her husband. Oops – this might not be easy. Stacy gave Karen a tentative smile. The two of them hadn't seen eye to eye during the Lakeside renovation phase, but the older woman seemed to have mellowed since becoming a grandmother. Talk during the polenta and beef main course was all about babies. Stacy swallowed her last mouthful and sat back.

'So when are you two planning a family?' asked Karen, who was busy showing off the collection of baby photos on her phone.

Stacy laughed. It was an odd thought – a baby. 'We've got a wedding to plan first!' She glanced at Rico, and heck, what was he looking so uncertain about? Hadn't they agreed that they did both want to get married? They did both want to, didn't they? Oh, glory.

'Ro – tate!' yelled Ralph, and the guests obeyed. Stacy was glad of the chance of a different topic, and settled down to ice cream cake with two couples Rico's parents had been friends with all his life.

By the time they reached the coffee stage, the breeze had become a wind, still warm – warmer, even, and you could hear waves slapping against the landing stage further along the garden. Darkness had fallen, and the lights of Germany on the opposite bank looked almost close enough to touch. Yellow storm warning lights were flashing all the way round the lake, too. You didn't want to be out on a boat in this weather.

Something brushed across her leg under the table, and she peered down. The white cat glared up at her. If a cat could look baleful, this one did. She bent to give it a finger to sniff.

'You should go home, puss. It's going to rain soon.'

The cat streaked off in the direction of the boathouse, and Stacy sat straight. Hopefully the poor thing had a home to go to, because the storm was going to start any time. A rumble of thunder in the distance confirmed the thought the moment it entered her head.

The waiters were doing the rounds with second coffees and more liqueurs now, and Rico put his head next to Stacy's.

'We're in for a big one this time. As soon as we can, let's do a round out here and make sure everything's secure,' he murmured. 'Better to check now than have to fix something later in pouring rain. We should lengthen *Lakeside Lady's* mooring chains, too.'

The party broke up around eleven, and Stacy followed Rico down to the landing stage as the last guests were leaving. There was *Lakeside Lady*, bobbing on the waves. The cabin cruiser was higher in the water than she'd been this afternoon, even, and–

Ten yards from the boat, Stacy jerked to a stop. She was walking in water.

It was happening. Flood waters were creeping towards his lovely new hotel, and it was going to get a whole lot worse before it got better. Rico swung round to Stacy, who was struggling out of her sandals.

'Leave them on, Stace. You don't want to tread on anything sharp that's been washed around in the water. Can you go back to the terrace and get them to make sure everything moveable's inside, and ditto for the rest of the garden? I'll deal with the boat.'

'Be careful, Rico.'

She fled, and Rico paddled on, the first heavy raindrops plopping down around him. He checked the buffers between the jetty and *Lakeside Lady* were secure, and slackened the chains a few inches. Surely that would be enough. He'd better take as much as possible off the boat, though. He gathered an armful of life vests, hurried up the path to dump them on dry land while he went back for the rest of the moveable items like cushions and the boathook, then secured the tarpaulin over the seating area. There, he'd done all he could. The rest was in the lap of the gods – and now the rain was really getting started.

Sirens wailed on the main road as he ran through stinging raindrops back to the hotel, fighting the wind now, his arms full of boat paraphernalia which he abandoned in a corner of the bar. The fire brigade was in for a busy night; cellars in buildings that were even closer to the lake than they were would need pumping. Was it too much to hope that theirs wouldn't be among them by the morning? Trees and branches would be crashing down on roads, and the rivers, already running full with snow melt, would have to carry rainwater too.

Ralph was on his way back up from the cellar. 'Dry so far, but that won't last, Rico. I've switched off the electricity down here. You don't want to short-circuit the entire hotel if the water does rise in the night.'

He clapped Rico's shoulder, and went to stand at the French doors between the bar and the terrace as the heaviest rain Rico had ever seen battered down. Rico joined him, and they stared out wordlessly. The hotel had survived many a storm over the years. Hopefully this wasn't one too many.

Chapter Eleven

Saturday, 19th May

Rain was running down the kitchen windows when Stacy trailed through to the kitchen the following morning. You couldn't see the level of the lake from here, but it must have risen. Hopefully not into the hotel… a quick cuppa, then she'd be right downstairs to see what was going on.

A scribbled note beside her phone was all she'd seen of Rico that morning. *Gone to lay sandbags with Ralph and Guido. Three of us is plenty, don't worry.* Stacy pressed the note to her chest. At least it didn't say, *Gone to bail out the cellar...* Heaven knows what time Rico had got up. It was awful; he was the love of her life and she never woke up beside him these days. He was so uptight about the hotel's problems, and with all the parents added to the mix, their relationship was being shoved into second or even third place. Rico was the type to brood, too. No wonder they were having communication problems, and Mum with her wedding agenda wasn't helping. Stacy sipped grumpily, glancing at the clock on the microwave. She was supposed to be meeting Mum and Dad for breakfast at nine, but it wasn't even half past seven yet and she was starving. She'd have something now, and join her parents for a coffee – which would be in the restaurant today. The terrace would be afloat in all that rain. And hopefully not literally.

Julia came in clutching a magazine. 'Where is everyone?'

'Laying sandbags. Rico left a note to say they wouldn't need us, though – three's enough, apparently.'

'Sweet,' said Julia. 'At least you got a note.'

Stacy met her eyes, and they giggled.

The sound of children laughing was coming from the bikers' flat when she set off downstairs in search of Rico. Oops, she hadn't checked on the Moretti family again. Might be an idea to see if they were coping. She knocked on the door on the other side of the fourth-floor landing.

'Hallo! Sorry, too much noise.' The young father looked much more cheerful today.

'No problem – it's lovely to hear them enjoying themselves,' said Stacy warmly. 'Are you okay with the shampoo and so on?'

'Yes – my daughter hates the combing, but we do it anyway. The rest of us, we are fine. Home tomorrow.'

It was as well they had the run of the flat, thought Stacy, as she carried on downstairs. Being stuck in a hotel bedroom with two small kids and a bottle of anti-louse shampoo wouldn't have been much fun. She opened the door into the reception area and was immediately met by a humming noise. Stacy stood still. Oh no – was that what she thought it was? She charged round to the cellar stairs where the sound was coming from.

Ralph was on his way up, followed by a fireman. 'We're pumping,' he said, patting her shoulder as he reached the top. 'It pushed up through the drains. Don't look so worried, Stacy. There was about five centimetres, but it's nearly gone now and the pump will keep it like that.'

'We'll be round regularly to check you,' said the fireman, barely looking at her as he strode to the door.

Goosebumps formed on Stacy's arms, and she crossed them round her middle. This really was happening. The lake – that huge lake – had flooded. How incredible.

'They're setting up pumps all over Grimsbach,' said Ralph. 'He – the fire brigade chap – reckons we'll see the lake rise until the middle of the week, then it'll start falling again. Problem is, it doesn't fall fast when it's this high. We'll have floodwater for a while, I'm afraid.'

'Where's Rico?' said Stacy. She could imagine how worried and cross he'd be right now.

Ralph jerked his head towards the terrace, where fat raindrops were splashing on the decking. 'He's moving *Lakeside Lady* into the boathouse. He's not a happy bunny, but maybe you can cheer him up.'

Upstairs, Stacy pulled on her rain jacket. Heavens, what should she wear on her feet? It was still warm, in spite of the rain, and there was nothing worse than bare feet in wellies. Beach shoes, that would do. She stuck her feet into them and ran back down.

And oh, my… Stacy stood at the door out to the terrace, her heart thumping. The lake had risen dramatically. The path to the boathouse was under water, and they had no lawn left at all. The lake was lapping at the edge of the terrace decking, and the hedge looked like an island poking up through the water. She pulled up her hood and scurried out into the rain.

There was no sign of either Rico or *Lakeside Lady*, so she splashed round to the boathouse. Good job she was wearing capri trousers. Luckily, the water level at the top end of the boathouse was still half a metre below the end of the platform where the cabin cruiser was moored. Rico was on board, attaching the chains to the mooring rings.

Stacy crouched down. 'Is she okay?'

He grimaced. 'She'll live. I wish I'd done this last night, though. The tarpaulin came loose and a ton of rain got in. Took me ages to bail her out. We don't use this boathouse enough, and it's nothing but laziness. Well, I've paid for it today.'

His shorts and T-shirt were sodden, and Stacy had never seen him look so thoroughly fed up. Talk about sick at heart...

She put a hand on his shoulder. 'We'll get through this, Rico. Okay, the weather hasn't done us any favours, but we have a good hotel and good people to help. Not least of all your dad.'

The corners of his mouth were still turned down. 'I'm going to get the boatyard where she spends the winter to collect *Lakeside Lady* and keep her until the flood's past. It's too dangerous, leaving her here when we don't know what driftwood or junk might be washed against her and damage her.' He stepped out of the boat and stood beside Stacy on the jetty. 'It's all such a bugger. Things were going so well, and now this.'

'I know. But this is a once in twenty years kind of thing. Okay, we might lose some money because of it this year, but we're still shaping up to be a lot more successful than the last couple of years, aren't we?'

He didn't look at her. 'But not successful enough.'

Stacy was silent. This was about taking time off for his degree. The maths wasn't rocket science – if the hotel continued to pull in the profits it had made for the past few months, they might manage a substitute for Rico. As things were, the flooding might put some guests off, and there was all the added expense, things like having the fitness room equipment in storage. This flood was an 'act of God', and the insurance was unlikely to cover all the costs.

'Rico – we'll either manage to get you back to uni this autumn, or we won't and you'll have to postpone your course until next year. But brooding and making yourself miserable won't help.'

For several seconds he glared at her, then his mouth stretched in a reluctant grin. 'You could have been my mother speaking there.'

Stacy blew him a kiss. 'Consider yourself told, then. And talking of mothers, mine will be wondering where on earth I've got to. Come on – you should change out of those wet things. Look, the rain's off.'

Rico secured the tarpaulin over *Lakeside Lady*, and Stacy grabbed his hand as soon as he was standing beside her.

'Rico, we're still on the same page about getting married, aren't we? I wish it wasn't so difficult to find a spare moment to talk about it.'

He blew out a huge sigh. 'Tell me about it. I think we should elope, myself.'

Stacy grinned. That sounded like a man who definitely wanted to get married. She stood on tiptoe and nuzzled his neck. 'Let's steal five minutes before we go back in, shall we?

Saturday mornings on reception were more than hectic. Alex pushed his hand through his hair while he was waiting for the printer to spit out a departing couple's minibar bill.

Nearly half the guests were checking out today, which meant this afternoon would be even more stressful, with new guests arriving. Thank God Maria was here to help on the desk.

He handed over the bill, and the guest wielded his credit card. Alex gave the couple his best smile as they left, then turned to the next pair waiting to check out.

Maria was on the phone, and she pushed it into his hand. 'A guest is speaking English – she's upset, and I can't understand what she wants.' She moved over to deal with the waiting guests.

Alex took the phone into the office. Better to deal with this out of earshot of other guests. He perched on the table. 'Hello? Can I help you?'

'I can't get out! The door's locked and the key's gone!'

It was Timea Roberts. Alex's head reeled – how could she have locked herself in her room? The doors were the old-fashioned kind with a mortice lock – you had to physically turn the key both in and outside the room to lock up.

He gripped the phone. 'Don't panic, we'll get you out. I'll be up in a moment with the spare key, okay? Remind me which room you're in?'

'203. Thanks.'

Alex went back to the desk and opened the key cupboard underneath. Oh. The two guest keys allocated to room 203 were both gone. It was a single room so, theoretically, one key should still be here. He thought on his feet – they had to get Timea out before she had hysterics. Housekeeping had keys too, and Vreni was on today. Alex rang the number, but for whatever reason, no one answered. Probably the phone was on the cart and Vreni was cleaning a shower, or something. Okay, plan B. Was there a plan B?

He went back to the office and connected to room 203

again. 'Sorry, Timea, I'm having a problem putting my hands on the spare keys. How many did you have?'

'Two. I put one on the hospitality tray so it didn't get lost and used the other – and now they're both gone! He's locked me in here!'

'*What?* How on earth–' Alex grabbed his self-control before it flew out of the window. They could sort that out later; the important thing was to get Timea out. 'Never mind. Have you tried calling your parents?'

'They're not answering.'

Of course they weren't. Alex tried too, with the same result. Hell on earth. But someone had locked that door, because it wouldn't have locked itself. He called Rico, gritting his teeth as his phone rang on, and on, then Ralph's voice boomed in his ear.

'Alex? Rico's in the shower.'

'I need a spare key for 203. Timea Roberts is locked in, we have no keys down here, and Vreni's not answering.'

'If you open the key safe, and then open the back wall – there's a catch on the left – you'll find the extra spare keys. Some are missing, though. I'll see if I can track down housekeeping.'

Alex did as he'd said. The back panel of the key safe was stiff and he scratched a finger in the process, but eventually the panel creaked open and – result! A key for room 203 was hanging on its hook. Alex grabbed it and ran. He arrived on the second floor to find Ralph and Stacy hurrying along the corridor from the side stairs.

Stacy took the key and knocked on the door. 'Timea? The key's here now.'

Alex shifted from one foot to the other. 'Stacy, do you need me? It's busy downstairs.'

She nodded at him, a grim expression on her face. 'Go – thanks, Alex.'

He headed for the stairs and ran back down. Well. That had been an interesting fifteen minutes.

Stacy slid the key into the lock and turned it. 'I'm coming in, Timea.' The girl was standing by the bed, her cheeks tear-stained and her eyes wild. 'It's Dad! He locked me in – he can't do that! I'm not going back with them!'

Stacy put an arm around the girl and hugged, feeling Timea's body tremble while she told the story of the spare key on the hospitality tray. There was no proof that Mr Roberts had maliciously locked the girl into her room, but someone had, and what other explanation was there? She stared around the room. The hospitality tray held only the usual bits and pieces, and there was no key in the door, either. Stacy let go of Timea and searched around the table and the floor. A locked door and both keys missing... what was going on?

'How can you be sure it was your parents, lovey?'

'He's done it before, in London. He's a control freak and it got worse after I was ill.'

Stacy bit her lip. Over-protective was one thing, but this was a stage too far. She looked at Ralph. 'Can you see if they're in their room, please? 204.'

Ralph vanished, and loud banging on the neighbouring door reverberated down the corridor. Stacy winced. The Roberts weren't there, evidently, and crumbs, hopefully no other guests were having a lie-in. And talking about other guests, she'd left Mum and Dad in the lurch again. Gawd.

Ralph put his head back round the door. 'I'll go down and

see if Maria knows where the Roberts are.'

'Can you tell my parents I'm tied up, please? They'll be in the restaurant.' Stacy made a face at him over Timea's shoulder. Mum would be having kittens again.

Ralph left her alone with Timea, who was sitting on the bed now, dabbing her eyes with a crumpled tissue.

Stacy sat down beside her. 'Okay. You and I are going to have a good search to see if those keys really are gone, then we'll get you some breakfast. Do you want it sent up, or shall we go down?'

Timea's chin jutted into the air. 'We won't find any keys here. And I'll go down for breakfast, please.'

Stacy almost laughed at Rico's expression as she filled him in about what was going on. They were standing in the doorway of the restaurant, where Timea was at a window table having breakfast with Alonzo, who'd been given permission to leave his post and join her, sitting opposite. According to Maria, Mr and Mrs Roberts had left the hotel nearly an hour ago.

Rico exploded, and she pulled him away from the door so that Timea wouldn't hear.

'Holy *shit*, Stace, what on earth were they thinking? Was she supposed to sit in there quietly until they got back? And do we now have to employ bar staff to look after guests whose own family have basically abducted them?'

'I know, it's unbelievable. We have to help Timea decide how to deal with this. She said she wasn't going back with them, but that was in the heat of the moment when we got the door open.'

Rico chewed his top lip. 'They're booked in for another

week, so she can take her time to decide. If they locked her in, she'd be within her rights to report it to the police.'

'All we can do is wait until they come back. Shall we offer Timea a different room? We can easily switch the singles around before the new guests arrive.'

Rico moved back into the restaurant. 'Good idea. Why don't I see what she thinks about that, and you can join your parents? Dad took them up to ours after breakfast.'

'I'll do that. Here's hoping that's the end of the excitement for today.' Stacy waved to Timea, and headed for the stairs. The end of the excitement was wishful thinking, wasn't it? What would happen when Mr and Mrs Roberts came back was anyone's guess.

Upstairs, she found her parents and Ralph looking very cosy, gathered round a laptop on the kitchen table.

Janie looked up. 'Ralph is showing us photos of other times the lake has flooded,' she said. 'Other lakes and rivers, too. We never hear about this at home.'

Stacy gave them a smile and put the kettle on. Mum was engrossed in Ralph's catalogue of natural disasters in Switzerland, bless her. Nothing like gaping at other people's misfortunes… but that wasn't fair. Mum was a kindly soul, and everyone was fascinated by stuff like that, with a kind of 'there but for the grace of God' feeling in the background. Dad was all agog too.

And please, please, she had to get her parents back in a good place about this visit, and the wedding, and Rico's family. Stacy sipped her tea, thoughts whirling. Mum had been so happy and enthusiastic about her fatal engagement to David. David could do no wrong, in those days. What was so different now when it was Rico, who was a hundred times the bloke David Dastardly was?

Chapter Twelve

Saturday 19th May

A watery sun was making steam rise on the road when Rico set off with Stacy and her parents for an afternoon walk through the village that day. After the morning's drama, it was good to do something more peaceful, like inspect the flood damage. Timea was in the spa, and Ralph was on call to be ready for any upset when Mr and Mrs Roberts returned. They still weren't answering their phones.

Two by two, with Stacy and her mother in front, they wandered along the main street, where the inhabitants of Grimsbach were clearing up a muddy mess. Pumps were running in all the buildings bordering on the lake, bringing the floodwater out through fat hoses running all along the street and emptying it into already overfull drains. Rico's breath caught as they approached what was normally a harmless little stream that crossed some fields before passing under a stone bridge and into the lake. Today, it was a muddy, angry torrent carrying logs and branches as well as assorted rubbish. Sandbags were piled at each end of the bridge to stop flood water spilling over onto the road, but it was seeping through anyway.

'I'm impressed how your emergency services are dealing with this,' said John. 'Do you know what the forecast is for the next couple of weeks?'

'Mainly dry, they said this morning. How much worse this gets depends on the remaining snow melt.'

Janie turned round, her brow creased. 'Oh, how worrying. The uncertainty–'

Stacy's frustration was almost palpable even at two metres away, and Rico stepped forward and put a hand on her shoulder as they stood on the bridge watching the stream hurtle down to the lake. What was it she'd called him once? A worrywart, that was it, and Janie was another.

Stacy shrugged his hand away. 'Mum, for heaven's sake, put your Pollyanna hat on. You don't need to remind us. Let's try to play the glad game and concentrate on the few things we *can* do, huh?'

Janie's face closed, and Rico leapt in to cover the aggro that had sprung up. Stacy had dealt with a lot this morning already, no wonder she was tense. He managed a reassuring – he hoped – tone. 'It'll be all right, Janie. We'll manage.' And he had to believe that too.

'Rico's right, love,' said John.

Janie gave them all an uncertain smile, but she didn't say anything else. Rico caught Stacy's eye, and they grimaced at each other. An awkward silence reigned as they walked on to look at the lake path, now under several centimetres of water. Seven or eight small boys in wellies were tearing along it on their bikes, shrieking with laughter as they flung up spray, and somehow, their happiness was contagious. All the adults looking on were smiling.

Janie smiled too. 'This is where my Scottish granny would have said, "We never died a winter yet".'

'I'm never sure what that means,' said Stacy.

'It means that things might be bad, but they won't kill us.' Janie linked her arm through Stacy's. 'And I suppose she was right. Sorry, Stacy. And Rico.'

Rico stifled a sigh. Blue water in the sunshine... how innocuous it looked. And no, a few centimetres in the cellar and a hotel that couldn't function properly wouldn't kill them, though they would make life difficult. But at least Stacy's mother appeared to have given up on the wedding plans – for the moment, anyway. Apprehension thudded back into Rico's middle. It wasn't much fun when you didn't know when, where or how you'd be getting married.

By three o'clock they were back at Lakeside, and Rico went to check that everything that could be done for a hotel flood on the Saturday of the Whitsun weekend, had been done. Monday was a public holiday, but he was going to have to talk to the fire brigade early next week, to discuss the ethics of running a large spa room with four tubs, all containing gallons and gallons of water that needed to be changed regularly. Not that they were short of water, of course; the problem was drainage. For the moment, the hotel was full, with slightly over half the guests this week booked in for the Spa Experience package, which included unlimited use of the dubious tubs, the out-of-order sauna, and the non-existent gym. They would have to look at some kind of refund for these people. Now that the sun had come out again, the guests were all happy enough today taking stock of the novel situation of a rising lake on the premises. Cameras were clicking and no one had complained so far, but that would only be a matter of time. They were still on day one of the flood.

He glanced into the small spa, where the hairdressing and manicure sections were all occupied, and faint music was coming from the massage room across the hallway. These wouldn't be affected, but they were leased out – Kim and the others paid rent per hour for the use of the rooms, and charged their own customers, with Spa Experience guests having their beauty treatments and massages subsidised by the hotel. Channelling people in there instead of the tubs might placate the guests, but would make no difference to the hotel's finances.

Flavia was covering reception now, and outside a few guests were having a drink on the terrace. Timea was perched at the bar with a long drink, chatting to Alonzo. At first glance she seemed her usual bright self, but what must be going on in her head? There was still no sign of her parents, but surely they'd be back soon. Alonzo was primed to let them know the moment Mr and Mrs Roberts hit the hotel, anyway. Rico gave the pair a wave and went back into the hallway, almost bumping into Stacy, who had her car key clutched in one hand.

'I'm off to the bakery. Mum wants to treat us to something yummy for afternoon coffee. Everything okay here?'

Rico told her his thoughts about the tubs, and her shoulders drooped. 'I hadn't thought we might not be able to drain the tubs. I suppose we should refund the price difference between regular hotel rooms and Spa Experience rooms. What a bummer.'

Rico shoved his hands into his pockets. 'Well, if they can't use half the facilities… We'll see what the experts think next week.'

'Yes. See you upstairs in ten minutes, huh?' She ran out

to the car park.

Rico went over to the desk, where Flavia was tidying up. 'Four sets of guests are still to check in,' she said. 'They're all Swiss, so hopefully they'll arrive soon. I–'

The arrival of Mr and Mrs Roberts interrupted her. The pair slunk through the hallway looking neither right nor left, both slightly pink. Rico grabbed his courage and stepped forward. God only knew what kind of messages Timea had left on their voicemail, but he was going to deal with this right here and now.

'Mr and Mrs Roberts? Can you come into the office for a moment, please?'

He waited until they were sitting down, then sped round to the bar for Timea. Her face crumpled the moment she saw him.

'They're back, aren't they?'

'Yes. Look, the day after tomorrow you'll be eighteen and legally an adult. I think we should play this very quietly until Monday. You have a different room, and we'll be there for you tomorrow if you need us. Tell them you're disappointed, but take the higher ground.'

'I don't want to talk to them. I might say too much.'

This was what he was afraid of, a full-blown family feud starting on the premises. Rico licked his lips. 'You have to see them. Please, Timea. Do your best.'

To his relief, she followed him to the hallway. Rico pulled a face at Flavia, and led the way to the office.

Mrs Roberts looked up. 'I'm sorry, Timea, but it was for your own good. We knew they'd let you out, but you have to realise you can't do what you want. You have to be careful.'

'That's not what the doctor said, Mum, and you know it. I'm furious, but I suggest we sleep on this. I'm going to my room.' She met Rico's eyes. 'Thank you.'

He waited until she was gone, then turned to the couple in front of him. 'I'll need the keys to 203, please. Timea has a different room now. She'd have been within her rights to call the police, you know. I don't want this happening again, but I'm sure it won't, so let's leave it there. Now, we noticed it's Timea's birthday on Monday – do you have anything planned? We were wondering about a birthday breakfast for her?'

The couple had both flushed bright red at the mention of the police. Mr Roberts moved in his seat and cleared his throat. 'We were going to let her choose an outing.'

Rico relaxed. Somehow, he'd managed to defuse the situation, for the moment at least. 'A birthday breakfast would fit in with that. Shall we see tomorrow what Timea wants to do?'

Mr Roberts stood up. 'Thank you. Maybe we went too far, but we worry about her.'

'I understand, but she's an adult– or she will be on Monday. She needs your love and friendship, not suppression.' Crap, he sounded like an agony aunt now. Or an agony uncle.

He escorted Timea's parents to the lift, then went back to the bar to give Alonzo the rest of the weekend off. With him in tow, Timea would be well guarded against further kidnap attempts.

Rico trailed back to reception, a slow grin pulling at his mouth. To think he'd wondered if running a hotel would be boring. IT had never been anything like this.

Stacy hurried into the hotel with her box from the village patisserie. These guys made the best torte for miles around.

She was carrying enough calories here to keep them all going for a week, but a gooey treat in the middle of a flood was exactly what they needed.

Rico was standing more or less where she'd left him in the hallway, and she gave him a little push. 'Are you putting down roots?'

He laughed. 'I hope you've brought me double rations. I think I deserve them!'

Stacy listened to the story of the Roberts' return while they were going up in the lift, then stood on tip toe to kiss him on the fourth-floor landing.

'Well done you. Come and have some calories.'

It was lovely to see him looking so pleased after the stress of the past few days, and he did seem to have dealt with the situation very competently. Stacy took her box of pastries into the kitchen. They could see what help or support Timea needed while she was still here, and her parents too, for that matter. She slid the cakes onto a large platter that had originally belonged to Rico's mother, and took it out to the balcony. Guido and Julia were still in St Gallen, but Ralph was there with Mum and Dad, and they were all poring over a large road map of Switzerland spread out on the balcony table. Wow, Ralph was doing a fab job keeping Mum and Dad entertained today.

He folded up the map. 'It's good to see Edie's platter still being used. She used to put cold meat on it – it's a sign of the new Lakeside, isn't it? Same hotel but different.'

Stacy dispensed coffee and handed round cakes. This was lovely, a real oasis of peace. The three parents were getting on well at last, though it would have been better if she could have included Julia and Guido in that too.

Janie waved her cake fork at the building. 'It's a lovely

hotel. You know, I was thinking. A friend of mine was at a spa hotel in Austria last year. I think you could adapt some of the things she did there for Lakeside.'

Stacy felt her hackles rise. Adieu peace... Could Mum not sit still and eat her cake for five minutes without having a go? First she was downright rude to Julia, then she wanted to take over the wedding, and now she was applying indirect criticism. Rico and Ralph both had their faces buried in their coffee cups, so she had to be the one who answered that.

'Like what, Mum?'

Janie hadn't noticed the lukewarm reception her remark had provoked. 'Well, they had special healthy choices for spa guests only on the menu, for one thing. Vegan stuff in particular. And they had a fruit bowl for the guests at the reception desk, and the chef did a talk once a week, about diet, or a demonstration of something.'

Stacy forgot her annoyance. These were really good ideas. A fruit bowl with a couple of apples and pears would cost next to nothing, and would give the hotel just the right look. She turned to Rico.

'Yes,' he said, staring into the middle distance. 'Food talks – and we could expand on that. You could do one or two health talks as well, Stace, and so could the masseuse. Lots to think about – thanks, Janie.'

Janie beamed. 'They had bikes for the guests to hire out, too.'

Ralph slapped his knee. 'Brilliant – Rico, we should get onto that straightaway. We're ideally situated here for bike paths.'

A glimmer of hope ignited in Stacy's mind. This was more positive than a sauna they couldn't use and a defunct fitness room. If they could turn this weather-disaster round,

Rico might be able to start his degree in the autumn after all.

His expression said it all. 'I'll do that first thing on Tuesday. There's a place in Arbon you can get good second-hand bikes.'

Ralph was off in the middle distance too. 'Get kids' bikes as well. And – you could do a guided bike tour now and then, and that could be open to non-guests as well. Or a guided walk, come to that.'

Janie wasn't finished yet. 'They had a lovely spa shop, too. You could sell some scented massage oil and bath stuff in the spa room.'

Stacy almost choked on her coffee. 'A spa shop! And we could include hand creams and make-up too. I'll talk to Kim about that. Mum, you've earned your keep today. These are brilliant ideas. Rico, why on earth didn't we think of all this?'

'The power of brainstorming,' said Ralph, putting his empty plate down and reaching for Janie's cup. 'I'll bring you more coffee, Mrs. You deserve it.'

Stacy leaned back in her chair, ideas for spa shop items whizzing through her head. As soon as the holiday weekend was decently over, they could start. But – improving the hotel was only part of what was going on in their lives, wasn't it? The wedding was the bigger problem, and Mum had such a bee in her wretched bonnet about it. And with the family, as well as Timea and Co, to keep an eye on, not to mention the water level and the pumps and all the other day-to-day issues, there was no saying when she and Rico would have the time or the peace of mind to have a serious wedding talk, which should after all be a happy kind of planning occasion, not squeezed into ten minutes at the end of the day when they were both exhausted.

She stood up to help Ralph fetch more coffee, and

stopped short. Oh God. Dad's face. He was staring at the mountains in the background, his mouth slack, and the look in his eyes was nothing less than heartbroken. And – Stacy's heart thudded. He hadn't spoken since she'd arrived with the cakes, had he? Not one word.

Chapter Thirteen

Sunday 20th May

'Oh, Alex – I can't believe tonight's the last *Fiddler on the Roof* performance. The season's just whizzed by. And goodness knows when I'll get another solo like this one.'

Zoe was hunched over her breakfast coffee mug, and Alex kissed the top of her head on his way to the toaster.

'Next up, your audition, babes. You'd better get practising for that.'

Zoe brightened. 'I've started already. There are two set pieces, and I can choose another, and they'll ask me to play something right there and then, too.' She gazed dreamily out of the window. 'Can you take me up to St Gallen this afternoon? Someone will give me a lift back after the concert.'

An idea zinged into Alex's head and he almost punched the air. 'Sure. Zoe – how about we stop by Mum's on the way there, and you can play her your solo? She'd love that, and it wouldn't take long.'

'Uh-huh. I'll have a quick run-through of a few things now.'

She took her mug into the spare room where she practised,

and closed the door behind her. Alex bit into his toast and chewed glumly. It was as if his life had two halves. One contained Mum and his job and his friends, the other was filled with Zoe. And for some reason, the two halves weren't gelling together. His working life didn't meet Zoe's, their friends were all either his friends or her friends, and moving in their parallel spheres wasn't enough today. For instance, Zoe had never suggested she came and played for Mum – it simply hadn't occurred to her. They were separate people leading separate lives from the same flat. But he loved her...

Arpeggios and twangs came from the spare room as Zoe tuned her violin, and Alex took his coffee to the window. The view here wasn't as spectacular as Mum's was, but you could see a bit of the lake. The usual worry niggled away at him, stronger than ever. Maybe pandering to his mother wasn't the right thing to do? He was helping her to stay at home, but perhaps he should be motivating her to go out and take baby steps back into a more normal life? Or big steps – what did he know? Nothing, that was the problem, and he'd need to tell her about Stacy's plan to help, too – but he would leave that until he knew what his boss was going to suggest.

Zoe's head appearing round the kitchen door made him jump.

'Hey – why don't you stay for a bit at the rehearsal? You haven't heard my solo as part of the rest, have you?'

Warmth flooded through Alex. She did care. She was just – dedicated, that was all. One-track, married to her vocation.

And where did that leave them as a couple?

It was odd, sitting in the almost-empty theatre, watching snatches of a whole. All the songs were performed, but the singers wore normal clothes and not their costumes. The lights were used, though, and it was amazing to see. For her solo, Zoe played at the back of the stage behind a curtain, and what the audience saw was her silhouette as she moved across the stage. Tears came into Alex's eyes as he listened – this was such an amazing musical and Zoe made it even more special. She gave the music an eerie kind of magic that hung in the air when she was playing. He wouldn't forget this, not ever.

What would he do if she went to Zurich?

'She's amazing, isn't she?' said a voice behind him when Zoe's solo and the following song ended.

Alex twisted round to see Phillip, whose injured thumb had given Zoe her chance. 'I know. She nearly had me in tears a moment ago.'

'Mm. She'll go far. We're lucky to have had her this long, and I reckon we have you to thank for that, mate. You're the reason she took the job with us.' He clapped Alex's shoulder and moved away to mutter with someone on the other side of the aisle.

Alex sat rooted to his chair. He and Zoe had met over a year ago at an art exhibition in Zurich, where she was studying and he was spending a weekend with friends. They'd hit it off straightaway, finding a shared interest in city break weekends and jigsaws, of all things. He'd gone back to Zurich the following weekend and they'd spent most of the time in bed. They'd been inseparable after that, and when the job in St Gallen came up, Zoe had grabbed it.

The million-dollar question was, had it ever been more than a stopgap for her? He was holding her back now, and she wouldn't put up with that much longer. Whatever she felt for him wasn't going to be enough long-term; Zoe was aching to return to Zurich and more chances for her music. And he mustn't try to stop her.

Sunday was always a lot less hectic than Saturday in the hotel, thankfully. Rico came up from checking the pumps in the cellar and went over to the desk, which Flavia was manning – should that be womaning? – as needed today. The 'Ring for attention' notice was up beside the buzzer, and all was calm. Good. He tapped into the computer to check what the day was supposed to deliver. No arrivals expected, no one checking out. Even better. A nice quiet day.

The lift doors opened and a forty-something couple came out and moved towards the spa rooms. Rico looked up, but the pair were deep in a hissed conversation in Swiss German.

'...still think we should tell someone.' The woman was frowning. She didn't look as if she was having the most relaxing holiday ever.

Her partner, a tall, broad man with a mop of greying hair, treated her to an exasperated look. 'For God's sake, how many times? It's probably nothing, and it certainly isn't anything we should tell anyone about.'

Rico pricked up his ears. Anything a guest discussed in that tone of voice was worth knowing about, if it was to do with the hotel. He tapped swiftly into the guest list on the computer. Judging by the ages and language, this must be Marco and Jasmin Schneider, who'd checked in yesterday. Rico cleared his throat, and both guests jumped, then squinted at him with guilty expressions. Brilliant. They'd been so involved in whether to complain, they hadn't even clocked his presence behind the desk. The invisible hotel manager...

He gave them a nervous smile. 'Morning. You're the Schneiders, I think? How was your room?'

The pair shot a look at each other. Ah... there was something.

Marco Steiner came over to the desk. 'The room's great. My parents were here seven years ago and loved it, so this was an easy choice when we decided to have a break in the area. We're about to try out your tubs.'

There was nothing about the man's voice to ring alarm bells, but his wife was looking uncertain. Rico put on his best managerial manner. 'The tubs are a new addition, and it's going well. Are you sure your room's okay? Only I couldn't help overhearing...'

Marco gave a laugh. 'Oh, that was nothing to do with the room – or the hotel. Don't worry. We'll be recommending the place to our own kids when we get home, won't we, Jas?'

Jasmin was nodding. 'Yup. You have the best breakfast buffet I've been tempted by for years, and that terrace is to die for.'

She, too, seemed completely sincere, and Rico gave up. The snatch of conversation he'd heard was just that – a snatch, and they could have been talking about anything. Still...

The couple moved off into the spa, but Jasmin Schneider looked back before she followed her husband in. Her face was thoughtful. Rico drummed his fingers on the desk. He'd better mention this to Stacy. It wouldn't hurt to keep an eye on the Schneiders, make sure they really were happy with their accommodation. Some people were reluctant to complain.

Upstairs, Stacy was filling the washing machine, and Rico fished the detergent out of the cupboard for her. Holidays at home strikes again... Next hols, they'd go away somewhere. He tidied a few things into the dishwasher as he told her about the Schneiders.

She scowled at the washing machine. 'Not much to go on, is it?'

'I know. We can't do anything, but let's keep an eye out, huh? Where are your parents?'

'In a hot tub. Rico, can you corner Mum about something to let me get Dad to myself for a bit, later? I'd like to have a chat, and with Mum there he barely gets a word in these days.'

Rico stood straight. Cornering Janie would be easier said than done. 'I'll do my best. Any idea how I could start?'

Stacy winked at him. 'Don't worry. I have the perfect plan.'

'Stacy? What on earth are you doing?'

Stacy pulled the vacuum cleaner past the lift to give her parents space to step out. She'd been cleaning the rooms the Moretti family had used. Housekeeping had enough to do without deep cleaning up here, and they might get some cyclists in tonight, looking for rooms. She explained quickly, and Janie tutted.

'It doesn't seem like a very managerial thing to be doing, dear.'

Annoyance flared up in Stacy. Why did Mum have to grab every opportunity to criticise? She barely managed a pleasant reply, but aggro wouldn't help.

'That's hotel-keeping for you. Anyway, didn't you use to clean the shop, back in the day?'

'That was before we had proper cleaners in every week.'

'Go on,' said John. 'You still whizz round with the vacuum cleaner, you know you do.'

He winked at Stacy, and she smiled back. This was where she grabbed her chance.

'I'll tell them at the desk that the rooms are good to go, then I'll be with you in ten minutes – I need to ask a favour, Mum.'

Janie beamed. Stacy ran downstairs, a picture of the Morettis when they left – dry, deloused and much more cheerful than when they'd arrived – sliding into her mind. Happy family, thanks to Lakeside.

Flavia was tapping something into the reception computer, bless her. She was a brilliant all-rounder, equally at home in the restaurant, bar, and front desk.

Stacy stopped at the front side of the desk. 'I've cleaned the Moretti's rooms, so the flat's ready for bikers. Any idea where the Roberts family is?

Flavia giggled, then replied in German, 'Timea and Alonzo are in the bar – he's totally smitten, isn't he? And Mum and Dad Roberts are having coffee in the restaurant. We've had two complaints about the lack of sauna and fitness room, by the way. I told them you'd see them about it next week when we'd know more.'

Horrors. The refunds were starting already. Stacy put that to one side for the moment. A word with the two senior Roberts was what she needed to do next.

She found them with empty cake plates, and signalled the waiter to bring more coffee.

'On the house. Have you sorted things out with Timea? We're wondering about her birthday.'

Mrs Roberts pulled at her neckline. 'I think so. I called my sister last night and she read the riot act with me. Timea wants to go to the Rhine Falls, and Alonzo is coming too – in fact, he's driving us. A special birthday breakfast would be lovely, thank you. We'll foot the bill, of course.'

'And we'll supply a cake and a bottle of prosecco, and a little present, too. Shall we say half past nine?'

Mr Roberts had never sounded glummer. 'Perhaps you should ask Timea about that.'

Stacy left them to it. You couldn't exactly call them happy bunnies, but relationships between Timea and her parents did seem to have changed for the better.

And if only she could say the same thing about Mum and Dad. But she was going to do something about them before she did a single other thing. Stacy dived into the spa. A quick word with Margrit should fix things…

Her parents were on the balcony when she arrived back in the flat.

'Mum – that favour. Could you possibly pop down and talk to Margrit in the spa about your spa shop idea? She's going to start organising ours this week, so a few pointers about the one you mentioned would be great.'

Her mother was delighted, as Stacy had known she would be. She closed the flat door after Janie and joined her father leaning on the balcony rail. The Alpstein range was caught in haze today, the Appenzeller countryside too. It was another scorcher.

Stacy took a deep breath. 'Dad. Rico's downstairs too, so we can be nice and private. Please don't tell me nothing's wrong because a) I'm a nurse and b) I've got eyes in my head and c) I'm your daughter and I love you. What's going on?'

His head dropped, and for a moment Stacy was afraid she'd pushed too hard. Then he reached for her hand.

'You'd think I'd be happy, wouldn't you? My girl engaged to a nice bloke and settled in a lovely place, my son about to be a dad and my shop back in profit. But it's all a bit much, sometimes.'

Stacy looked at him sharply. 'Are we talking about Mum and her famous organisational skills?'

He smiled briefly. 'I suppose so. She couldn't be more excited about being mother-of-the-bride, not to mention a grandma, but when you get down to it, there isn't a lot she has to organise because of course you and Rico and Gareth and Jo are the ones doing the organising nowadays. Your mum's desperate to do things, but...'

Stacy was silent. They had a prime example of a mother and a father trying to do too much for their daughter right here in the hotel, but you couldn't compare the Roberts family to her own, could you? Yet here she was, feeling antagonised by her mum in much the same way as Timea was antagonised by hers. And unlike Mrs Roberts, Mum had no sister to read the riot act.

'I'll have a word with Mum. And you should too.'

Tears glistened in his eyes. 'She doesn't listen. She means well, Stace.'

'I know, but we have to make her listen. Of course she's excited about the wedding, I am too, and she can organise the Elton Abbey part pretty much as she wants it, but...'

Suspicion was niggling away in Stacy's head. Dad had been married to Mum for over thirty years; he knew her as no one else did. Mum hadn't changed – she'd always been excitable and OTT and they loved her for it. Okay, she'd gone a bit overboard this time, but – was that enough to make Dad look like a whipped dog so often? No, there had to be more than that.

The flat door banged open, and voices in the hallway announced the arrival of the Swiss side of the family.

Stacy patted her father's shoulder. 'I'll make sure I have that word with Mum, huh? And we'll talk again, Dad.'

Chapter Fourteen

Tuesday, 22nd May

Stacy stood on the front steps waving madly as Ralph's car, with Guido and Julia inside, left the hotel grounds and turned towards the motorway and the long drive home to Lugano. Regret rose in a huge lump in her throat. They were gone, and she hadn't been able to fix Mum's relationship with Julia.

They'd spent Monday afternoon on a family boat trip down the lake to the flower island of Mainau, famous for its gardens. But while they'd all been together, first on the boat and then strolling round the island, Mum and Dad and Julia and Guido hadn't done much socialising, somehow. You couldn't expect everyone in an extended family to get on, and nothing would be easier than making sure the two women didn't often meet, but… it would have been nice to feel that Mum and Julia at least liked each other. Stacy slumped as she followed Rico back inside.

The other problem was, not having expected her parents to be here this week, she was working, and she hadn't been able to find someone to take on all her shifts in the tub room. Margrit, the other spa nurse, had taken over yesterday, but that didn't work every day. Stacy sighed. She wouldn't be able to clean Julia and Guido's room until lunchtime. On the upside, Mum and Dad could move upstairs whenever the room *was* ready, which would please Mum. Maybe things would feel easier when they were all in the same flat.

Rico walked back inside with her. 'What are your parents doing this morning?'

'Spa morning, while the tubs are still operational, followed by lunch out somewhere. I'm glad they're up for getting out and about by themselves. I'll call the bike place, if you like, and if they have bikes that would suit us, Alex can hire the minibus at the garage and collect them this afternoon while I keep an eye on reception for him.' Stacy smiled at the receptionist. He was looking a bit fraught, but then it was a busy morning, with several sets of guests checking out after the Whitsun weekend.

Rico tapped into the bike shop's web page on his phone. 'It's a big place. I don't see a few second-hand bikes being a problem for them. You could get some trail maps of the area, too. No, scrap that – we can suss out some good routes and make our own maps.'

Stacy jotted this down in her notebook then returned to the tub room, where several hotel guests and four locals were in tubs already. It was good to see Rico more positive, and hopefully his phone calls would throw up some ideas about how to keep the tubs running. A larger dose of water purifier to avoid emptying them so often could be a solution, even if it wasn't the natural experience they were aiming for. There was no good answer, that was the problem. Stacy stopped beside Timea, up to her neck in water in the hottest tub. The girl's birthday breakfast yesterday had been a huge success – Timea had been almost tearful at the prosecco, balloons and cake, and Stacy had given her a voucher for two cocktails at the bar and a white T-shirt with the hotel logo on the front. And here were Mum and Dad, good.

'We'll have an hour here, darling, then get the bus up to St Gallen for lunch,' said Janie, leaning back in her favourite tub. 'I'll bring back something for dinner, shall I, and you can help me cook it upstairs for the four of us. I'm not used to an electric cooker.'

'Lovely. But it's five of us – Ralph's still here.'

Her parents both looked surprised. 'I thought he was going back with Guido and Julia?' said Janie.

'That was the original plan, but he decided this morning to stay and help with the extra work the floodwater's making.'

Stacy couldn't help the irritated, impatient feeling rising inside her yet again. If Mum and Dad had bothered to come and say goodbye to Julia and Guido, they'd have known what was going on. Somehow, she and her mother had lost the closeness they once had. It had started last December, when she'd gone back for Christmas and realised Janie was still holding on to the notion that her daughter was coming 'home' someday. The weekend in Elton Abbey to show off her ring had gone well, but of course Emily and Alan had been there much of the time too, and oh, how good it would be to chat to her friend again. It felt like a long time since she and Emmy had been on Skype for a proper chat, and with Mum and Dad here, it would be a while yet before she could sit down and pour her heart out to Emily.

Stacy turned back to her medical room, where a middle-aged woman was hovering by the door. Ah – this was Jasmin Schneider, one of the pair Rico had overheard the other morning having a cryptic conversation about not complaining.

'Hello – it's Jasmin, isn't it? What can I do for you?'

'We had our first go in a tub on Sunday – I don't need a blood pressure check every time, do I?'

'I guess Margrit checked you last time? If it was okay then, you're good to go. How are you enjoying your stay?'

A little frown gathered between Jasmin's eyes, then she smiled. 'We're loving it. This is such a lovely area and the hotel's so comfortable…'

Stacy waited. There was a 'but' coming; she could almost see it hovering in the air between them.

The older woman inched closer. 'But – this is none of my business and Marco says we should ignore it.' Jasmin pursed her lips.

Oh heck, what was coming now? Stacy put a hand on the older woman's arm. 'Why don't you tell me, and if I think it's nobody's business too, we can both ignore it?'

Relief flashed across Jasmin's face. 'That would be good. It's just – I don't always sleep well, and twice now I've been up in the night. I went into the en suite, and both times I heard the couple in the room next door having a really quite acrimonious argument in their en suite, crying, raised voices, and last night there was a bang too, or a thud, as if someone had fallen over. I know everyone argues with their partners, but… I was worried.'

Stacy stared into the middle distance. Whatever she'd expected, it wasn't this. A bit of subtle investigating would be the best thing here. But very subtle, because as Jasmin said, everyone argued sometimes. But not everyone did it twice in three days in the en suite in the middle of the night.

She cleared her throat, trying to sound like an experienced hotelkeeper. 'Did you only hear it in the en suite?'

'Yes.'

'Okay. Leave it with me, and off you go into a nice

hot tub!' Help, she sounded like some starchy matron at a boarding school now.

As soon as she could, Stacy went into the guest list in the computer. The Schneiders were in 103, so their bathroom shared a wall with 104, where a couple called Leslie and Yvonne West were staying. The Wests were here for a week from Bristol, and they must be… Stacy tapped her finger on the mouse, mentally picturing the new guests. Were they the fifty-something couple who usually breakfasted right at the back of the terrace?

Someone called from a tub, and Stacy went back to the main room. She'd have a word with Rico later, and they'd decide together what – if anything – they should do about this.

A round of the tubs later, Stacy went into the medical room to call the bike shop, who were only too pleased to look out some bikes for her. They agreed on a price range, and Stacy went to give Alex his instructions, pleased that her German had coped with the phone call.

Alex made a note, then squinted at her. 'Have you had a chance to talk to your nurse friend about agoraphobia yet?'

Stacy shook her head. 'I did call, but she was away over Whitsun. I'll have another go today, and let you know.'

She waved her parents off shortly before midday, then went to look for Rico – they might be able to grab a moment for the much-postponed wedding talk, not to mention what to do about the Wests. But Rico and Ralph were busy sandbagging the terrace, and Stacy's stomach clenched. The needs of the hotel, not to mention her parents, were pushing the wedding into the background, and if she wasn't careful,

Mum would go back to England and arrange the whole thing without consulting them, date and all. Why was life so complicated?

Margrit arrived to start her shift, and Stacy sped upstairs to prepare Julia and Guido's room for her parents, trying not to think that it would have been more helpful if Mum had offered to do this, instead of providing a meal that Stacy would have to cook on her scary electric cooker. And oh dear, what a terrible daughter she was, thinking like that.

She was heading downstairs again to talk to Margrit about ideas for the spa shop when raised voices in the hallway had her scurrying into reception.

'…all you can hear in our bedroom is that pump! It isn't good enough – I want to speak to the manager!' A middle-aged man was standing with a clenched fist on the reception desk, a woman nodding beside him, and Stacy recognised them as new arrivals from Saturday. Gawd, this was turning into One of Those Days.

She hurried over to help Alex. 'Herr and Frau Schwarz, isn't it? I'm so sorry you've been inconvenienced. Which room is it, Alex?'

'Are you the manager?' demanded Mr Schwarz, and Stacy tried to look assertive.

'I'm his assistant – let me have a look for you. We can get him if I can't help.'

'It's 101,' said Alex, staring at the computer screen.

Stacy went round the desk to look. The hotel was full, and room 101 was on the first floor, directly above the part of the cellar where the pump was situated. Her brain whirred – but thank heavens, with Mum and Dad moving out of their room today, the perfect solution was right in front of them.

She gave the irate guests her best smile. 'We'll move you

to another room this afternoon. Are you on your way out?' Hopefully they were…

Frau Schwarz glanced at her husband, who still wasn't looking happy. 'We're getting the boat to Friedrichshafen. We won't be back until this evening.'

'Why don't you let me move your things for you?' suggested Stacy. 'Then your new room – on the third floor and well away from the pump – will be ready for you on your return.'

'We have things in the safe in room 101, and we have to leave now to catch the ferry,' said Herr Schwarz. He still sounded grumpy.

His wife gave his arm a little shake. 'We can fetch them when we're back.' She turned to Stacy. 'Can't we?'

'Yes, of course,' said Stacy. 'You can collect your new keys here at reception, pick up your valuables, then go on up to your new room. It's 306.'

The couple departed, and Stacy breathed out. That had been exciting, but at least they'd solved the problem. 'I'll pack my parents' things, then housekeeping can get in to clean that room while I'm packing for Herr and Frau Schwarz,' she said to Alex. 'And as soon as we've made the switch, I'll take over the desk and you can get off and pick up the bikes.'

She trudged across the hallway and pressed the button for the lift. No way did she feel like running upstairs right now.

Rico dropped his phone on the kitchen table and stretched, staring out of the window. As far as the spa was concerned, it was good news and bad news. His calls to the tubs company and the fire department had ended with the agreement that the tubs should be used for half-days in the meantime, to reduce the drainage problem. They were going to have to give hotel guests booked in for the spa package a sizeable discount, and as the problem was likely to last for several more weeks, their takings would definitely be affected. *Adieu* master's course for the foreseeable. Bummer.

A bang from the bikers' flat next door followed by loud laughter and a door slamming broke into his gloomy thoughts. It was after four already – where had the day gone? He should check what was happening downstairs.

Stacy was at the reception desk. 'How did the calls go?'

'The tubs are on part-time duty for a bit. Should we make that mornings or afternoons?'

Stacy put her head to one side. 'How about ten until three? That's our busiest time. Mind you, a lot of people come between five and seven, too.'

'Let's alternate, then. One day ten until three, the next, two until seven. We can try it for a few days, then take stock. And the fire service bloke said it would be for four more weeks at least, although they're expecting the flooding to end before that.'

Stacy agreed glumly, then smiled at the four burly young men who came out of the lift and joked their way into the bar area.

Rico stared after them. 'Are they the guests in the bikers' flat? They're a bit noisy, aren't they?'

'Are they? I haven't seen them. Alex booked them in.' She clicked into the bookings file. 'They're from Switzerland and the Czech Republic. One night.'

'Oh, well, I suppose we'll survive. I'd better see if Dad's finished on the terrace. He had to go for more sandbags.'

Stacy was staring after the bikers, and Rico left her to it.

He wasn't enjoying this feeling of having so much to do they didn't have time for the important stuff like having quality time together, or the wedding discussion they still hadn't had.

There was no sign of Ralph outside, and the wall of sandbags at the edge of the terrace was still incomplete. To Rico's dismay the wooden decking was looking distinctly waterlogged, and the lake was set to rise until tomorrow at least. He pulled out his phone and called Ralph.

'Rico – I was about to call you. I'm at the Alpstein. They have an emergency, one of their pumps failed. Can you and Alex come over to help? We need every pair of hands we can get here.'

Rico pushed the wet terrace to the back of his mind. 'Alex is still out buying bikes, but I'm on my way.'

He dived back through reception to tell Stacy what was going on, then jogged along the main road to the Alpstein, an old traditional hotel specialising in Swiss cuisine. They had always co-existed well – Lakeside's 'English' concept and now the spa meant they were never going to poach each other's guests. He turned into the Alpstein grounds and saw a long line of people passing sandbags from a lorry down to the bottom of the garden – which was almost entirely covered in shallow blue water. Yet more water was gushing from a hose coming from the side of the building, hampering the sandbaggers quite considerably. A fireman at the gate directed him into the back of the lorry, and Rico climbed up and set to work. This wasn't looking good.

Chapter Fifteen

Tuesday, 22nd May

Stacy stared unhappily after Rico as he jogged through the front door and vanished in the direction of the Alpstein. A pump failure was an absolute worst-case scenario – could that happen at Lakeside too, suddenly, without warning? Flood water seeping in through drains in the cellar, inching up the walls, damaging the electrics, people from the village running to fight what must be a hopeless battle. Water had no mercy. She listened to their own pumps droning away, so much in the background now she barely noticed them. A couple of guests came to reception, wanting to settle their extras account before their departure early the next day, and Stacy forced her mind back to running a hotel.

By the time the guests had paid and moved on into the restaurant, Stacy's parents were walking up to the desk, red of face but beaming.

'We had such a nice lunch in St Gallen, dear,' said her mother, fanning herself with her hand. 'We went into the tourist information and they recommended a restaurant a lovely bus ride away, right up on a hill, and it was marvellous. We could see for miles over the lake, and it was much cooler than it is down here.'

'I know the place you mean,' said Stacy. Thank heavens they'd had a good day. The querulous tone was gone from Janie's voice. 'It's amazing at night, too, when you can see the lights all around the lake in the distance.' She handed over a couple of keys. 'I've moved all your things to our flat, so you can go straight up and settle into your new room – you know which one.'

'Good. And we're making saffron risotto for dinner,' said Janie. 'I've bought–'

'Oh – Mum, we should postpone that until tomorrow. Rico and Ralph have gone to the Alpstein to help with a flood emergency, so I'll have to hold the fort here in the meantime, because when Alex gets back with the bikes he'll–'

Loud and raucous laughter rang out from the terrace. Stacy froze, but the noise died down a few seconds later.

'Goodness, that sounds rather lively, dear,' said her mother, accepting the keys to the flat. 'All right, then – I'll pop the shopping in the fridge, and we'll have a think about dinner for us three as soon as you come up. Be as quick as you can, we've hardly seen you all day!'

Stacy watched them enter the lift, a curious mixture of frustration and love swelling inside her. It must be hard for them, coming to terms with the fact that their only daughter's home was so far away, but Mum especially seemed determined not to acknowledge that Stacy had a life of her own here. Or was she being too harsh? It was natural they wanted to see as much of her as possible during their visit.

Margrit came out of the spa rooms clutching a plastic folder, which she waved at Stacy.

'I've put all the ideas for a spa shop in here. They're in order of how well I think they'd work for us. Have a look and see where you think we should go from here.' She slid the folder over the desk and returned to the spa rooms.

Stacy pulled out the two sheets of A4 and read. Wow, this was good. Margrit had listed everything they could sell, things ranging from small bottles or jars of salts and other water supplements – glass bottles because they were more environmentally friendly – to more touristy items like local wine or honey and magnets or notepads with an image of the hotel. This was like what Jo and Gareth had done with Mum and Dad's stationery shop. They'd thought outside the box and come up with something a little bit different, and while Pen 'n' Paper wasn't your average stationery shop any longer, it was turning a good profit. Stacy leaned on the desk, planning. They could start small, put a few items on a table somewhere in the spa rooms, see how much interest there was, and expand accordingly. All they'd need to start off was bottles for the salts, etcetera. Nice one. Cheered, Stacy put the folder to the side for Rico to look at later, and turned to greet a couple coming in for a meal on the terrace.

Alex wheeled the last two bikes into their new home in the boathouse, drove the minibus the two hundred meters along the main road to the village garage and jogged back to the hotel, enjoying the evening sun on his back. Being receptionist here wasn't at all bad; certainly a lot more varied than his last job in an engineering company. He ducked into the staff loo to wash his hands, and was on his way back to reception when a hopeful and furry white face appeared from behind a large rubber plant.

'Hey! Puss!' Alex strode towards the invader, but the cat saw him coming and streaked past in the direction of the terrace. Shit. They had a guest with a shedload of food allergies this week, hopefully she either wasn't on the terrace or wasn't allergic to cats too. He stood at the doorway out to the terrace, but the cat had vanished.

As usual, most of the guests had gathered here for a drink before their evening meal. The four young men from the bikers' flat were huddled round a table at the edge of the bar, and Alex noticed dismally that water was beginning to seep through the sandbags in that area. This flooding was bad news for Lakeside; they were going to lose money over it and if the rumours were to be believed, the hotel had been snatched back from the very brink of ruin. Was his job here even safe? But surely there couldn't be much more snow left in the mountains to melt and fill the lakes; they'd had nearly 30°C for days on end. Laughter came from the bikers' table, and Alex glanced at the four young men, who all had large beers in front of them. They were motor bikers, not cyclists, which was unusual for the hotel. The laughter died down again, and Alex did a quick round of the terrace. The cat definitely wasn't here, which was fortunate because Frau Mercer with the allergies was sitting near the bar with her husband. Satisfied, Alex went back to reception, where Stacy was recommending a restaurant in Arbon to two of the guests. A champagne cork popped in the bar as the couple were leaving, and Stacy smiled at Alex.

'It's prosecco all the way this week, isn't it? That's the guests here for their tenth wedding anniversary. Ten years is almost an achievement nowadays, isn't it? Thanks for collecting the bikes, by the way.'

'No problem. Shall I take over here until Maria arrives?' The sound of clinking glasses was coming from the terrace now, and Alex sighed. Would he and Zoe celebrate ten years together? It didn't sound likely.

'Wait – they might need your help at the Alpstein. I'll call Rico and ask.'

She pulled out her phone as male voices boomed through from the bar, singing 'happy anniversary to you' to the tune of *Happy Birthday*. Loud cheers followed, and Alex frowned. That was the bikers, and as far as he knew, the anniversary couple didn't know them.

'Shall I check they're okay out there?' Alex was on his way before Stacy's nod came along with loud cheers from the terrace.

His heart in his mouth, Alex ran outside. The bikers were grouped around the anniversary couple's table, swinging their beer mugs and laughing. They were drunk, and the couple looked both furious and apprehensive. The barman was on his way across the terrace too, and Alex took a deep breath. Firm but good-natured, that was the way to go.

'Thanks, guys, well sung, but let's have some quiet now,' he said, trying to grin and look resolute at the same time. To his relief, the bikers retreated to their own table, slapping each other's backs.

Alex grimaced at the embarrassed couple. 'I'm so sorry about that. They're a bit the worse for wear. Are you–'

He staggered backwards as something gripped his shirt collar and pulled. Horror filled Alex – hell, no, one of the bikers was back, breathing down his neck. The hand slid along to grab his shoulder and shake him painfully while a slurred voice spat in his ear.

'Do. Not. Apologise. For. Us.' The man, a large and hairy six-footer, thumped the table with his other hand.

Alex jerked away. Seconds later, the remaining bikers were surrounding the table, and glasses flew to the floor and splintered. A fist met Alex's head, and he saw stars. Screams came from all directions as chairs and tables crashed to the decking. The bar staff surged forward to grab the bikers, and Alex crawled behind the bar, his head throbbing. He could hardly see out of one eye, and oh God, oh God, a seething mass of bikers, bar staff and guests was surrounding the anniversary couple's table, where the pair were clinging to each other – and the man had blood running down the side of his head. Alex moved towards him, then a hand on his back and a fierce shove catapulted him across the decking, and he rolled under a nearby table.

Quick, quick, where was his phone? He scrabbled in his back pocket then flipped the case open, his fingers sliding on the screen as he tapped, and shit, no – Stacy was being pulled into the middle of that brawl. A scream, and hell, she was down on the decking and–

'Police – quickly! We have a fight at the Lakeside Hotel!'

Rico stood straight, massaging his back. It was over half an hour since he'd arrived, but the procession of sandbags heading down the garden still wasn't enough to build the barrier they needed to keep the water back. More reinforcements arrived from the village and joined the team on the lorry, and Rico jumped down to help divert some of the bags to the cellar entrance. His muscles ached with the unaccustomed heaving and throwing, and heaven help them all if Lakeside landed in this state. Hopefully, that wouldn't happen – the hotel grounds here at the Alpstein were bordered by a now extremely swollen little river running from the hills to the south into the lake, which meant a lot more water was rushing past this hotel than Lakeside.

He wiped his face on his sleeve. Grab a sandbag, pass it on. And another. And another. It felt like he'd been doing it for hours, and Rico had never been so glad to hear a shout from ahead. 'The new pump's working! We're done!' He helped pile the remaining bags to one side in case they were needed in the future, and went round to what was left of the Alpstein terrace, where beer was being served to the helpers.

Ralph clapped his back. 'Makes you realise things could be much worse at Lakeside, doesn't it?' he said in a low voice.

Rico raised his eyebrows in silent agreement, sipping slowly. The cold beer felt good, sliding down his throat. He checked his phone – almost seven. They should get back to Lakeside; Stacy and Janie were supposed to be cooking dinner. He drained his glass, then twisted round as a police car wailed along the main road, followed by another. Rico spared a moment to be glad it wasn't fire engines, racing to deal with a broken pump at Lakeside.

He was about to suggest that they headed home when one of the sandbag volunteers yelled from the front of the building. 'Rico! Ralph! Two police cars have turned in at Lakeside!'

Hans, the Alpstein owner, ran out of the building and spoke almost simultaneously, his phone pressed to one ear. 'Rico – you need to go back. It's a fight – people are hurt!'

Rico pushed his glass into someone's hand and ran.

Chapter Sixteen

Tuesday, 22nd May

Rico connected to Stacy's mobile as he raced away from the Alpstein, but it rang out unanswered. That wasn't a good sign... Please be okay, Stace. He shoved the phone back into his pocket and pelted on, his lungs bursting. Two police cars were parked in front of the front door at Lakeside, and an ambulance wailed up beside him as he crossed the driveway. Rico's heart nearly stopped. Shit, oh shit. Was Stacy hurt? Or a guest, or…? He dived inside, a paramedic close behind him.

The disturbance was in the bar. Rico charged straight through and jerked to a halt in the doorway, panting. Where was Stacy?

Ralph appeared beside him, breathing loudly. 'I'll deal with the police. You find Stacy.' He approached the four police officers in the middle of a noisy crowd of guests and staff.

Rico scanned the terrace. One guest had blood running down the side of his head, and a paramedic was ushering him to a chair. Was anyone else hurt? Heart thudding, Rico stepped further into the room. 'Stacy?' His voice came out a shaky croak.

'She's over here.' Alex waved from behind the deserted bar, a cloth clutched to one eye, and Rico stumbled across the room.

Stacy was huddled on the floor, tears tracking down pale cheeks. Horrified, Rico dropped to his knees and grasped her shoulders gently.

'Are you hurt? What happened?'

She gazed at him with wide, tear-damp eyes. 'It was those bikers. I couldn't stop them, Rico. I made things worse. Now Alex is hurt and one of the guests, and my legs have gone all wobbly on me.'

Rico leaned against the bar. 'Are you okay, though?'

She pressed both hands to her cheeks, nodding, and Rico felt a pinprick of relief in the middle of his fear. She was conscious and talking, though he had never seen her so distraught.

'She got caught up in the shoving that went on earlier, and she fell and crawled back here,' said Alex.

Rico gathered Stacy in his arms, and she cuddled against him. He spoke to Alex over the top of her head.

'What happened to your head?'

'One of them punched me and caught my eye. It's not too bad, though. I can see again.'

'Go and let one of the paramedics have a look. And Stacy needs checking too.'

Stacy pulled away from him. 'I'm fine, honestly. They should check the others first. And I should go and help that guest–' Her voice was shaking.

'The paramedics are doing that.' Anger was flooding through Rico. What kind of person would shove a woman around?

One of the police officers came over, his expression grim.

'One of those bikers has a bloody nose, and I'm sure half your staff will have bumps and bruises, but apart from that bloke with a cut head, everyone seems whole. Don't worry. We've arrested four men and they'll be taken to the station to make statements, but by the look of them they won't be doing much in the way of sensible talking until tomorrow when they've sobered up.'

'Good,' said Rico. 'I'll have their things packed up and sent over. They can pick up their bikes when you've finished with them, but I don't want them setting foot in this hotel again.' White-hot anger coursed through him. A drunken rabble at the hotel was something they'd never had to deal with and he was bloody well going to make sure this was the last as well as the first time.

He stood to the side as the bikers were led out, protesting loudly, then waved to one of the paramedics. 'Another patient for you over here.'

Stacy struggled to her feet. 'I'm not hurt.'

The paramedic came over and took Stacy's arm. 'Let's go somewhere quiet and have a quick look, shall we?' She led Stacy over to a chair behind the bar.

Rico looked round. The staff were busy setting tables and chairs upright, helped by some of the guests, while others had sat down again.

He grabbed a glass, and rang on it with a teaspoon to get attention. 'Ladies and gents, thanks for your help – disturbance over. If all the guests would go through to the restaurant, we'll supply you with drinks on the house while the staff clear up out here. Normal service will have resumed by–' He pulled out his phone. Gawd, it was only half past seven. It felt like it should be midnight at least. '–eight o'clock. Thank you.'

The guests straggled off to the restaurant, and Rico went to check on Stacy. Relief poured through him – she was standing up talking to the paramedic, and she had more colour in her cheeks. And that was the important thing, wasn't it? That Stacy was all right.

Rico came in as the paramedic finished her examination, and Stacy almost laughed. Almost. He looked like how she felt – knackered, but incredibly relieved things were no worse.

'All in one piece,' said the paramedic cheerfully.

Stacy grimaced. 'I'm fine. Apart from my shattered nerves.'

Rico put an arm round her. 'Let's get you upstairs.'

Stacy was glad of the support as they trailed through reception, where Alex was behind the desk, fielding approaching guests through to the restaurant instead of the bar. And oh, poor Alex. The Lakeside reception was going to be manned for a day or two by a bloke who looked like he'd done several rounds in a boxing ring, and lost. All she could hope was it wasn't as painful as it looked.

Rico was beckoning to his father. 'Dad, could you find someone to take Alex home? He shouldn't drive like that. And tell him he can have tomorrow off, huh? I'm taking Stacy upstairs.'

Stacy pressed the button for the lift. 'Heavens – I'd completely forgotten about Mum and Dad!'

Rico hugged her hard. 'I'd forgotten about them too. Oh, Stace. I wish we could be alone for a bit and have that talk we've been putting off for days.'

She nodded into his chest. They could wish all they wanted, but with Mum and Dad here, the talk wasn't going to happen – and Mum was going to hit the roof as soon as she saw her darling daughter, wasn't she?

To Stacy's surprise, she was only half right about hitting the roof. Janie took one look at her and immediately went into 'mother in a flap but coping' mode, fussing around Stacy and ordering John to fetch water, wine, arnica for any bruises, and a cardigan in case Stacy was cold. Stacy relaxed back into the sofa while Rico was ordered to one side, and actually, it was kind of nice to allow Mum to comfort her and take charge. Rico looked on for a few moments, then turned to her father.

'Okay. John, you and I can be kitchen people. Stacy should have something to eat. There's spaghetti sauce in the freezer, and we'll open a bottle of Merlot or something that's not too heavy. A small glass'll do you good, Stace. Dad'll cope downstairs for a bit.'

He handed her father a bottle and corkscrew and went through to the kitchen. John stood in the living room doorway, wielding the corkscrew and barking out question after question about what had happened downstairs. Stacy let Rico answer most of them, aware that Janie was drinking in every word.

'How dreadful, darling. I won't have a moment's peace now, thinking about you working in conditions like that.'

'Mum–' Stacy passed a hand over her face. Bye bye Mum coping. Arnica and hugs yes, guilt-tripping Rico, no. This was so not what she needed.

Fortunately, Rico was up to it. He came back to the living room and sat down on the sofa beside Stacy. 'Janie, it was a one-off. I've lived here all my life. We've always had bikers in summer, and we've never had trouble before. It won't happen again.'

'And I hope you'll make sure of that,' said Janie stiffly. She cuddled Stacy close. 'Sip your wine, darling.'

Stacy accepted the glass from her father. This would go straight to her head.

Rico took a glass too and clinked with her. 'Spag in ten. I'll give Dad a call and see what's going on.'

Stacy inched closer so that she could hear what Ralph said too. He sounded pretty cheerful.

'No problems now, Rico. Is Stacy okay?'

'She will be. I'm making her something to eat. I'll be down soon.'

'No need, son. I have everything covered. I'll join you when we get the bar open again.'

Stacy heaved a sigh of relief. It really was over. Rico ended the call, then ushered her through to the kitchen where he dished up spaghetti bolognese. They all sat round the table, and Stacy couldn't help laughing as her father began a story about Janie's reaction when Gareth and Jo told them they were going to be grandparents. Rico patted her leg under the table, and she gave his hand a squeeze. This was better.

Rico watched as Stacy forked up her spaghetti. The thought of what might have happened to her was enough to put him right off his, but it would only worry her if he didn't eat too, so he did.

Ralph came in and lifted the pan lid. 'All quiet downstairs, you'll be glad to hear. Good, you've left some for me.'

Rico got up to fetch his father a plate. Ralph clinked glasses all round and started on his spaghetti.

'We gave out forty-three free drinks to the guests,' he reported. 'We'll need to give the staff some kind of bonus too, Rico.'

'Double time for that shift?' suggested Rico, thinking glum thoughts about their bank balance. Tonight was going to bring in no profit at all. It wasn't what they needed, but there was nothing anyone could do about it.

'Good plan,' said Ralph. He put his fork down. 'Okay, people, I've been thinking, and I've come up with an excellent idea – at least, I think it's excellent.' He was looking at Stacy.

'Am I getting the feeling I might not like this?' said Rico.

Ralph leaned back in his chair. 'I'm sure you'll let me know if you don't!'

Everyone laughed, including Rico. 'Spill, then,' he said to Ralph, dividing the remainder of the wine among the five glasses.

'Okay. I need to get back to Lugano soon. Stacy, why don't you and your parents come with me? That would let you have a little break, and recover from the upset here. We could go tomorrow – I think we can safely leave Rico in charge.' He winked at Rico.

'I remember Stacy raving about Lugano and the Ticino,' said John, looking interested. 'It would be great to see another part of Switzerland, wouldn't it, dear?'

'I'd love to,' said Janie. 'And it would be so good for Stacy, too, after all this.'

Rico's heart sank to Australia. With Stacy in Lugano, there would be no chance of getting things straight between them. They could talk this evening, yes, but one chat wouldn't cut it, especially with Stacy exhausted. He was shattered too, come to that, and his shoulders were feeling the effects of all that sandbag hauling. He caught Stacy's eye, trying to look happy and encouraging. If she wanted to go, then of course she should.

She blew a kiss at Ralph. 'It's a great plan, Ralph – but I'll amend it a tiny bit. You and Mum and Dad go tomorrow. Rico and I will both come for a day or two on Sunday or Monday. I'm not going to swan off and leave him alone here – and there's nothing wrong with me that a good night's sleep won't fix, don't worry.'

Relief catapulted Rico's heart in an upwards direction again. He leaned back in his chair as Stacy stood firm against the protests of all three parents. In the end, the decision was what Stacy suggested – the parents would go to Lugano, leaving on Thursday instead of tomorrow, and he and Stacy would join them the following Monday.

John stood up and lifted the empty plates. 'You three go and sit down comfortably. Janie and I will do the clearing up, won't we, dear?'

Rico didn't argue. He followed Stacy and his father through to the living room, surprised when Stacy closed the door behind them. She went to perch on the arm of Ralph's armchair and spoke in a low voice.

'Ralph, I'm worried about Dad. There's something big bothering him, but he won't tell me what it is. Do you think you could have a man-to-man word while you're away? He might be more likely to open up to another guy.'

Ralph looked uncertain. 'I'll do my best, but…'

Rico knew what he was thinking. Getting John away from Janie for long enough to have any kind of conversation wouldn't be easy. His thoughts raced. 'The hairdresser on the corner of the small piazza – don't they speak English?'

Ralph laughed. 'They do. Good thinking, son. Stacy, leave it with me.'

Rico stood up. 'I'll go down and do a round and thank the staff, and check all's quiet.'

145

He ran downstairs, feeling literally lighter. They would do this. They'd be okay, he and Stacy. With four whole days home alone, they'd get their wedding plans agreed on and they'd sort anything else that needed sorted, too.

He strolled through the bar and the restaurant, chatting to guests and staff, promising thank-you rewards and organising the clearing of the bikers' flat first thing in the morning. A quick call to the police revealed that the four men were currently snoring in the cells. He stopped at the end of the terrace, where dark water sat where no water should be. The lights of Germany looked close tonight, but the water level hadn't risen much that afternoon. He pressed a sandbag with one foot, and a little pool of water squeezed out, so the lake hadn't fallen, either. The danger wasn't past. He turned back into the hotel.

And now he would tuck Stacy up in bed and start that chat with her. Tell her he loved her, anyway. With new energy, he jogged up the four flights of stairs to the flat, but was met by Janie in the hallway.

She put her finger to her lips. 'Shh! Stacy's fast asleep in bed.'

Disappointed, Rico wandered through to the living room. Ah well. There was always tomorrow.

Chapter Seventeen

Wednesday, 23rd May

The only thing that hinted at yesterday's riot this morning was poor Alex's face. Stacy pushed through the door from the stairwell into the front hall, and stopped dead. Alex's left eye was swollen to a slit, and to say that the side of his face was multi-coloured… well, that was bang on, and it was going to get worse before it got better, too. She approached from his left, and he didn't even see her until she was right in front of him.

'Alex, for heaven's sake, what are you doing here? I thought Rico gave you the day off? That eye needs regular ice packs on it until the swelling goes down.'

He jutted his chin out, then winced. 'It's no worse for me than it is for a couple of the others. I want to work. Please.'

Stacy could relate. Mum had tried her best to persuade her to stay in the flat with her feet up, and Stacy had said more or less exactly the same as Alex had now. She wanted to check her staff were okay, and anyway, she hadn't been injured. Unlike the guy behind the desk.

'Okay, but you're to take time to have that eye iced in the spa every two hours. More often if Margrit thinks you need it. Scoot off and see her, and I'll watch the desk for a bit.'

Alex slunk into the spa, and Stacy took his place. It was almost ten o'clock, and the guests were going to and from breakfast or setting out on whatever trip they'd decided on today.

Jasmin and Marco Schneider passed by on their way from the terrace, and they all exchanged smiles. Marco was a touch tight-lipped, and Stacy watched the couple as they stood at the stairwell entrance, talking intently. After a few moments Marco went on upstairs, and Jasmin trailed back to the desk, frowning.

'Morning. We heard there was a brawl here last night – how awful for you. Are you all right?'

'We had a fright, and one of the guests and our receptionist were hurt, but they'll be fine in a day or two. You're lucky you weren't here.' Stacy paused. What with one thing and another, she hadn't done anything about Leslie and Yvonne West, the couple Jasmin had heard arguing at night.

Jasmin was hesitating too. 'Marco wasn't pleased when I said I'd told you about those other guests. He feels it's none of our business.'

'I haven't seen them since we talked about it. Did you hear anything last night?'

'No. I slept right through. It was wonderful. But – crying and shouting like that, I don't think we – I mean, I don't think it should be ignored.'

'You're right, and I'll make a point of checking with the woman today. If she's…' Stacy hesitated for the right tone. 'Abused' was a strong word to use when she didn't know what was going on. 'If she's having a problem, maybe I can help her.'

Jasmin looked blank. 'Sorry, I must have given you the wrong impression. It wasn't the woman I heard crying. It was the bloke. They were both shouting, but mostly her, and he was crying.'

Shock rippled through Stacy. That was – unexpected. 'You're sure?' It wasn't unheard of, of course.

'Positive.'

'Okay. Leave it with me. In that case, I'll talk to my partner about it first. I'll get back to you if we need any more info, and if you hear nothing, you can assume it's been dealt with.'

'Thanks. That'll please Marco, too. He didn't want me in the middle of any – nastiness.' Jasmin swung round and started up the stairs.

Stacy tapped her fingers on the desk. She had made a dangerous assumption, hadn't she? It was a good thing Jasmin Schneider had stopped by. But why would any couple behave like that on holiday? It was one thing to disagree with your partner about where to go or what to do, but to come and stay in a hotel, supposedly to enjoy yourselves, and then have such an argument that your bloke ended up in tears was unusual. And it had happened twice that they knew of, in the middle of the night. Stacy shivered. Some couples thrived on arguments, of course. But what Jasmin had described didn't sound like your regular marital spat, did it?

Alex reappeared, and Stacy left him to it and took her folder into the spa for a word with Margrit about the spa shop project, her lips twitching wryly. Running a hotel was many things, but boring wasn't one of them, was it?

The tubs were filling up nicely, and Stacy joined Margrit at the back of the room, where they could keep an eye on everything. She pulled out the list Margrit had made. 'I think we should start with the easy things, like the purifying salts – we have a good stock of these for the tubs already. We can buy little bottles for them and get them on sale straightaway. Any idea where we could get those?'

Margit laughed. 'There's a certain Swedish warehouse… I'll have a look on their website, shall I, and if they have anything I can go and get some. Shall we start with fifty and see how it goes?'

'Yes – and get some ribbon or something to make the bottles look funky and spa-like. And some labels and price stickers, and a few marker pens. I'll look and see what other things we can put in them, too – some nice smelly bath additives would be good. Let's aim to get something on sale next week. Rico and I are away from Monday to Wednesday, though.'

'That doesn't matter. Housekeeping has additives for the bedrooms, and the bottles will be quickly filled once we have them. We can put them on a trolley in a prominent position in here. Flavia has lovely, elegant handwriting, so I'll get her to do the labels. We can make a feature of the "homemade" look.'

Stacy made her way back to the front hall. If only everything was as easily sorted as the shop.

Rico listened to the story of the crying guest the Schneiders had heard, then plumped down on the bed. It wasn't what he'd expected when Stacy pulled him into their bedroom for 'a quick word'.

'And she's absolutely sure? I don't know, Stace. It seems terribly intrusive, shoving our noses into someone else's business. There could be something going on in their lives that explains why he was crying in the night.'

'Like what?'

'Like… Illness? Or maybe someone died and he's gutted. You know how stuff like that always seems worse in the middle of the night. And she could be getting impatient and just wants him to cope with it.'

'That sounds heartless too. We could grab him when he's alone, say he looks a bit down and is there anything we can do. That wouldn't be too intrusive. If there is anything off about it, though, he might respond better to a bloke doing the asking.'

Rico wilted. This was so not what he'd thought he was getting into when he decided to run the hotel. 'Okay, okay. I'll do it. But I'll wait until a good chance presents itself, okay? Any idea where they are? The Wests, I mean?'

'On the terrace having breakfast. I had a quick look on the way up. You could do a round of "good mornings" and see what you think.'

'I'll go and say good morning, but I'm not promising more.' Rico swung into the en suite to check his hair, then stomped out. It didn't feel like the best kind of start to the day.

Downstairs, one of the waiters pointed out Leslie and Yvonne West. The couple couldn't have looked more ordinary. Both mid-fifties, both with greying hair, both well dressed and both sipping coffee. Neither speaking, hm… Rico stood at the bar pretending to scroll on his phone, trying to work out what the hell he was going to say to this couple. 'Excuse me, we've had a complaint about you guys arguing at three a.m.' didn't cut it, somehow.

He started a slow stroll round the terrace, stopping for a word here and there and keeping an eye on the Wests. They still weren't talking. He happened to be walking in their direction when Yvonne West stood abruptly and stomped off. Rico blinked. Now that was a little odd. She hadn't said a word to her husband, who was gazing across to the lake. You'd have thought that 'see you upstairs' at the very least might have crossed her lips. Rico strolled on.

'Morning. It's Mr West, isn't it? Is your room all right?'

The man started, then cleared his throat. 'Oh – ah – yes, it is. Lovely. Thank you.'

Rico rubbed his hands together, trying to look as if he was the manager enjoying his job. 'Going to be another scorcher, I think. Where are you off to today?'

Leslie West shrugged. 'Dunno. My wife decides all that – I'm sure she has some kind of plan. We went to Appenzell yesterday.'

'Great little village and gorgeous scenery up there, isn't it?' Jeez, he was behaving like a caricature of your friendly local hotel owner.

'It was too hot for Yvonne. We didn't stay long.' Mr West's mouth drooped.

The guy was trembling. Stacy was right, there was something odd going on here. Rico grabbed his courage before it deserted him completely. He slid onto the chair Yvonne West had vacated.

'Mr West – um, Leslie... You seem a little tense. Is everything all right? Can I do anything for you?'

Now it was Leslie West who stood up abruptly. Rico scrambled to his feet too, and they walked out together.

'Let me know if I can help you with – anything,' he said, as they arrived at the lift. It was waiting, and Leslie West got in with a muttered 'thank you'. Rico trailed on to reception. That hadn't gone well, had it?

It was late afternoon before Rico saw the couple again. Inspired by the Wests, he and Stacy took her parents up to the Appenzellerland for the day, dropping Ralph off at his cousin's home en route. Janie was enchanted by the alpine scenery and the little villages they passed through, and John took about a million photos as they toured around. Rico even drove up the Schwägalp pass to the cable car base station, and they went up for an expensive coffee on the summit of the Säntis, where you could gaze through panoramic windows all the way to the Bernese Oberland on the other side of Switzerland. Stacy took the wheel on the way home again, and Rico smiled benevolently at Janie and John. At least these two were more appreciative about the Appenzeller countryside than Yvonne West appeared to have been.

'Drinks on the terrace in half an hour?' he suggested, as they walked across the hotel car park.

'Good idea. I'm for a quick shower first.' Stacy lifted her hair from the back of her neck.

'Me too. Thank you, Rico. And Stacy. That was a lovely day.' Janie marched straight to the lift, John following silently as usual.

Stacy followed on, her shoulders drooping, and Rico hurried to keep up. Poor Stace. But Dad would get to the bottom of whatever was going on with John. Come to think of it, Dad might have been a better person to talk to Leslie West. The two were the same generation.

'I'll get them to reserve us a table outside. See you upstairs.' He gave Stacy a hug as the lift arrived, then trotted out to the terrace and oh, hell. Leslie West was propping the bar up, a large glass of what looked like whisky in front of him, and by the way he was hunched over it, it might not have been his first. Rico reserved a table, then slid onto a stool beside the older man.

'All right, Mr West?'

Leslie West sniffed. 'All wrong, Mr Weber.' His voice was slurred and much too loud.

'Anything I can help with?' Rico signalled for a mineral water. He'd better be careful here; they didn't want another scene with a drunk and belligerent guest on the terrace. People were shooting them apprehensive glances already.

Mr West took a large slurp of his drink. He burped, and the fumes spread across the bar. Yes, it was whisky. Rico's mind raced – how was he to get this man safely upstairs without causing even more of a scene?

'Never get married, son. Nothing you ever do is good enough, and by the time you realise you want out, it's too late.'

Ah. Tricky. Rico fixed on a sympathetic expression. 'Have you been married long?'

'Five years. I thought she was the best thing that had ever happened to me, but that was my mistake. Worst day's work I ever did, signing that register.'

With all his heart, Rico wished Stacy was here too. She was so much better at things like this.

'I think you have to talk to Mrs West about it. She–'

'She wouldn't listen and then she'd hold it against me and use it to put me down even more than she does already. She knows when she's onto a good thing, does Yvonne. It's not me, mind. It's my bank balance. She takes and takes and takes.' Another slurp of whisky disappeared from the glass.

Rico wiped his forehead. Hell on earth. When this guy sobered up and remembered he'd said all that – if he remembered – he was going to feel even worse than he did right now. 'Is there anything I can do to help, Mr West?'

And unless this man said, yes, you can do such and such, he was going to exit this dire conversation and get Stacy. Mr West gave him a filthy look, then drained his glass and thudded it down on the bar. 'I'll have another one in here!'

Rico shook his head at Alonzo behind the bar. More whisky would only make the situation worse. He was still wondering how to say 'no' in a pleasant, calm way that wouldn't enrage Mr West any further, when footsteps tapped up behind him. Yikes. Here was Mrs West.

'For pity's sake, Leslie, what's this?'

She grabbed her husband's arm and shook it, pulling him off the stool. Rico had to grab the man to stop him falling.

'Steady, Mrs West. He's a bit…'

'He's a drunk. It's hopeless. Leslie – for God's sake, get a grip. And get yourself upstairs.'

'Mrs West, maybe if you talk to your husband… Can I do anything?'

'It's not talk he needs, believe me. And no, you can't. Thank you. I'll manage.'

Leslie West was cowering beside his wife, his jaw slack and lips trembling. Rico winced as the man stretched a hand towards him, then withdrew it at a hiss from his wife. How much of this was down to the whisky and how much was down to fear? It was impossible to tell, but this was where he was going to get heavy.

Rico stood up. 'I think I should fetch my partner, Mrs West – she's the hotel nurse. Your husband may need some help. Am I right?' He gave the man as significant a look as he could, but Leslie West made no reply.

Mrs West's mouth was a thin slash. Seconds ticked by, then: 'He needs to sober up before anyone can do anything, so I'll get him to bed now. Tomorrow, do what you like.' She about turned and tapped off again, her husband stumbling in her wake.

Rico called after them. 'I'll see you tomorrow morning, Mr West.'

Neither replied to this, and Rico took a large slug of his water. Well. Yvonne West was right about one thing, anyway, her husband did need to sober up. And he would definitely check on the man tomorrow.

Chapter Eighteen

Thursday, 24th May

Stacy stood arm in arm with Rico at the front door, waving until Rico's car with Ralph at the wheel and Janie and John inside exited the Lakeside gates and disappeared along the road, en route for the motorway and Lugano. She and Rico would be carless at Lakeside for the next few days, because of course Guido and Julia had driven back to the Ticino in Ralph's car on Monday.

She grinned at Rico. 'Alone at last!' And what a good feeling it was.

He dropped a kiss on her head as they went back inside. 'You, me, a few dozen guests, the entire staff–' he swerved round a couple of firemen in the entrance hallway '–not to mention all the mixed bods that are in and out these days checking the pumps and delivering sandbags…' He scratched his head. 'Have I missed anyone?'

Stacy giggled. 'I think you've covered it. But you know what I mean.'

And oh, how relaxing, they had the flat to themselves. Stacy took the lift up and tidied around the kitchen, making plans for the morning. Rico had gone to see to if Mr and Mrs West were downstairs, but the minute he arrived back they were going to have the biggest air-clearing session ever. Somehow, it was easier to be optimistic now they were definitely alone – the incident with the bikers had shown her how much Rico cared about her, even if he wasn't saying much. The uncertainty that had sprung up between them over the past week or so was nothing more than a misunderstanding. Mum and her wretched wedding plans, that was what had started it all.

She was standing on the balcony when her phone buzzed. What on earth? Rico was calling her... Stacy tapped connect.

His voice was low. 'Stace. I'm getting a coffee for Leslie West. He says his wife's disappeared. He's in a bit of a state, can you come and take a look? We're on the terrace, I found him wandering around like a lost soul, looking for her.'

'On my way.' So much for the air-clearing session...

The two men were at a table near the entrance to the terrace and one glance told Stacy that Rico was right. You didn't need to be a nurse to see that Mr West looked like death warmed up. The combination of too much whisky and the strain of the moment seemed a fatal one, and hopefully not literally.

'Morning, Mr West. Rico tells me you can't find your wife?' Stacy sat down beside the man and put her fingers on his pulse. It was rapid, his skin was hot, and his eyes were bloodshot. A large glass of water was what he needed most now, and some paracetamol.

He barked out a laugh. 'She's gone.'

For a heart-stopping moment Stacy wasn't sure what he meant. Was the woman... No, she must still be alive – mustn't she?

Mr West wasn't finished. 'And she's taken everything with her. Her luggage, our tickets, everything.' He burst into tears.

'Can we take this to the medical room?' Rico stood up, and Stacy helped him support the broken man back inside and through the spa, where fortunately, not many guests had gathered yet. In the medical room, she took his temperature and blood pressure, both on the high side, and handed out a couple of paracetamols along with another glass of water.

Rico beckoned her to the door. 'What do you want to do with him?'

'He needs to lie down for a while. Why don't you take him to his room, then you'd see if his wife really has legged it while you're tucking him in. I can pop up and check on him in an hour or so.'

Leslie West agreed to this, and Stacy went up in the lift with him and Rico as far as the first floor, where the two men got out, leaving her to return to the flat. Heck… What was going on with that couple? If Yvonne was the one doling out abuse of whatever kind, why had she left Leslie here? A punishment of some kind? That wasn't impossible.

Rico strode in ten minutes later. 'He's asleep. No sign of her, and her clothes and one case have gone. I suggested trying to call her when he's feeling better. Their flight isn't until Saturday so she might come back, though God knows where she's gone off to. I called Alex on the way up here, but he didn't notice her leaving. She must have gone really early.'

'Oh, Rico. Let's never get like that, shall we?'

He sat down and gripped her hand on the table top, his expression an almost comical mixture of hope and apprehension. 'Stace – things have been a bit weird lately. What happened to us?'

Stacy held on tight. 'We didn't have time – or no, we didn't *take* time – to tell each other what was going on in our heads. I even wondered if you were regretting our engagement, but I'm guessing I was wrong about that.'

He kissed her hand. 'Totally wrong, but I can see it was my fault and I was doing the same thing. I got stressed about the lake, and the wedding. Let's talk now, though. Stacy – where do you want to get married?'

Stacy barely stopped her mouth falling open. 'Where' was the one question she hadn't expected. She had assumed they'd be traditional and marry in Elton Abbey, but the fact that Rico was asking seemed to indicate he was having different thoughts.

She spoke carefully. 'For me, I don't care. But you know Mum, she wants a big affair with half the village and all the trimmings.'

'That's what I thought. But in Switzerland, you need to have an official civil ceremony too, even if you have a church wedding afterwards. It's different to England, where you can only have one or the other. I'd really like to get married here, and maybe have the church bit in England?'

Stacy frowned, her mind racing. 'Have I got this right – if we had a church wedding in England first, we couldn't have anything at all official here?'

'That's right. What we could have is a civil ceremony here, then a church blessing in England. That's what my parents did.' His eyes were fixed on hers, and Stacy's heart went out to him. How could she have doubted his love?

She tilted her head to one side. 'I don't see why we can't do that too. That way, Dad can still walk me down the aisle, we'll have all the bridesmaids Mum's heart desires and a big reception afterwards. Easy-peasy.'

Relief – mingled with apprehension – chased across

Rico's face, and Stacy gave his hand a little shake. 'Aren't we daft, getting into such a muddle about something so completely uncomplicated?'

'Stace, I have the feeling when it comes to weddings, your mum thrives on complicated. Will she be okay about this?'

Stacy opened her mouth to answer, then closed it again as Rico's mobile shrilled out. He pulled it towards him, then wrinkled his nose. 'It's Alex. I'd better take it.' He tapped to put the phone on speaker, and Stacy could hear the excitement in the receptionist's voice.

'Rico, I've just this minute heard the lake has fallen two centimetres since last night! They reckon another three weeks should see it, um, back in the lake, so to speak!'

Something akin to peace surged through Stacy. When you considered the size of Lake Constance, two centimetres was a huge amount of water. Now all they needed to do was get the hotel fully functioning again.

Rico ended the call and beamed at her. 'Bottle of fizz in the fridge for tonight?'

'Sounds like a plan. And I've had another one – another two, in fact.'

He kissed her hand again, then moved up to her neck, and Stacy heaved a huge sigh. This was so good… 'Stop distracting me. Okay – plan one. We'll tell Mum what we're thinking about the wedding but we'll say we don't want to get concrete about dates and so on until the end of the year. We're in no rush, are we?'

'Sounds excellent. Plan two?'

'This one's business. The bikers' flat. I was thinking…' Stacy lifted a used envelope from the working surface behind her and grabbed a pen from the drawer. 'Before we opened the spa, you put one-night cyclists into normal rooms and charged them normal rates, didn't you?'

'Yes. It was a good way to fill up any empty rooms.'

'Right. And the flat they get now has four basic rooms which we give them pretty cheap for one night, plus they get the use of the living room and kitchen and so on.' She drew a rough plan on the envelope. 'Okay – my idea would be to upgrade the existing bedrooms to our usual standard, and turn the living room into another two. Make them more expensive, and that way we're less likely to get troublemakers like those bikers.'

Rico pored over the envelope. 'Brilliant – you see, this is why you're so good at this. Fabulous ideas all over the place. We'll be getting the cellar spruced up again when the flood water's down, so we could do this at the same time. It wouldn't be a big job.'

He cupped her face with both hands and kissed her thoroughly, and Stacy's head reeled.

'Hey – I'm supposed to be checking on Mr West in about ten minutes, remember?'

Rico's phone interrupted whatever he'd been going to reply to this, and he gave her a wry look.

'Alex?'

'Bloke from the town council here to see you, Rico. They're assessing flood damage.'

'Be right with you.'

Rico's shoulders sagged, and Stacy laughed. 'Work first, play later. I'll put that fizz in the fridge, shall I?'

Whistling, she loaded a few stray glasses into the dishwasher. Right, this was a good day for a long overdue Skype call to Emily back home in Elton Abbey. Stacy sent off a quick message. *Are you around to Skype today?*

Now to see what was happening with Mr West. Her phone

pinged as she was running downstairs. Oh – it was Alan.

Hi there. Emmy flattened with summer bug. She'll call u in a day or 2.

Oh, poor Emily. Stacy stood in the first-floor corridor and messaged back. *Hugs to both xxx* What a good thing Alan was there for Emily.

And she was here for Mr West… Stacy tapped softly, then put her head into the room, but Leslie West was fast asleep with his mouth open, snoring softly. Stacy left him to it. She'd better write up a medical note for him downstairs, though, in case he needed a doctor later.

'Stacy! The new ear thermometer's arrived and I don't think it's working properly!'

Sabine, one of the spa attendants, cornered her the moment she set foot in the spa, and a little flame of happiness warmed through Stacy. It was lovely to be needed. This was her place.

Chapter Nineteen

Thursday, 24th May

Rico fitted out Herr Ammann from the council with a pair of Lakeside Hotel wellies, as the cellar floor was still covered by a centimetre or two of water that the pumps didn't reach. He led the way through the unusable sauna and the ex-fitness room, the pumps a constant drone in the background, but they'd become so much a part of hotel life that Rico barely noticed them now. And hopefully, the same could be said for the guests. They'd had no further complaints about noise, but then they hadn't put anyone in the room directly above the pumps since the first guest had objected.

'In comparison to the Alpstein, I suppose we've got off lightly,' he said, as the councillor made notes on his clipboard.

'You have. It's a real mess there,' said Herr Ammann. 'If that's everything inside, let's go through the garden – or as much of it as we can.'

Rico led the way to the low bank of sandbags at the end of the terrace. Not many guests were out on the terrace at the moment; the sun was having a break and there was quite a breeze off the lake. He peered over the sandbag wall, then punched the air and grinned at Herr Ammann. 'It's retreating!

We didn't have all that grass yesterday.'

The older man guffawed. 'I'm not sure I'd call twenty centimetres "all that grass".' Another note went on the clipboard before they splashed round to the landing stage, where the jetty was still underwater, and on to the gardens at the other side of the hotel, unusable as guests would be over their ankles in mud the moment they ventured onto the lawn.

Back at the front door, Herr Ammann shook hands. 'You'll hear from us in a week or two. There's a fund to help those affected by the flooding make good the damage. It won't be a huge amount, but every little helps.'

Rico lifted a hand as Herr Amman drove away. A fund... that sounded hopeful. And now he would set up a meeting with Andi the builder, to plan the alterations upstairs, and he'd grab the next fireman who appeared, to ask how long the pumps would be necessary – if there was an answer to that one. At long last, things were looking up for Lakeside. And things were looking up for him and Stacy too, and that was the important thing.

Rico jogged inside feeling more cheerful, connecting to Stacy as he went. 'How was Leslie West?'

'Asleep when I last saw him an hour ago. Are you coming up? You could swing past his room for me if you are.'

Hm. Rico jogged on, grinning at Alex on the desk as he passed. The receptionist's bruises were getting more colourful by the day, with green, purple and yellow splodges over one side of his face. That must be painful, but Alex was a trooper. Hopefully he'd be a bit less multi-coloured by Saturday, when the main guest changeover took place. Rico arrived at the Wests' room and stood at the door, listening. Yes, someone was moving around inside. Rico tapped.

The door jerked open so suddenly Rico stepped back.

Yikes. Leslie West was one big scowl – not what you'd call a happy bunny, but then, who would be in the circumstances?

'How are you, Mr West? Do you need anything?'

'Apart from my wife, my tickets home and my credit cards, you mean? This is all your fault.'

The lift doors opened further along, and Rico strode into Mr West's room. He wasn't about to start a barney in the corridor for all to hear.

'Have you tried to contact her?'

'Of course. It went straight to voicemail. And she hasn't opened my message, either.' Leslie West sank down on the bed. 'What am I going to do? I've next to no cash on me.'

Rico took the chair by the desk. It was hard to get his head round someone behaving like this.

Mr West wasn't finished. 'She did the same thing two years ago. But that was in the UK so I could go to the bank and get another card. She came home in a few days that time.' He brightened visibly at the thought.

All Rico could do was stare. Why didn't this bloke grab what was left of his dignity, and leave the marriage a long way behind him? But possibly that wasn't so easy when you were the abused party.

'Can I suggest you call your bank? See what they say as far as the cash situation is concerned, and take it from there. You can have whatever you need on tab from the hotel in the meantime, but if you have to buy another plane ticket… Maybe you should phone the airline as well.'

'All I want is my wife back.'

Rico stood up. This was going nowhere, and he had no idea how to help the man. 'I'll ask my partner to come by later and see if you need any more medication, shall I?'

He escaped, and ran on upstairs. It was hard to be

optimistic about Yvonne West turning up again… Hopefully Mr West's bank would be more help than he'd been.

By twenty to five that evening, Alex was drumming his fingers on the desk, waiting for Flavia, who was doing the evening shift on reception today. His head was aching, but he'd forgotten his painkillers, so there was nothing he could do about it until he was back home. Alex glared at the courier who was coming in the front door, whistling loudly. That was going right through his head…

The courier was oblivious to the discomfort he was causing. He slapped a brown envelope with the logo of a well-known bank onto the desk. 'Afternoon. Delivery for Mr Leslie West. Needs a signature.'

Alex nodded glumly, then jerked upright. Yikes, here was Stacy on her way out of the spa, he'd better not let her catch him drooping all over the place again. His boss did an abrupt U-turn to end up beside the courier on the other side of the desk.

'I'll take this, Alex.' She turned to the courier. 'Would you like to come with me? This is for a guest and it's, um, confidential.'

The two of them vanished upstairs in the lift, and Alex wilted again. Fifteen minutes to home time.

Stacy was back in five of them, ushering the courier through the front door again before joining Alex at the desk. 'Mr West's having a bit of a personal issue, Alex. We should make allowances if he doesn't seem himself.' Her brow wrinkled. 'You don't look great either. Are you all right?'

'Nothing a headache pill won't sort. I'll get one at home.'

Stacy was still peering, and it was all Alex could do not to take a step backwards. Nothing like having your boss gawp at you with a nurse-on-duty expression as she took stock of your bruises. Those bikers had left their mark in more ways than one.

'Poor you, but I rather think you're at peak bruising. I'll fetch you a pill now, shall I?'

She spun round and vanished into the spa before Alex had time to object, and praise be, here was Flavia. He gave her a quick update on what to expect that evening and headed for the staff cloakroom, where Stacy joined him half a minute later.

'Here you go.' She handed over a small white pill and a glass of water, and Alex swallowed obediently.

Stacy perched on the window ledge. 'I managed to get hold of Margrit's community nursing friend today. She thinks your mother should go to her doctor. He can set up some support services or therapy for her.'

Alex slumped. 'She won't hear of that. I don't know how often I've suggested it, pushed her, even, but no. She's coping, according to her. I don't know if I should read the riot act and go on strike, or what…' To Alex's horror, tears welled up, and he blinked furiously.

Stacy was shaking her head. 'I don't think you should, or not without taking proper advice first, anyway. Your job is to be her son, on her side. Let me think about it again. The other thing this woman mentioned was a visiting service. You don't need a doc's referral for that, and it's for all lonely older or disabled people. That might be an easier place to start. They work parallel to the Red Cross. I can give you the number for them.'

Alex hesitated. A visiting service might be more acceptable to his mother. Hope flared in his chest. 'Tell you what, I'll go by on my way home and see what Ma thinks about that. Thanks, Stacy.'

He grabbed his jacket and hurried out to the car park, managing a smile for Timea Roberts and Alonzo, who slid into a staff space as he arrived at his car. Alex pulled a face at Alonzo's back as the other man rushed round to help Timea with her bags. Nice to see a man happy with his girlfriend. Mr and Mrs Roberts were apparently resigned to Timea going everywhere with Alonzo now, and when was the last time he'd had a lovely afternoon out with Zoe? Maybe they could do something next week. But first things first. Alex pulled out of his parking space, his mother's problems again uppermost in his head. A visitor, hopefully a nice lady who would dish out support and advice as well as visiting, might be acceptable to Mum. Might…

Half an hour later, he knew how wrong that was. His mother exploded at the mere suggestion.

'A stranger? Come to visit me like I'm some poor old soul who needs help to cope with her life? I can't believe you even thought I might want that. I'm financially independent and I'm happy with my life the way it is, thank you very much.' Denise turned away, her lips pursed tightly.

Alex tried again. 'Of course you're coping, but I want you to get out as well. Meet people, socialise. You miss so much, staying at home all the time. You'd have loved *Fiddler on the Roof*, for instance.'

Denise stood up, her cheeks blotchy. 'I saw it years ago. I thought you understood, Alex. My life, my choice. Just go, please. And don't come back until I say you can.'

'Ma, whatever you decide is fine by–'

'Go!'

She didn't want him to see her cry. Sick at heart, Alex left, not even daring to hug her as he usually did. He blew her a kiss instead, but she wouldn't look at him. Shit. That could not have gone worse. He drove home, only to find a large suitcase in the hall.

'Zoe?'

She whirled up to hug him, then whirled away again. 'Good, you're back. I'm going to Zurich to stay with Susanna for a day or two – she can help me practise for the audition, and you're working all weekend anyway.'

Susanna was her clarinettist friend who was living the dream with a flat near Zurich. Alex leaned in the doorway, watching as she packed her violin. Ma had kicked him out, Zoe was abandoning him and he still looked like a failed boxer. Life was as grey as it could get.

Chapter Twenty

Saturday, 26th May

Stacy walked through reception, and thank heavens, things were getting back to normal at Lakeside. Alex was at the desk and coping well with the Saturday morning changeover. His bruises were going down, though he still bore more than a passing resemblance to Mike Tyson after a hard match, and most of the guests were teasing him about it as they checked out. Hopefully the new guests checking in this afternoon would be equally unfazed.

Stacy stuck her head into the spa, but Saturday mornings were always quiet there, and she wandered back to the hallway and straightened the brochures on the coffee table. This was a good idea of Alex's; loads of guests sat down here now to have a browse or plan their day. The lift whined into action upstairs, and she started back to the desk. Leslie West would be leaving soon, and after everything that had gone on with the man, saying goodbye personally was near the top of her to-do list this morning. His wife had never reappeared, though the bank had sorted out the credit card problem. Ah – here he was. Stacy slid round to stand beside Alex, her heart sinking when Leslie West approached with a tight smile on his face.

He slapped two keys down on the desk and spoke directly to Alex. 'I need to settle my mini-bar bill.'

'Certainly, Mr West.'

Alex printed out a receipt, and Stacy held her breath. The usual 'I hope you enjoyed your stay' wasn't appropriate for this guest.

'Have a good flight home.' Alex handed over the receipt. Mr West inclined his head, including Stacy in his glance, then turned away without speaking.

Stacy joined him as he walked to the door. She could understand he was hurting and embarrassed, but none of this was Lakeside's fault, and she didn't like to see a guest leave the hotel with so much bitterness and resentment still in him.

'I hope things work out for you, Mr West. Is someone meeting you at Heathrow?'

'My sister. She never liked Yvonne.'

It was now or never. Stacy followed him out to the front drive where his taxi was waiting. 'Mr West, it isn't my place to tell you what to do, but there are people who can help you cope with what happened.'

He wrinkled his nose at her. 'Help me cope with abuse, you mean. I don't see it like that.'

'I'm sure talking things over with your sister will help. All the best, anyway.'

The taxi drove off, and dejection rolled over Stacy. Life was never simple, was it? And neither was hotel-keeping. This was their first failure, if you could call it that: a guest who left feeling worse than he had when he arrived here. Not everyone's problem had an instant solution, of course, but hopefully there wouldn't be too many more of this kind.

Back inside, Mr and Mrs Roberts were standing at reception, surrounded by their luggage. Timea was nowhere to be seen, and here was another not your run-of-the-mill set of guests going back to England today.

Stacy gave the couple a careful smile. 'I hope you enjoyed your stay, after, um, you got things sorted with Timea?'

Mrs Roberts smiled unhappily. 'We did, but I don't think I'll ever stop worrying about her. She's off to uni after the holidays, and she says she's going to look for a flat-share. We won't have a moment's peace.'

A picture of her mother slid Stacy's head. 'I don't have children yet, but I'm sure all mums worry. Mine still does, anyway! But kids learn to look after themselves, and that's what Timea's doing. Where is she?'

'On her way down, I hope. Alonzo's driving us to the airport.'

Mr Roberts' face was tripping him, and Stacy fought back a wild urge to laugh. Glory – parenting wasn't for wimps, was it? Timea stepped out of the lift, and shot Stacy a rather watery smile.

'I'm glad I can say goodbye to you – thank you so much for all your help, and the lovely breakfast you put on for my birthday. I wish I didn't have to leave Alonzo behind, that's all…'

Stacy hugged her. 'You know something? A friend of mine came here last year and fell in love with one of the bar staff. They're planning their wedding in England now. So never say never, Timea.'

She took them to the door, then waved as the family vanished through the gates in Alonzo's car. A summer barman and a guest... Maybe there would be a happy end for Timea and Alonzo too, but they'd probably never know.

Rico came up from the cellar as she went back inside. 'All quiet?'

'Yup. It's odd, isn't it, how people are here for a blink of time in their lives, and then they're gone?'

He gave her a quick hug. 'Very philosophical, Mrs. You need a coffee. Let's have a break before the afternoon onslaught begins, huh?'

Alex handed over his fourth set of room keys that afternoon, and the new guests – a young couple plus the woman's grandmother – headed for the lift. He stared after them. Hell, he'd thought things were hectic this morning, with half the hotel wanting to check out at the same time. Guests checking *in* were ten times worse because they all had questions about the hotel, the spa, the area, what restaurants – and if he heard another 'what does the other guy look like?' joke... Alex touched his eye gingerly, and winced. It was only three o'clock, he still had four more sets of new guests to check in and knowing his luck they'd all arrive at the same time. At least he had Rico on call if the queue became too long.

And here was another query. Alex fixed on his best smile and answered a series of questions about the spa – it was all in the brochure he'd already given the couple, but this was part of the job, wasn't it? The guests went off, satisfied, and Alex gave himself a pat on the back.

Stacy stopped on her way out to the terrace. 'You're doing a great job, Alex. I'll bring you a coffee, shall I?'

At least he had good bosses here, but at the moment they were the only people who thought he was doing a good job. Alex doodled on the phone pad. Ma still wasn't speaking to him – he'd called twice, and both times she'd answered then cut the call before he'd had the chance to say more than hello. His texts remained unanswered, too. Should he try flowers? As for Zoe, she'd be up to her ears in music and wouldn't be giving him a second thought. She'd sent pink hearts in answer to the two messages he'd sent her, but it was more than his life was worth to try calling her when she was in the middle of her music. Alex heaved a sigh. There was a saying that if you loved someone, you had to let them go, otherwise you'd lose them. That was how it was with Zoe, but... Misery welled up again. He would lose her anyway, wouldn't he?

He used the lull in arrivals to sip the coffee Stacy had left him, then found a smile for the next guest approaching, a forty-something bloke in a smart suit.

'Afternoon. Ronald Steiner. I have a single room booked for four nights.'

Alex found the booking, and after the usual check-in formalities he handed over a key and the spa information brochure. Herr Steiner, who was from Austria if his accent was anything to go by, was looking up and down the hallway with a bemused expression.

'This place isn't the way I remember it from my last visit six years ago.'

'No – they've changed the concept. We're a spa hotel now, with emphasis on wellness.'

'Is there still a conference room?'

Alex gaped. Not as far as he knew, but that might not be far enough. Rico was coming out of the restaurant, and Alex beckoned him over to help Herr Steiner, then went on to check in the two middle-aged ladies who were waiting.

A few minutes later, when the ladies and Herr Steiner had all gone off to their rooms, Rico joined Alex behind the desk and rummaged in one of the drawers.

'That chap used to hire the small conference room – the

one we did away with – for his company's annual end of the year meeting with their Swiss branch,' he said, producing a folder of plans. 'It was a good money-spinner, two days a year. I'm wondering if–'

A loud scream came from above, then another. Alex jerked upright. He met Rico's eyes, then they both dashed for the stairs, where the screams were still ringing up and down the hotel, coming from the second floor, by the sound of things. They barged through the fire door shoulder to shoulder and stopped dead outside room 205, where Herr Steiner was standing waving his arms and an elderly woman was clutching her bathrobe shut at her neck while a young woman tried to comfort her, and a young man was expostulating loudly with Herr Steiner.

A cold, sick feeling thudded into Alex's gut. This was the couple plus grandmother he'd checked in half an hour ago. And Herr Steiner, who he'd checked in ten minutes ago, and... Oh no. Hell... Could he have given two people a key to room 205? Because that was what it looked like.

Alex stood mutely beside Rico while indignant explanations came from four people simultaneously in two languages. The grandmother, Mrs Rose from Norfolk, had been having a nap on her bed after the journey from England when she'd opened her eyes to see a large-sized Austrian in her room, taking his jacket off... A quick glance at the room keys and yes, both were for room 205. Alex could have sunk through the floor.

Hot shame flushed through him as Rico coped with his mess; it didn't take him two minutes to have all the guests laughing. He ushered the little family into 205 and dispatched Alex downstairs with Herr Steiner, to work out what was going on with the rooms. Alex tapped into the computer and oh, jeez, Herr Steiner was supposed to be in 201, Timea's first room. He handed over the correct key, his cheeks flaming. Impossible to know what Herr Steiner was thinking, but he wasn't laughing any more and he wasn't saying, don't worry, easy mistake, or anything like it. Alex opened the key safe. He couldn't have given Herr Steiner a key from hook 205... It was three hooks to the left of 201; he'd have noticed that. Wouldn't he?

Footsteps sounded on the stairs, then Rico joined him at the key safe. 'The most likely thing is a key was on the wrong hook, and that could have been any of us. You should still have checked the number on the actual key, of course, but if you were rushed I can see you might not have. I don't think there's any harm done, but try not to do it again!'

Misery nearly choked Alex. Rushed had nothing to do with it. He'd been sunk in self-pity about Zoe and hadn't been paying attention, that was what.

'I won't. Sorry.'

Rico swung into the restaurant to organise afternoon tea on the house for Mrs Rose and her family. Alex patted his cheeks – a splash of cold water would have been good, but he didn't dare leave the desk while Rico was on the prowl. Gawd. Maybe he wasn't cut out to be a hotel receptionist. He hadn't exactly shone over the Timea episode either; neither of his bosses knew that she had told him she was going off with Alonzo that first time... Now this. Alex blew his nose, and turned to find an elderly couple waiting to check in. He smiled determinedly and stabbed at the keyboard. He would check this key ten times, you could bet on that.

'I hear you had an interesting afternoon.' Stacy put her head round the door of the staff cloakroom when Alex was getting ready to go home.

'You could say that. Four of the guests now give me hard stares every time they pass reception. I don't know whether to apologise again, or smile on regardless.'

Stacy laughed. 'Oh, smile on regardless. Don't worry, Saturday's always the busiest day, and we all make mistakes. I've talked to Rico, and you can have tomorrow off, Alex. Go and see your girlfriend in Zurich, or something. You've had a lot on your plate with your mum, and everything here, not least of all the fight on Tuesday evening. A day off for taking one on the chin for Lakeside is the least we can do!'

She wasn't giving him a choice, was he? Was this really like she said, or was she getting rid of an incompetent receptionist for a day? But he'd take the time off either way, even though Zoe was in Zurich with no time for him, and Mum wasn't speaking to him. Alex straightened his shoulders. Self-pity wasn't an attractive look. He had Monday off as well; he would go to Zurich and listen to Zoe practise and mooch around in the city.

'Thanks. Mum still isn't taking my calls.'

'Oh dear – I hope she'll come round soon. I wondered if you'd agree to me calling by to see if she'd speak to me? It's my fault she's so angry with you.'

'To be honest, I don't think there's a snowball's chance in hell she'll let you in, but…'

Stacy pulled a face. 'But I can't make things worse than they are already, can I?'

Alex shrugged. Hopefully not…

Chapter Twenty-One

Sunday, 27th May

Sunday morning church bells were pealing in the village as Stacy left Lakeside the next day. Hopefully Alex had gone to Zurich to see his girlfriend; it sounded as if the relationship was a little shaky. And hopefully too, Denise Berger would agree to a quick chat. Guilt wormed into Stacy's middle to join the apprehension there already. The rift between mother and son was partly down to her, and it wasn't a good feeling. But this was the best time to drop by, according to Alex, so fingers crossed.

In Rorschach, she parked in a visitor's space under a block of flats near the top of the hill behind the town. Stacy gazed around appreciatively as she locked the car. Even here at street level, the view was lovely, so it must be amazing from the flats on the top floor. Oh, glory, please let this visit go halfway well at least. Helping people who needed help but didn't want it was the hardest thing on the planet, and so far all she'd done was make things worse for Alex and his mum.

Upstairs, she leaned on the doorbell and waited. Silence. But Denise must be at home. Stacy stood close to the door, listening. Still silence. Heck… Well, she'd try again. A gentle knock and a few words might be better than another blare on the bell, though. Stacy breathed out, summoned her best German, and tapped on the door.

'Mrs Berger? Denise? I'm Stacy Townsend from the Lakeside Hotel. Alex's boss.'

Footsteps behind the door. 'You're the one who wanted to send some charity-visitor, aren't you?'

The voice was bitter, and Stacy flinched. Well-intentioned or not, that hadn't been her best idea, had it? And maybe coming here wasn't, either.

'I'm sorry. Alex is worried about you. Please let him come and see you again. He's miserable.' Nothing like a bit of emotional blackmail, and what a horrible person she was, resorting to it.

Denise Berger wasn't falling for it, anyway. 'He should have known better. I don't need help, and I definitely don't need charity. I'd like you to go, please.'

'I will. But please let Alex come back, Mrs Berger. If we can do anything, let me know.'

No answer came, and Stacy turned back to the stairs. This whole episode hadn't been her finest hour, had it?

Back at the hotel, Rico emerged as she was pulling into their usual parking space.

'I was watching for you. I see it didn't go as you'd hoped? You did your best, Stace. You can't win 'em all, you know.'

Didn't she just. Stacy took the hand he was holding out. 'Are we going somewhere?'

'Come and help me check everything's okay at the landing stage and boathouse. We don't want anything floating away if a storm comes up while we're in Lugano.'

They walked down to the lake, and Stacy told him about her visit to Denise – not that you could call it a visit, when she hadn't even clapped eyes on the woman.

Rico pulled her in for a hug. 'It's up to her and Alex now.'

He went into the boathouse, and Stacy sat down on the wall separating the path from the hotel garden. The ground was still saturated here, but at least it was ground now, and not lake. Another couple of centimetres less water would make an even bigger difference. Stacy raised her face to the sun. This was lovely. A horn tooted as one of the passenger boats passed by further out on its way from Rorschach to Arbon, white paintwork shining brightly in the sunshine, and further away, the car ferry was crossing the lake to Germany. It was picture perfect, and if only the past week had been as great as the scenery in front of her.

Stacy slid further back on the wall. 'Rico! Tourist boat alert. The wash'll be here in a minute.'

He reappeared as the first wave caused by the passenger boat arrived, and they sat on Stacy's wall with their feet held up, laughing as waves sped across the path for a few moments before dying away. Stacy stood up, cheered by the little incident. That had been fun, and they needed more fun in their lives. Roll on tomorrow and the trip to the Ticino.

Inside, a beaming Margrit beckoned her into the spa.

'Flavia and I have been busy – come and see our shop!'

Stacy pulled Rico into the spa with her, and wow – busy was right. Flavia was arranging the 'shop' on a trolley covered in a blue cloth at the back of the room. The bottles were in two sizes that Margrit said were small and medium, all filled with either blue or green salts, each with a blue bow tied around the neck and labels written in Flavia's flowery handwriting.

Stacy clasped her hands under her chin. 'That looks fabulous – a great beginning for the Lakeside Spa Shop!'

'We can expand it to include the other things as we get them,' said Margrit, showing Stacy her list. 'I ordered some lavender and delphinium soaps, and some white face flannels – we can make little gift packs with them, in baskets, maybe. And Flavia found some lovely flowery cards – is it okay if we get some of these too, until we get the ones with a pic of the hotel?'

'Sure, we can have both. Get small quantities at first, until we see what sells. And let's put some shower gel in bottles too.' Stacy cheered up about three hundred per cent. Something was going well. Brilliant.

A loud slap, a shriek and a giggle behind them was followed by laughter from the large tub, and Stacy whirled round to see a pair of swimsuit-clad guests about to get into the water, the woman – a thirty-ish blonde with hair piled on top of her head – laughing and rubbing her backside while her partner grinned at the other tub occupants and raised his hand again. The woman pushed him away.

'Whoops.' Margrit trotted down the room. 'Hi there – it's your first time here, isn't it? You get a quick medical before we let you loose in the water. You can follow me.'

She led the pair, who were arm in arm and giggling now, into the medical room and closed the door.

Stacy's lips twitched at Rico's bemused expression. 'Margrit will cope, don't worry. We have to be prepared to have all sorts in here, and there's nothing in the rules to say you can't kid around with your partner.'

'As long as they stop at kidding and don't disturb people who're here to relax.' Rico took her hand again and pulled her to the door. 'Come on, you. We have cases to pack for tomorrow.'

Alex trailed out of Zurich main station into brilliant sunshine and several dozen tourists milling around peering at maps or their phones. So much for his plan. He'd taken Stacy's advice and come to visit Zoe, but after a rapturous greeting when he turned up at Susanna's place, she'd kicked him out.

'We're practising like mad – you could go into town, and I'll join you somewhere for an ice cream at four o'clock, huh?'

So here he was, doing what she'd said. Problem was, the shops were shut on Sundays, so all he'd be able to do was sightsee around the place and mingle with the tourists for the next three hours. Yet again, he was occupying second place in Zoe's life.

He crossed the Limmat, the wide green river that flowed out of Lake Zurich and on north-west of the city to join the larger Aare, and wandered along in the direction of the lake. This part of Zurich was nothing if not picturesque in the sunshine, and dozens of others were doing the same thing. Alex heard English, German, Italian and something he didn't recognise before he'd gone twenty yards. Most people were clutching phones or cameras and clicking away in all directions. The three big churches on the Limmat banks were getting a lot of attention, especially St Peter's with its enormous clock, and the Grossmunster with the twin towers. He glanced across the water to the third church, the Fraumunster, and sniffed. The Fraumunster had a tower and a clock too, but it wasn't as dramatic as the other two. Competition was fierce around here. Bit like him and Zoe's music, when you thought about it, and like the Fraumunster, he wasn't competing very well. Music came first, didn't it?

On an impulse, Alex marched over the Münster bridge and stood in front of the Fraumunster. It was an ordinary grey church building with tall stained-glass windows which, seen from the street, were nothing but different shades of grey. Inside, though, it was different.

He wandered round the building to the big wooden door, and slid into the church. It was peaceful in here, and cool. A hushed murmur of voices filled the air while footsteps thudded gently on the ancient stone slabs. Alex walked down the main aisle then up the few steps into the chancel, and as usual, dropped into the nearest chair and sat gaping. The tall, arched Chagall windows, so colourless from the street, were shining in full glory here with the sunlight behind them. Each had a predominant colour – green, red, yellow and two blues, and to say they were spectacular was doing them an injustice. The motifs were modern and the colours vibrant, vivid, indescribably alive, and the chancel was filled with people sitting gawping – as he was. He would never see enough of this. The green was his favourite, then the smaller of the two blue ones. A Japanese couple further along the row got up to leave, and Alex shifted to let them pass. The woman's hair, long and dark, swung over her face as she walked. Like Zoe's. He blinked up at the windows again.

They looked so normal from the outside. Like Zoe looked like a normal, attractive girl. But when you were sitting here on the inside, these windows were seriously and scarily amazing. Like Zoe when she was playing her violin. And one day, people would sit listening to her play, and they'd have exactly the same awed expressions the people in here had when they looked at those windows.

And where would that leave him?

Chapter Twenty-Two

Monday 28th May

The train drew out of Zurich main station, and Rico settled down beside Stacy, who had the window seat. The last long train journey they had taken together was to get his scan results in Chur last winter. He'd spent the outward leg in a state of frozen terror, and on the way back he'd been intoxicated with sheer relief and love and prosecco. This would be a more peaceful trip, and they should make the most of their last few hours being a twosome before all their parents descended on them. Or to be more accurate, before they descended on all the parents.

Stacy pulled out her phone to check her messages. 'Do think they'll cope without us at Lakeside?'

Rico gave her a little push. 'You're being a worrywart again and for once I'm not being a worse one. The lake's going down and the pumps are off. We've got Margrit in the spa, Alex on reception and Peter will manage the hotel as well as the restaurant if anything comes up. And we're only a phone call away if they need us.'

Stacy dropped her phone into her bag. 'I guess. I wish I'd been able to help Alex and his mum more, though.'

'I know. It's tough for him. But he's going to be a good

receptionist, isn't he? The guests like him.'

'When he gives them the right keys they do, yes. I don't think Mrs Rose will ever forgive him for her fright on Saturday!' Stacy giggled, then turned to the window, her face pink with excitement. 'And we're on proper holiday, so let's make the most of it. I've never seen any of these places we're passing through today.'

Rico swung forward to kiss her. This was the life.

The train gathered speed, and he took a slug from his water bottle. 'The journey takes longer by train, but soon you'll see the famous Gotthard tunnel instead of the San Bernardino.'

Stacy shivered. 'My blood still runs cold when I think about what happened when we came out of the San Bernardino tunnel last year. I could have lost you forever.'

'But you didn't. And no snow today, so forget it. In a minute or two you'll see Lake Zug on this side. Zug's such a nice old town – we'll go there one day.'

He sat back, watching Stacy look out of the window as they passed through the usual Swiss urban environment before things became more rural. Soon the waters of Lake Zug were sparkling beside the train line, and a few minutes later they stopped in the little town. He would definitely bring Stacy here one day; you didn't see nearly enough from the train. She caught his eye at one point and smiled dreamily, and Rico basked in being alone with her. Pity they were going to land in the middle of a mass of parents, aunts, uncles and problems in the Ticino…

He cleared his throat. 'Next stop Arth-Goldau, and after that there's long stretch where we're right beside Lake Lucerne.'

Stacy opened a map on her phone. 'You're as good as a

geography lesson!'

The scenery was lovely, though, and Rico enjoyed seeing it all through Stacy's eyes. The train passed through the lakeland of central Switzerland, where green hillsides were dotted with little houses and villages. Patches of woodland provided a darker contrast, and all with a backdrop of higher peaks, some still white on top – it was glorious alpine scenery, and how lucky were they with the weather? Rico stared out as they came to Lake Lucerne – it was high too, with stretches of the bank still sandbagged. The flooding had affected most of Switzerland.

When the train was swallowed into the Gotthard tunnel, Stacy opened her rucksack. 'This one's longer than the San Bernardino, isn't it? Let's have lunch.'

Rico accepted a chicken sandwich and waved it at the blackness on the other side of the window. 'It's the longest train tunnel in the world.'

'I didn't know that. Longer than the Channel Tunnel?'

'Yup. Not a lot longer, mind you. Okay, let's discuss how and when we're going to break it to our folks – your mum especially – that we don't want to plan a wedding until next year.'

'I've been thinking about that. Let's wait until we're all together, having dinner or something, and bring it up while everyone's full and happy. And don't worry – I've got a trump card to play. Mum's going to love it.' She beamed at him.

Rico reached for his water bottle. 'What's the trump card, then?'

'Wait and see! It popped into my head yesterday, and it's a corker. This is going to be a walk in the park.'

They sat chewing as they trundled through darkness

then emerged into the hilly woodland scenery of the Ticino. Another half hour and the train was squealing to a stop in Lugano. Rico hefted their bags onto the platform and looked around for his father. Had he brought everyone? But of course he had.

'Stacy, darling – lovely to see you here too! And oh, you were right – isn't this an amazing place?'

Janie grabbed Stacy for a long group hug with John while Rico and Ralph slapped each other's backs in their usual greeting. Determination rose in Rico. He wasn't going to let Janie upset things, now that he and Stacy had eventually decided what to do about the wedding. He wouldn't put it past her to try and talk Stacy round to her ideas. Fingers crossed Stacy's mysterious trump card was enough of a corker…

It was sunshine all the way when Stacy left Julia and Guido's spare room the following morning, Rico's hand clutched in hers, and yay, Lugano was the best place ever for a holiday from hotel-keeping. With Mum and Dad in Ralph's flat several floors below in the apartment building, they were all nicely spaced out and it meant a more peaceful start to the day for her and Rico.

She stood on tiptoe to kiss Rico while the lift transported them to the ground floor where they were due to meet the three parents for a day's sightseeing. They were all waiting, Mum bobbing up and down on her feet and Dad and Ralph with long-suffering and faintly resigned expressions respectively. Oh dear, poor Ralph. She hadn't been able to ask him yet if he'd spoken to Dad, but if he had, it hadn't made a difference. Dad was still looking fed up.

Stacy pushed back a wave of misery. Her mother could be so overpowering. Mind you, yesterday evening had gone well. Ralph had left the four of them alone for the first meal, which they'd had in a restaurant near the lake, and to Stacy's relief no one had uttered the word 'wedding'. That was more than likely down to Dad – he must have had a stern word with Mum about it. Stacy smiled wryly. The missing conversation had been the elephant in the room, but it had given them peace to enjoy a lovely evening together. Tonight, she promised herself. They could talk after dinner – unless of course Janie brought it up before then. Stacy took her place in the seven-seater Zafira Ralph had borrowed from Guido – and thank heavens he had. Five in a regular car would have been a sweaty squash in this heat.

First stop was the Swiss Miniature Park at Melide, where visitors could walk round an outdoor exhibition of small-scale versions of the most famous landmarks and buildings in Switzerland. The three men broke away from Stacy and her mother almost as soon as they entered the park, discussing ratio and build and other technical bits and pieces.

Stacy laughed. 'Boys and their toys,' she said, linking arms with her mother as they stopped to admire a model of Chillon Castle, set on the banks of a little Lake Geneva. 'It's a good thing there's plenty to interest us non-technical people too!'

It was the right thing to say. Janie was beaming her way round the pathway. She stopped at the Bundeshaus, the Swiss parliament in Berne, suddenly thoughtful. 'Stacy, should we–'

Whoops. Time to deflect Mum before she got started. 'Mum, if this is about the wedding – can we do that after dinner tonight when everyone's there? Rico and I have such a good plan to run by you all.'

'Oh – all right,' said Janie. 'I thought with us girls together we could–'

Stacy wagged a finger, feeling like the world's worst conspirator. 'It's a family thing, Mum, we should all be there. For me?'

The beam was back. 'Of course, darling. I can't wait to hear what you've thought up!'

The men were stuck at the model of Zurich Airport, pointing out various miniature planes to each other, and Stacy led her mother to a shady bench. The climate here was Mediterranean, hardly surprising with the border to Italy a few kilometres along the road. Stacy's phone pinged as a text came in. Ah – it was Emily.

Hi Stace, better now – can we Skype today?

'It's Emily,' said Stacy. 'Let me send a quick answer.' She tapped swiftly, squinting to see the screen in the brightness. *Out for the day with Mum and Dad. Will text when I'm home on my laptop. Might be latish xxx.*

The answer came promptly. *No probs*. Stacy sent a thumbs-up to finish off, and put her phone away. They had a couple of things to get through before she and Emily could talk.

Butterflies were crashing around in Stacy's tummy by the time they were at the coffee stage after dinner that evening. They were in an outdoor restaurant across the road from the promenade along the banks of Lake Lugano – such a different lake to their own Constance. Here, darkly wooded hills came right down to the water on all sides, and the lights on the summits of the high twin peaks flanking the bay twinkled out in the gathering dusk. Monte Brè, where Rico had taken her and Emily for lunch last autumn, was on Stacy's left, and how good would it be if Emmy was here to support her about the wedding? But there was no Emily, and Janie was throwing frequent loaded looks in Stacy's direction. Now to bite the bullet.

'Rico and I have decided what we're going to do about the wedding,' she said, trying to sound casual and confident. Please, Mum, don't get upset... Rico grasped her hand on the table top, and Stacy squeezed back as she outlined the double-venue plan. Her father was nodding encouragingly, and Mum was listening keenly, but the frown lines between her eyes were deepening every second.

'But Stacy – that means you won't be getting married in Elton Abbey.'

'That's right – we'll have the civil ceremony in Grimsbach, then a blessing in Elton Abbey. We want to have something proper in both places, Mum.'

Janie's lip was trembling, and her eyes were suspiciously bright. John leaned towards her. 'We'll still have it in the church, love, and we'll still have bridesmaids and flowers and what have you. Won't we, Stacy?'

'Absolutely. Mum, it's the only way if we want an official ceremony in both places – and we do.'

Janie said nothing, and Stacy's stomach churned. She'd been afraid Mum would go off on a tangent about cakes and dresses and menus before they'd explained everything, but this silent tearfulness was even more difficult.

Stacy tried an encouraging smile. 'You could even have two wedding outfits. You get to be mother of the bride twice!'

Light dawned on Janie's face. 'Oh! Of course. Good. For a moment I was thinking we wouldn't see you being married.' She dabbed her eyes, and Stacy sent a 'help me here' glance across to Rico.

He rose to the challenge – almost. 'You can help us decide on everything for the blessing, Janie.'

Stacy bit back a laugh. If she knew Mum, no one else would be doing much deciding about the Elton Abbey part of the celebrations. But now for the really tricky bit. Go, Stace.

'We want to wait before we set a date, though,' she announced brightly. 'I thought we could talk about that around the end of the year, Mum.'

'What? But that means you won't be getting married for over a year!' said Janie. 'We can't organise a wedding in five minutes, you know that.' Her shocked dismay would have been comical in other circumstances.

'Well, no. But we don't want to get married until after next summer season anyway.' Stacy took a deep breath. This was where she played the trump card. 'And I thought it would be so nice if Jo and Gareth's baby was flower girl or page boy, and if we planned for, say, late summer next year, the baby would have a chance to learn to walk first.'

Rico twitched beside her, and Stacy hid a smile. He always went pink when he was trying not to laugh.

A dreamy expression replaced Janie's shocked one, and Stacy knew the argument was won.

'Darling, that's a lovely idea. And of course by the end of the year I'll have more time to make plans – Jo will need a lot of help at the beginning.'

'Exactly. Win-win all round.' Stacy felt Rico's foot rub her leg under the table, and she smiled at him sweetly. Another problem solved.

It was almost eleven before Stacy was back in their room

at Julia's, ready to call Emily. Janie hadn't wanted to stop, once they started with wedding plans. Good thing the UK was an hour behind Switzerland.

Emily's face loomed excitedly on the screen, pale, but with huge, bright eyes. 'Hi, Stace – everything okay? And. You. Will. Never. Guess!'

Stacy knew that look. Something had happened. 'You won the lottery? Met Justin Bieber? Found a new job?'

'Wrong, wrong, and wrong. We've found the most amazing house – a house, Stace, with a garden!'

'Wow! In Elton Abbey?'

'Yes – it's in the estate behind the road the library's on. Dad's loaning us part of the deposit until Alan's working. It's semi-detached, three beds, a fab kitchen, and a great garden at the back – we can move straight in and start having babies!'

'Sounds amazing. Do you have photos?' Stacy was surprised – and ashamed – to feel a little twist of nostalgia in her gut. It was everything she'd dreamt of, once upon a time. A nice house, an interesting career, and a family running around in the garden. And a husband, of course. The house part had vanished when she fell in love with Rico and Lakeside, and she wouldn't change a thing, but – remembering the old dream was somehow bittersweet.

The next ten minutes were spent in house talk, but eventually Emily came round to the hotel. 'How's Lakeside? And Rico?'

'The flood water's going down, and Rico's fine – at least he's been worrying his socks off, you know what he's like – but it's okay now.'

'He should go back to uni and start his master's – that's what he wants, isn't it?'

'Yes. Problem is, we're going to lose money over this flood, and employing someone to do Rico's job would be expensive.'

'Couldn't you be acting manager? You'd still be on hand if someone medical was needed, and you could get another tub attendant.'

'I wish I could, but my German isn't good enough yet, especially on the phone. I'd spend all day asking people to repeat what they'd said, and getting the receptionist to check letters. No – maybe Rico can go next year.'

It was a pity, she thought, as she closed the laptop after their conversation. But some things you can't change, and this was one of them.

Chapter Twenty-Three

Tuesday, 29th May

It was after eight o'clock when Rico woke, and what did you know, sunshine was streaming through the crack in the curtains already. He slid across to Stacy, still asleep beside him, one arm looped over his hip and an adorable little pout on her lips. She must be dreaming… He kissed her nose, then moved down to her neck.

'Mmm.' She shifted, pulling him closer without opening her eyes.

Rico froze for a second, listening. Nothing. Guido and Julia had left for work already. They had the flat to themselves and an hour and a half before they were due to meet Janie and John. This was what you called having a good holiday… and Stacy seemed to be agreeing with him.

By ten to nine they were having breakfast in Julia's tiny kitchen.

Stacy shook muesli into her bowl and added yoghurt. 'Sex really gives you an appetite, doesn't it?'

Rico reached over to nuzzle her ear. 'An appetite for more?'

She pushed him away, giggling. 'No – for breakfast! Then I need a shower to make me respectable enough to go shopping with my parents.'

Rico gave up, and started on his muesli. 'I think I'll give Alex a ring and see how they're getting on at Lakeside. Got to keep the staff on their toes, you know.'

Stacy cast her eyes to the ceiling. 'If you say so.'

Rico scraped his bowl clean, then tapped to connect to the Lakeside reception, putting the phone on speaker so that Stacy could join in too.

'Hi, Alex – how's things?'

'Good. The lake's down another three centimetres. And we have four new guests having spontaneous holidays, so with the people coming on Wednesday, we're full for the next week.'

'Brilliant. Did you–?' A shriek and loud laughter came down the phone, and Rico raised his eyebrows at Stacy. Alex's voice was muffled, as if he'd covered the phone while he talked to someone. He waited.

'Sorry, Rico. A guest asked about hiring bikes.'

'What was all that shouting in the background?'

Alex laughed. 'That was Mr and Mrs Paxton on their way into the spa. They're what you might call enthusiastic spa-goers.'

'I hope they're not disturbing anyone?'

'No complaints so far. Most people seem to like them, and they don't half liven the terrace up. I wasn't here, but Alonzo said they organised a great pub quiz last night.'

Rico exchanged a glance with Stacy – a pub quiz was a good idea, but...

Stacy leaned forward. 'Alex, how's you mum?'

'Still not answering calls, but she does read my messages now, though she doesn't reply to them. I'll give her another day or two before I try breaking down the front door.'

Someone else arrived at reception then, and Rico disconnected, not sure if he liked the idea of guests 'livening up' the terrace when he wasn't there to keep an eye on things.

Stacy stood up. 'I guess it's good news that Alex's mum is reading his messages. I – yikes, look at the time!' She fled into the bathroom.

To Stacy's surprise, her mother was waiting alone on the ground floor when she and Rico arrived, exactly three minutes late.

Janie beamed at her. 'Ralph and your dad have gone off for a boy's day out, so it's just me for the shopping trip today.'

Stacy tried not to laugh at the relief on Rico's face.

He didn't miss a beat. 'Then why don't I leave you two to have a girl's day at the shops while I catch up with Guido at the boatyard?'

Stacy tucked her arm companionably through Janie's as they started into town. This was great. Ralph would have loads of time to get to the bottom of whatever was troubling Dad. She waved to Rico, who was at the corner already. Talk about not seeing someone's heels for dust…

And – she wouldn't tell Rico, of course, but shopping with your mum was actually more fun than shopping with the love of your life. Naturally, Mum insisted on going into a posh wedding-outfit kind of shop, but one look at the prices there had her whizzing straight back out again.

'Goodness, darling, I wouldn't like to get outfits for three bridesmaids in there! We'd need to remortgage the shop.'

Stacy grinned. She was having three bridesmaids, was she? Good to know. They adjourned to a department store and had a lot of fun trying on hats, 'just to see the styles, darling', then stopped for lunch at a café a little way up the hill, where it was cooler.

After lunch, they caught a tourist boat up the lake to Gandria, a tiny village right on the border with Italy. It was late afternoon before they were walking back to Ralph's flat, with Stacy feeling as if they'd had a much-needed day out of time. They hadn't talked about anything deep, but sometimes a day like that did you all the good in the world.

The lift dropped Janie on Ralph's floor and Stacy went on up to Guido's flat, surprised to find Ralph sitting with Rico in Guido and Julia's kitchen.

Rico poured her an iced tea. 'Get that inside you – you look like a lobster.'

Stacy sipped. It was divine. 'Gee, thanks, darling. The Rico Weber school of charm and romance… you can't beat it.'

Ralph roared. 'Never mind, Stacy – I'll make you a nice white wine spritzer when you've finished that.'

'See?' Stacy tapped Rico's leg with her foot. 'That's how you do it. Be like Ralph, huh?' She smiled sweetly at Rico, then turned back to his father. 'Did you manage to talk to Dad?'

'That's why I'm here. I did, but I'm not sure it was helpful. He admitted he's been feeling down recently, but he insisted it was all because of his coming retirement, and feeling old and useless now he's about to be a grandfather.'

Stacy slumped in her chair. 'That's ridiculous. He's always been positive about retiring and I can't imagine what's changed. As for useless – he'll be rushed off his feet soon, what with babysitting and Mum going bananas making wedding celebrations.'

'That's what I said. He cheered up afterwards, but I'm sure that was because he didn't want to continue the conversation, not because he felt better. Sorry, Stacy.'

She patted his hand on the table. 'Thanks for trying. I'll have one more go myself before they leave.'

Ralph stood up and opened the fridge. 'You can always depend on my brother to have wine in the fridge.' He wielded the bottle opener. 'Don't fret, Stacy. Your dad's a grown man. You might have to leave this one to him and your mum.'

Stacy nodded. It was true. You could only do so much for your parents, couldn't you?

Alex accepted the bike maps two of the guests were waiting to hand over, and rolled his eyes as the couple melted away to the lift. How anyone could go biking in this heat and enjoy it was beyond him. Okay, he had another half hour before Maria came to relieve him on the desk. Better get things a bit tidier before she arrived.

He sat down in the office to sort through the pile of biking trail maps the couple had been looking at – they were going out tomorrow too, crazy fit people – when Margrit ran out of the spa, her face aghast.

'Alex? Oh, there you are.' She came right into the office and closed the door behind her. 'Someone's been taking things from the spa shop!'

He pushed the maps to the side and stood up. 'What? Are you sure? When?'

'Come and look – I don't know what to do. It must have been between ten and three, because that's when the tubs were in use today. Four bottles of shower gel are missing. I sold three this morning, but when I went to restock the trolley, I saw that seven are gone.'

Alex stared. Shit. Was one of their guests a thief? 'I

suppose someone didn't take them and leave the money with someone else?'

'That was my first thought too, and I asked Sabine, but – nothing. This is dreadful.'

Alex gaped at the trolley. It was on the side wall, away from guests going to and from the showers or medical room but still in view no matter where you were standing in the spa. It would have needed the most colossal cheek to pocket four bottles and leave with them. Unless…

'Could someone have nipped in after three? Who was here then?'

Margrit dabbed her cheeks with both hands. 'You're right. That's much more likely, isn't it? I was in the medical room because we had a delivery after lunch and I was putting everything away. Oh, Alex. What a horrible thing to happen.'

Alex thrust his hands into his pockets. 'Should we call the police?'

Margrit was nearly in tears. 'No. I'll talk to Stacy first, but I'll wait until she's home tomorrow night. I suppose it's remotely possible that someone took them while Sabine and I were both occupied with something else, and decided to pay later. Meantime, I'll lock this trolley in the medical room overnight.'

She kicked the brake off and wheeled the trolley away. Alex returned to the desk, frowning. A little gaggle of guests came in, among them Mr and Mrs Paxton, the loud and giggly couple who were still being loud and giggly. Not their usual Lakeside guests, but that was a snooty thing to think. There was no reason in the world to think they had nicked four bottles of shower gel. It could have been anyone, and come to that, it needn't even have been a hotel guest. But he'd keep his eyes wide open from now on.

Chapter Twenty-Four

Wednesday 30th May

Janie took Stacy's arm as they walked along beside Lake Lucerne. 'Lucerne's a lovely place too, darling. Look at those mountains. I can't believe how close they are!'

'The Pilatus,' said Stacy, gazing at the peak towering on the other side of the lake. Like Lugano, Lake Lucerne was a complete contrast to Lake Constance. Here, they had a big bustling city as well as mountains right by the water, and a lot more tourists, too. 'Another time, we'll go up in the cable car and see the view from the top – Rico says it's spectacular. Look, a little further along here you'll see the old wooden bridge.' She led her mother past a photo-snapping party of elderly people and on towards the old town and the bridges.

Rico had suggested the stop-off in Lucerne on the way home from the Ticino. It meant a detour, but he and John wanted to go to the Transport Museum. Stacy and her mother had looked at each other, for once in complete accord.

'We'll have a wander in the town,' said Stacy. 'You can show me the museum another time, Rico, love.' This mini-break was turning into more of a mother-daughter bonding time than a romantic break for her and Rico, but that was okay. Now they'd got the wedding non-plans sorted, they were free to enjoy themselves, though come to think of it, Mum had been unusually quiet today, which meant she was mulling something over. Poor Mum. She was such a traditionalist; she'd probably had her daughter's wedding planned from the moment of birth, if not conception, and now those plans were – not quite ashes, but definitely different.

They came to the road bridge where the river Reuss joined the lake, and Janie pulled out her camera. 'I'll take one of you with the wooden bridge in the background, shall I? Cheese, darling!'

Stacy obliged, and they walked over the bridge, Janie taking photos in all directions.

'We'll cross back over the old bridge, and you'll see the painted panels hanging from the roof,' said Stacy. 'They're not originals, because almost the whole bridge burned down in the nineties, but they rebuilt it.' Now she sounded like a tour guide, and an inefficient one at that, when you considered it was only the second time she'd been to Lucerne. Janie was lapping it up, though. They crossed the wooden bridge arm in arm, and the happy look on Janie's face brought a lump into Stacy's throat. Mum would have been happy anywhere, as long as it was the two of them.

On the old town side of the Reuss, they found a shady restaurant terrace and ordered apple cake and coffee.

'I'm sorry if I was too full-on about your wedding,' said Janie. 'Your dad and I had a chat last night. We'll leave it to you. I don't want us to fall out, Stacy.'

The lump was back. Had that chat included Dad's retirement worries? 'We won't, Mum. And we'll need loads of help, with two celebrations to organise. Just – it's not quite time yet. I know the Swiss way might seem strange to you, but I want Rico to feel he's decently married too!'

'I see that now. I think – to be honest, Stacy, I'm not used to having so much time on my hands. With Jo and Gareth taking over the shop, I don't know what to do with myself half the time. It'll be better when the baby's here, but…'

And there it was. The reason for Janie's recent behaviour, and maybe the cause of Dad's misery, too. Stacy waved her cake fork. 'You need to find some outside interests. In a year or so you'll be retired full-time. You should have more in your life than the shop and your family.'

'I'm going to do some art classes in summer, and I thought quilting, too. I could do a quilt for each of my grandchildren.'

Stacy almost choked on her coffee. No pressure there, then. Her mother would never change.

'Sounds like a great idea. And you can do trips in the UK, too.'

'That's what your dad said last night. We're planning a few days helping your Aunt Sue in Edinburgh, after her operation. There's plenty of time before the baby comes.'

By the sound of things, Mum and Dad had started out along a better road. Stacy listened to Janie's plans for baby clothes and places to visit with grandchildren. Bless the baby. He – or she – was going to give its grandma a new lease of life. And its grandpa? Stacy thought back to John's expression when he thought no one was watching. Somehow, it might take more than a trip or two and some babysitting sessions to make Dad happy again. She would have that word with him ASAP. Today, if possible.

They strolled on though Lucerne, finding a wool shop on the way back to meet the men, and Janie bought some horrendously expensive wool to make a jacket and hat for the baby. Stacy winced as her mother wielded her credit card. Good job babies were small. Mum would be bankrupt in no time if they weren't. Still – it had been a productive couple of hours. Long might that continue.

Alex handed over the hotel's newest map of biking trails, and waved goodbye to the pair of guests about to push the pedals for the second day in a row. This was the couple whose grandma he had terrified into a near-death experience by sending a large Austrian businessman into her room on Saturday while she was asleep, but the pair seemed to have forgiven him. He wasn't so sure about Mrs Rose the grandmother, though. She was in the spa now, and she still gave him a funny look every time she passed the desk.

He crossed the hallway with some brochures for the coffee table, glancing into the spa as he passed. The shop trolley had been repositioned by the medical room door on the back wall, and Margrit was patrolling up and down between it and the tubs. She caught Alex's eye and grimaced. He knew what she meant. Stacy and Rico weren't going to be happy when they heard about the theft.

His phone buzzed and he slid it out hopefully, but as usual now, the message wasn't from his mother. This radio silence was unnerving; maybe he should get Zoe to try. But it didn't seem fair to haul her into his family drama when she was so occupied with Friday's audition. Alex chewed his bottom lip. They were both going to Zurich again tomorrow night when he'd finished work, and he'd stay until Sunday night and come back again for work on Monday. What Zoe would do depended a lot on what happened at Friday's audition. Fear gnawed further into Alex's gut. Zoe loved Zurich; he'd seen that clearly at the weekend. She'd grown up there, and somehow, she was more alive in the city, where there were more music people and more chances and more – everything. It was all showing him clear as day that he would lose her sooner or later, unless he moved to the city too. It was a problem he didn't want to face.

Alex went back to his phone. He would try his mother again. They hadn't spoken for nearly a week – suppose something happened? She could fall and break a leg or something, and who would help her then? He knew she hadn't, because she was opening his messages and she'd been active on social media, too, but how sad it was he had to stalk her on Facebook to find out if she was alive or not. Alex's thumbs hovered over his phone. Another *please call me* message was only going to get the same treatment as every other *please call me* message he'd sent her since the weekend. A change of tactic might work…

Going shopping after work. Need anything? He tapped send, then put his phone away to help a guest whose shower was playing up. This was the kind of thing that Rico would investigate before sending for a plumber, wasn't it? Alex called Flavia, who was working in the restaurant today, to listen for the reception bell, put the *Please ring for attention notice* on the desk, grabbed the tool box from the office and accompanied the guest back upstairs.

Ten minutes later, he was on his way down again with wet feet after successfully tightening the head on the shower hose. It was always a good feeling, when something went right. Maybe he could be good at this job after all. Alex made a note in the Repairs file for Rico and – oh! A message pinged in – from Ma.

A packet of carrot salad and a cucumber, please.

Alex waved a fist in the air. Brilliant. They were communicating. He sent a thumbs-up and *See you around*

17.30, then beamed at the harassed-looking couple approaching the desk with about six suitcases.

'You must be Mr and Mrs Rawlton? Your room's all ready for you.'

A packet of carrot salad and a cucumber wouldn't solve Ma's problems and they certainly wouldn't solve his and Zoe's, but life was looking a whole lot brighter. The status quo had been re-established. Progress of a sort, wasn't it?

It wasn't the homecoming Rico had expected – or wanted. He gaped at Margrit, who was almost in tears as she told them what had happened.

'Should I have called the police? Alex suggested that, but I wanted to talk to you first and I didn't want to spoil your break, you both work so hard...' She blew her nose.

Rico shook his head. They were in the medical room, with the door open as quite a few guests were in the tubs and Sabine was on a break.

'I guess the police couldn't do much,' he said. 'It was our fault for leaving the trolley in a place where someone had the opportunity to steal stuff. Well, that's one lesson learned.'

Stacy gave Margrit a quick hug. 'Rico's right. We have to arrange our shop in a way that doesn't give people the opportunity to steal.'

Margrit sniffed. 'Flavia suggested a locked cabinet – you know, the kind with a glass door. We were wondering too about making a list of shop items to put in all the rooms, with photos and descriptions of the products.'

'That's a great idea,' said Rico immediately. 'We can make that ourselves, and add to it as we go. Once we have a good selection ready we can laminate it, that way it'll last longer and people won't use it to scribble on, too.'

They left Margrit looking happier and headed back upstairs, where John and Janie were leaving the flat en route for an hour in a tub.

Stacy sighed after them. 'Oh, Rico. I wish I could help Dad more. He still looks terribly down.'

Rico hugged her. 'Tell you what. I'll occupy Janie for an hour tomorrow morning and let you have a quiet word with him. How's that?'

She grinned. 'Okay, tell me how you're going to occupy Mum. I'll need time to get Dad to talk to me.'

Rico stuck out his tongue. 'I'll grab her after breakfast and ask her advice on presents for the bridesmaids. I can take her into the village and show her the jewellery workshop there.'

Stacy laughed. 'Genius. Half an hour will be plenty, I guess. Thank you. How about a walk outside, now that it's cooler?'

Rico lifted the plane and car kits he'd bought at the transport museum and waved them at Stacy. 'Let's walk by Tobias and Kim's and hand these in for Elijah and Ben.'

She lifted her bag. 'You just want to play with them.'

'I don't – they might not even put them together tonight. I want to borrow Tobias's DVD of the Transport Museum and show your dad some of the things we didn't have time for today.'

The family lived in one of the residential streets behind the main road in Grimsbach. Kim and the children were in the garden when Rico and Stacy arrived, and the two little boys immediately started unpacking their kits.

'Help me, Rico,' said Elijah, pulling Rico to the garden table.

Rico helped him set out the twenty pieces, and in less than five minutes they had a miniature double-decker plane assembled. Elijah sped off round the garden with it.

Kim was slotting parts of Ben's vintage car together for him. 'These are great, Rico – nice and easy to make. Here you go, Benny-boy. One Rolls Royce.'

Ben crawled off, vrooming with his car, and Stacy and Kim went off to look at the vegetable plot. Rico accepted a beer from Tobias and sat chatting about boats and planes and cars as the little boys played around them. Family life, and this was what was in front of him, wasn't it? One day he and Stacy would have kids, all going well. A feeling of almost panic surged inside Rico. Kids would be great, yes, but… oh, first he wanted to go to uni and finish what he'd started there. What if Stacy wanted to start a family right after the wedding? Or even sooner?

On the way home he grasped what was left of his courage and asked her. Her look of horror was enough to reassure him about that, anyway.

'Kids? Now? You're as bad as Mum, Rico. I've thought about it, of course, but it's not time yet. Let's get the hotel going first, and then there's the small matter of getting married – and yes, I know kids are possible without a marriage certificate but let's be old-fashioned and do the wedding bit first, huh? Then we'll see.'

Rico walked on, her hand grasped firmly in his. No kids for a year or two, good. She'd said nothing about him going back to uni, though, and maybe that was a plan for later too. Master's courses were possible any time. Theoretically. He should be living the day, shouldn't he?

Chapter Twenty-Five

Thursday 31st May

Stacy linked arms with her father as the car, with Rico and Mum inside, exited the hotel grounds and turned left for the village and the jewellery workshop. That was Mum sorted for the next half hour. Now for her father.

'Let's grab a cold drink and find a nice bench on the lake path,' she suggested. 'It's still a touch damp down there, but most of the path's okay to walk on now.'

John gave her a wry look. 'I'm not daft, you know. But well done. Your mother didn't suspect a thing – you know her better than she knows herself.'

Oops. Maybe honesty was the best policy here. Stacy gave the arm she was holding a little shake.

'I wanted to have a good talk with you, that's all. Come on.'

They walked through the bar and Stacy poured two glasses of iced tea. The grass was still a swamp, but the lake path was better, and at this time of the morning, few people were around. They sat down on a red bench facing the water, and Stacy relaxed back. This was a good place. It was often easier to talk when you weren't actually glaring into the other person's eyes.

Her father sipped his drink, staring out over the lake. It was hazy today; Germany was barely visible. Stacy took a firm hold of her courage. If she didn't do this now, she might not get another chance. Mum and Dad were going home at the weekend.

'What's the real problem, Dad? I know you said it was all about retiring and finding a new way to live and organise the day and so on – but it's more than that, isn't it? Are you worried about your health? Is there anything we don't know about? Please, I want to help.'

He gave her arm a squeeze. 'Oh, I'm healthy, don't worry. As for finding a new way to live – it's not only me doing that, Stacy. I've reached a stage where I'm wondering why I spent the last forty years building something up, only to have it ripped down again.'

The bitterness in his voice was shocking, and Stacy sat frozen to her seat. She'd never heard him speak like that before.

'What do you mean?' Was this about his marriage? But he and Mum were everything to each other; no way could they be splitting up. *Surely...?* Stacy swallowed hard. You did hear about couples like that, spending decades together and then suddenly everything was different. 'Is it – Mum?'

'No, no. It's the shop, Stacy. Pen 'n' Paper. The business I spent my entire life building up, and within a couple of months, Gareth and Jo have turned it into something completely different. It's a – a craft centre now, not a stationery shop.' He slid down the bench, his chin trembling.

Stacy's heart ached for him. He'd always been a tidy, orderly kind of guy. The glorious chaos Gareth and Jo had created in the shop must be agony for Dad every time he saw it, but – nothing stayed the same.

'I can see that must be tough for you. I guess times change, though, and at least they've got the shop back in profit. Gareth and Jo have jumped into a hole in the market, and that's a good thing, isn't it?'

'You mean, I should stop being an old codger and get on with my life. And how am I supposed to do that?'

Thank heavens, the bitterness wasn't so deep he couldn't see a tiny chink of humour in his situation. Stacy finished her drink while she thought.

'Okay, you're retiring officially soon. We can't stop time, Dad. Let's have a think about how you and Mum can shape your lives afterwards, and talk again, with Mum too? You need a new focus.'

He sniffed. 'Easily said, harder to find.'

'I know. That's why we need time to think about it.' Stacy stood up and held out a hand. 'We're thinking about how to change things for the better, Dad. Not regretting what's happening and agonising over stuff we can't change, huh?'

The wry look was back. 'You should have gone in for psychology, miss. You're too good at this.'

Stacy looked back at the hotel. Lakeside, where she had a thousand and one things to juggle every day. Now, guests were gathering on the terrace, the housekeeping team was out watering geraniums, and one of the waiters was struggling with a sun umbrella on the terrace.

Go in for psychology? She grinned at her father. 'Sometimes I think I did just that, you know! Come on – Mum and Rico will be back in five and we can grab some lunch.'

Rico ran down to the jetty, ignoring the fact that a dozen

late lunchtime guests on the terrace were staring at the mad grin on his face. Let them stare... *Lakeside Lady*, a boatyard employee on board, was approaching the jetty at speed, returning from her sojourn at the yard in Rorschach, and how brilliant it was to welcome the family cabin cruiser home again. And even more brilliant to see how the flood water was receding – a mere centimetre or two a day, true, but steadily. According to the experts, it was set to continue like that. Oh, it would still take them several weeks to get the cellar dried out and refurbished, and the garden would be unusable for at least as long, but it was still a good feeling. The start of better times, hopefully.

Rico motioned *Lakeside Lady* into the boathouse and helped attach the mooring chains, noticing with amusement the bike sitting in the cabin cruiser. The boatyard guy passed it up, then stepped ashore.

Rico walked beside him up the path to the main road. 'I was going to drive you back to Rorschach.'

'No need. I've no objection to a ten-minute bike ride in the sun. Makes a change from bending over some problem or other at the yard.' The other man jammed on a helmet and cycled off, swerving round Andi's car driving through the gates.

The project manager parked his car and joined Rico as he walked back to the hotel. 'Thought I'd make you my coffee-stop today, as I was passing. And we could think about your refurbishment of the upper-floor flat? This flooding has created havoc in the business – there are so many projects we can't get on with at the moment, and yes, I know you won't want to start this one until after the season, but we could at least set up plans.'

'We can do more than that. The sooner we get this done

the better – we're compensating guests for pump noise and lack of amenities this summer anyway. Might as well add to the pain and get the profit on the better rooms ASAP. Come and have a look at the flat, then we'll set a date.'

They spent half an hour wandering round the bikers' flat, then fixed on the following week to refurbish and went down to the terrace. Rico fetched espressos and joined Andi at a table under a sun umbrella. It was yet another boiling hot day – the weather seemed to be trying to make up for all the rain and snow they'd had earlier in the year. The view from here could have been on a picture postcard – the lake sparkling blue shading into soft greys and greens of Austria and Germany on the opposite banks. Rico tapped his fingers on the table. *Lakeside Lady* was metres away… If they went out onto the water, they'd see the splendour of the Alpstein mountains on the Swiss side too. Was there still snow on the Säntis?

'Got time for half an hour on the boat?' he said spontaneously, draining his cup.

'Lead the way. I've got more time than I want, these days,' said Andi glumly.

Rico detached the mooring chains in *Lakeside Lady* while Andi lounged on the back seat. A cool breeze ruffled through Rico's hair as he took his place at the wheel and reversed out of the boathouse, and wow, this was amazing. It was so good to be out on the lake again, manoeuvring the cruiser round in a wide sweep then turning to head north towards Germany. Sunshine, blue water, the low thrum of the engine. This was the life.

Lakeside Lady lurched, and Rico grasped the wheel more firmly. The swell on the water was more than he'd expected, and Lake Constance could be deceptive. A massive amount of driftwood was floating around near the lake bank, too; he had to keep his eyes open to avoid colliding with anything that might damage – or even just mark – Ralph's precious cabin cruiser. But a few minutes later the mountains came into view behind them, and Rico switched the engine off and sat back to admire the panorama.

'Pretty good, huh?'

Andi's eyes were shining. 'You never get tired of it.'

And that was true, thought Rico. Depending on the weather, the Säntis and her sister-peaks could appear close by, far off, snow-covered, hazy, early-morning pink – the variety was endless. Some days they were shrouded in cloud, of course, but this wasn't one of them. For a few minutes they sat in silence, then Rico started *Lakeside Lady* again and turned back for the jetty. How lucky they were to live in a place like this.

'Rico, wait! There's a boat out there and I think it's in trouble!'

Rico jerked round, feeling the cabin cruiser slide to one side as he decelerated. Andi was pointing to the north, where a rubber dinghy was bobbing on the water several hundred metres away, the occupants waving madly. Rico spun the wheel round and sped toward them, and oh, no, the storm-warning lights all around the lake had come on and were flashing at the fast speed. That was the signal for boats to get out of the water right now. He should have checked the forecast before they'd set out. What a basic mistake, but at least they could help these guys in the dinghy.

Lakeside Lady raced through the swell as dark clouds gathered overhead, coming from nowhere. Abruptly, the sunshine was gone, and Rico swore under his breath. But they had to make time for a quick water rescue. It wasn't as if the other boat was far away.

Two adults and three children were in the rubber dingy, and as they drew alongside Rico saw it was deflating fast. They must have hit something sharp, and by the looks of things they weren't seasoned boaters. None of the children were wearing life vests, and the father was obviously struggling with the tiller.

Lakeside Lady inched alongside, and Rico cut the engine. 'Want a lift back?'

'Thank God you saw us,' said the mother. 'I thought we'd have to swim for it.'

'I can swim,' announced the oldest child, a boy of about eight.

'Well, you don't have to,' said Rico, leaning over to grab the dingy. 'You can come on board here, and we'll tow your boat back. We should hurry – there's a storm on the way.'

This last sentence was unnecessary. Thunder was growling over the lake, and Rico stared apprehensively at the sky. The pleasant breeze had turned into a brisk and ever-cooler wind, and the two boats rocked uncomfortably. In these parts, a storm could develop in minutes, speeding down the Rhine Valley and erupting over the lake. Why, why, why hadn't he checked the forecast before they started out? Spontaneity and boat trips could get you into trouble.

The little boy and his younger brother scrambled aboard immediately, but the youngest child, a girl of about three, clung to the side of the dingy, whimpering. Hard-heartedly, the father passed her up to Andi, and the little girl immediately lay down on the floor and screamed until her mother was in beside her. The father tossed up their rope, and Rico attached it to the end of *Lakeside Lady* while the man climbed aboard. More thunder, and – had that been lightning? It was high

215

time none of them were out on the water. Rico handed the four adult-sized life vests he had on the boat to the parents and two oldest children, and started for home, going as fast as he dared. Fortunately, the little girl was calmer now, although orange lights were flashing briskly all along the shoreline, and the constantly-rumbling thunder was close by. *Lakeside Lady* pitched uncomfortably from side to side, and shit, here was the rain. Huge, stinging drops pelted down on them, please, this mustn't turn to hail... He had to physically brace against the wind.

'Hold on tight!' Rico yelled over his shoulder. This was dire. It wasn't often a gale came up as quickly as this, but when it did, the waters here could be as rough as the sea. Waves of over a metre in height had been measured before now on Lake Constance; people drowned here every summer. Rico glanced uneasily at Andi and the youngest child, both without life vests – as was he – and at that moment a sudden gust caught him by surprise.

Lakeside Lady slewed sideways, and Rico hung on for dear life, using all his skill to keep the boat top side up in the water. A shrill scream came behind him, and he twisted round.

'Lisa! My God – my baby!' The mother scrambled to the side of the boat beside her husband, and both were grappling in the water.

Rico's blood ran cold. The smallest child was gone... and a bundle of clothes was thrashing in the lake. Without thinking, he grabbed Andi, shoved him behind the wheel, and dived into the deep, dark waters of Lake Constance.

In two seconds, the force of the swell had pulled him metres away from the boat. Rico trod water, twisting round desperately to see where the little girl was. Nothing. Where the hell had she gone? The water was surging; these waves must be close on a metre now – then all at once the child was bobbing beside Rico, and he grabbed her and held her head above water. Andi would bring the boat round.

Waves slapped into Rico's face as he struggled to hold the child, who was terrified and choking wildly. Where was *Lakeside Lady*? In the few seconds he'd needed to get a proper grasp of the girl, the boat had disappeared. No, there she was, but somehow, they were drifting further and further apart… The little girl was quiet now, and Rico knew that wasn't a good sign. He had to get them out of here. Another wave swamped them, and Rico spluttered, then yet another came and he was pulled to the side, then down, down through cold, deep water. The child slid from his grasp, and darkness was everywhere.

Chapter Twenty-Six

Thursday 31ˢᵗ May

Sudden rain splattered on the terrace decking, and the few guests still sitting there fled indoors. Stacy rushed out to help rescue the sun umbrellas and glassware.

'Golly, that came up quickly!' she said, when the outside bar was secured. A surprisingly chilly wind was whipping in all directions – you'd never think it had been so lovely just a few minutes ago.

'Can happen, in weather like this.' Alex had abandoned reception and come to help. 'Still, at least we're not in the middle of serving lunches.'

Stacy pushed damp hair out of her eyes and followed him back to reception. Her parents had gone to Chur for an afternoon in the old town there, and she'd spent the past hour upstairs on the laptop, ordering furnishings and knick-knacks for the soon-to-be-ex bikers' flat, only coming down when her advice on someone's blood pressure was needed in the spa.

'Do you know where Rico is?' It wasn't like him not to be around when a sudden job arose.

Alex looked blank. 'He was here earlier with Andi. He wanted to organise plans for the upstairs renovation. I guess they went up to look at the bikers' flat.'

That sounded possible. Stacy went into the diary to see what Rico had arranged – oh, next week; excellent. It would mean a bit of noise, but with any luck the new rooms would be ready for guests in a month or so. They could certainly use the extra income.

She went up in the lift to find Rico and Andi, but the bikers' flat – free of guests as usual during the day – was deserted. Stacy wandered round the living room. They'd need a skip for the rubbish, had Rico organised that? She came to a stop by the window, where rain was streaming down the glass.

And oh my *God*, there was *Lakeside Lady*, trying valiantly to draw up alongside the jetty. Stacy caught her breath. Several figures – two of them children – were on board. What was going on? She flew downstairs, and met Andi rushing in from the terrace, followed by a sobbing couple with two sodden and screaming children.

Andi's voice was shrill with panic. 'Call the lake police! Rico and a child went overboard. I couldn't get a signal out there!'

Stacy's legs collapsed beneath her and she grabbed the bar to stay upright. No, no, that couldn't be true. Rico… She staggered across to the rain-smeared French door. The lake was heaving, waves were rushing over the jetty, blown up by the wind. *Rico…* Stars danced in front of Stacy's eyes as she fought to stay conscious.

One of the bar staff was on his phone, passing on the information to the lake equivalent of coastguards, and Flavia was taking care of the couple and their children. Andi crouched down on the floor behind Stacy, his face white.

She spat the words at him. 'Why did you leave him out there? And where?'

He clutched his head with both hands. 'It wasn't far from the shore. A kid was swept overboard and Rico dived in to save her. But the water pulled them away, and I couldn't keep the boat steady, Stacy – I had to bring her in or we could all have been lost.'

Lost. But Rico couldn't be lost… Stacy clapped both hands to her mouth, her stomach heaving.

Margrit appeared at her side. 'Come with me, Stacy. We'll wait until the police come.' She led Stacy through to the spa and sat her down in the medical room.

'What can I do, Margrit?' Shivers were rippling through Stacy's body, her teeth were chattering and she had never felt so hopeless. Rico was out there in the storm, in the lake – and there was no way she could help him.

'Hang on, Stacy. Just hang on.'

Something hard was rubbing against his head, and Rico jerked back into reality. A dead tree branch, waterlogged and splintering, was prodding between his neck and head. He made a wild grab for it and hung on, and thank God, it was large enough to help him keep afloat. A couple of deep, shaky breaths, and his head cleared. Where was the little girl? A bundle of dark clothes was caught on a floating tree trunk nearby, and yes, yes, she was breathing. Rico kicked out, bobbing on the swell, coughing as a wave slapped over him, but he managed to reach the child. The little face was still, eyes closed, but shallow breaths were moving the small chest.

'Wake up!' Rico's voice was hoarse and wouldn't have wakened the lightest sleeper on the planet, but he managed to grab the girl and heave her more securely over the tree trunk. Rain was still pelting down; he couldn't see a thing. Where was the boat? Where was the bank? They had to get out of this…

Thanking his stars that the snowmelt water coming down the Rhine was still washing wood around, Rico grasped his courage and the last of his strength, and pushed the tree trunk in the direction of dry land. The lake bank was this way, yes, he could see the church tower in Steinach, over to the right. They'd been washed pretty far down the lake already. Kick, Rico. You can do this, because you have to. Think of Stacy, think of Dad. Of Lakeside. He bloody wasn't going to drown today and lose them all. A surge of cold, cold water and a wave pulled him beneath the surface again, and despair loomed anew.

His legs were going numb, he couldn't breathe, he couldn't see the lake bank, oh God, no. They weren't going to make it… But Andi would come. Or he'd get help. Rico's head broke above water, and he sucked in air. The tree trunk with the child was in front of him. Rico grabbed it, and kicked out again. Swim, man.

And oh, thank you, thank you. Sea grass was scratching at his legs, stinging like hell but it meant the bank was close by. Rico fought his way forwards, on, and on, and he had ground beneath his feet now. Land. They *were* going to make it. At least – he was. The child was sinisterly still. He grabbed the girl and hauled her through the shallower water until they were on dry land – land that must be in one of the nature conservation areas along the lake bank, because there was nothing here but trees and bushes and stuff floating on the water. A duck quacked an alarm nearby, and Rico laid the girl down and laughed hysterically. She was breathing, she was breathing. He pulled the child safely onto her side and crawled four steps further to find someone, but the world swam before his eyes, and darkness came down again.

Alex put his head round the door of the medical room to say the lake police were out in boats, searching, and would be in touch soon, then he disappeared again. The news was no comfort to Stacy. Rico and the child could have drowned in the time it had taken Andi to get the boat back and raise the alarm. Someone brought tea, and her teeth rattled against the cup as Margrit held it to her lips. The nurse sat cuddling her, and suddenly Stacy remembered her parents. They'd be wandering happily round Chur – should she call and get them to come home as quickly as possible? But she couldn't put them through a long train journey knowing that Rico was missing, and they wouldn't be able to help, anyway. Oh, how cruel that was, what a nasty, mean person she had turned into – of course Mum and Dad would help, in fact her mum here with her was exactly what she needed. Stacy bowed her head, eyes closed – what to do, what to do… then she knew. She would wait and see what the police said, then she would call Dad. And Ralph. She would have to call him too. Please God she wouldn't have to tell him Rico was– had they only found each other to be so cruelly separated, this time forever? What would she do if…? Stacy sobbed aloud.

'Stacy! They've been found – they're alive!' Alex was in the doorway.

Stacy leapt to her feet, then grabbed Margrit, her head swirling. 'Where is he?'

'They're taking them to hospital in St Gallen. They're both unconscious. Come on – I'll drive you there.'

Stacy stumbled to the door. Unconscious… the danger

wasn't over yet. Margrit ran after her and grabbed Stacy's handbag in the room behind reception.

'Take this – you might need something. Is your purse there – and your phone? Let us know as soon as you can how Rico is.'

The hospital in St Gallen was twenty minutes away up the motorway, and Stacy concentrated on simply breathing while Alex drove, right on the speed limit, weaving in and out of the afternoon traffic. Lorries and bikes and cars... the windscreen wipers flashing from left to right, back and back again, quick, quick. Please, Rico, be okay. He was getting medical attention; everything that could be done, was being done. Oh God. What if he was badly hurt? And the child? Had they gone in a helicopter? She hadn't heard one, but if the wind was blowing in the wrong direction, she might not have – and she didn't know where the two had been found. They could have been swept miles down the lake. Stacy sat twisting her hands together as Alex drove into the city. The little girl was going to the Children's Hospital in St Gallen, and the police were taking the parents there. Stacy was glad she didn't have to sit in the same vehicle. Rico had put his life in danger to save their child, and how quickly – how brutally lives could change. If Rico and Andi hadn't gone out on the lake today, those people could all have drowned – and Rico would be safe at Lakeside, moaning about the flood water and this new rain.

At the hospital, Alex let her out at A&E, and she ran inside while he drove off to park. The relief when she saw Rico, lying on a trolley talking to a nurse, was even greater than in January when his scan results had come. Stacy flung herself onto his chest and burst into tears.

'He's going to be just fine – but let him breathe,' said the nurse, pulling a chair over and sitting Stacy down on it.

Rico was hanging onto her hand. 'I'm okay, Stace. Except I sound like Kermit the frog with a head cold.'

Stacy managed a shaky smile – if Rico could joke about his croaky voice, she could smile, couldn't she? 'And the little girl?'

'Apparently she's stable,' said the nurse. 'Rico's going for a chest X-ray in a moment, then we'll see what's going on. In the meantime, we have to heat him up a bit.' She tucked Rico's arm back under the thermal blanket and left them.

Stacy sat shivering, her legs shaking visibly. Now that it was all over, she didn't seem to be in control of her muscles, but the nurse part of her knew that was down to shock.

'You look like how I feel,' whispered Rico. 'That was hairy, Stace. My life didn't quite flash before my eyes, but it bloody well nearly did. And I hope the kid really is okay. I guess Andi and the others got back in one piece? It was some storm.'

Stacy turned to see the window on the other side of the room. Rain was still streaming down, but the sky was lighter and the trees outside had stopped lashing about. And she had to sound normal here, for Rico's sake.

'They're all fine. I think Flavia's looking after the little boys. Reckon we'll get more flooding? I hope they don't have to reinstall pumps.'

'Shouldn't think so. One go of rain can't make that much difference.'

But normal conversation was more than Stacy could stand. 'Oh, Rico, I'm so glad you're safe!' It burst out of her before her brain engaged, and he reached out to take her hand again as the nurse came back in.

'Oy! Hand back in the warm, please – you can be soppy

tomorrow. Time for your X-ray, Rico. She put a hand on Stacy's shoulder. 'Why don't you go for coffee? There's a café by the entrance.'

Coffee was the best idea ever. Stacy fetched a cappuccino, and looked round for a table. Heavens, there was Alex sitting by the window; she'd completely forgotten about him. She sank into a chair opposite and filled him in.

'Thank God. I'll get back to the hotel, Stacy – text me when you're ready to go home, and I'll come for you. It doesn't matter if it's after hours.' He patted her shoulder and was gone.

Stacy drank her coffee, then fished for her mobile. Ralph should know what was going on and this was as good a time as any to call him. He picked up on the second ring.

'Hi, Ralph – just to let you know he's fine now, but Rico had a bit of a mishap with *Lakeside Lady* this afternoon,' said Stacy, then smothered a hysterical giggle when Ralph immediately went off in the wrong direction.

'Is she much damaged?'

Quickly, she told him what had happened.

Ralph was horrified. 'Good grief, he could have drowned. Are you sure he's in no danger? I'll come straightaway.'

'He's a bit croaky, but they said he'll be fine. It's panic over. He'd tell you not to come, Ralph.'

His voice softened. 'Thank God. But I'll come tomorrow – I'd like to see your parents again before they leave on Sunday. Tell Rico he'd better not have marked *Lakeside Lady*!'

He rang off, leaving Stacy smiling again. Rico'd have to think up a good reason for his trip on the lake… Okay, that was Ralph informed, and she should call Mum and Dad now too. They'd be heading home soon anyway, and while she didn't want to spoil their outing, it would be kind of nice to have them at Lakeside. Family was such a complicated business, wasn't it? Mum drove her bananas sometimes, but it was still a comforting thought, having her mum around when something went wrong. And she could tell them Rico was fine, so Mum was less likely to have hysterics in the middle of the main street in Chur. Stacy flipped her phone open and tapped connect.

Alex pulled up in a staff space in the hotel car park and shoved the door open, his stomach growling. It was nearly time to go home now and he hadn't had lunch yet. But at least Rico was all right. Or he would be. Alex sat still, his brain turning furiously. He'd told Stacy he would collect her at the hospital any time. The problem was, he and Zoe were planning on catching the train at seven tonight to get them to Zurich for the audition tomorrow. He was going to leave them all in the lurch at Lakeside for the next three days, and faithful receptionist or not, he had to do it for Zoe. What he needed was a good plan B for Lakeside, and what that was he had no idea.

Flavia was holding the fort at reception. 'Any more news?'

'Not since I left the hospital. Give me five to splash my face and I'll take over here. You're a star.'

She smiled. 'No problem. The little boys' aunt came and picked them up, but nothing else has happened here since you left.'

Back at his post, Alex was kept busy as what felt like every member of staff on the premises came to ask if there was any fresh news about Rico and the child. The guests were asking too – some of them had seen Andi return with the boat and the little family.

By half past five the hotel had returned to its normal weekday state, with guests coming in after a day out and going for a soak in the spa, and others exiting the spa and getting ready for dinner. The sun was out again, and people were having drinks on the terrace. Just like a normal day – except it wasn't.

For the tenth time at least, Alex checked his phone. Still no word from Stacy, and he couldn't stay on much longer. Should he call her? If he knew what time she'd be coming back he could organise something – or someone. He was supposed to be popping in to see his mother before the trip to Zurich, too. If–

The front doors swung open and Stacy walked in, followed by Rico and Tobias, Kim's husband. It only took a moment for them to be surrounded by staff, with 'how are you' and 'are you all right, Rico?' coming from all directions.

Stacy laughed. 'His voice is a bit iffy, but he's fine.' She smiled at Alex. 'I remembered Tobias works in St Gallen, so we cadged a lift home. You can get off now, Alex, I know you're away this weekend. Thanks a million for your help today.'

Rico clapped him on the shoulder. 'Yes, thanks, Alex.'

A lump came into Alex's throat. This was such a great place to work. He didn't want to follow Zoe's dream and live in bustling, vibrant Zurich, did he? Whatever happened now, both he and Zoe were going to be hurt and unhappy about part of it.

Chapter Twenty-Seven

Friday, 1st June

Stacy was still asleep beside him, and Rico lay watching her breathe. His Stacy, and yet again she'd been worried sick about him. As if the scare in January hadn't been enough... Rico rolled over carefully to see the alarm. Quarter past six, way too early to wake her after the day they'd had yesterday. Cautiously, he slid out from under the duvet. Arms and legs working, check, though his shoulders were stiff. He grabbed his clothes and trudged across the hallway to the family bathroom, where he was less likely to disturb anyone. All was silent in Janie and John's room, and unaccustomed fondness rose in Rico. Janie'd been like your typical mother hen last night, bless her. She hadn't known who to run after, him or Stacy. His own mum would have been the same, and thank heavens Mum hadn't had the worry yesterday. He would never forget the expression on Stacy's face when she came into A&E and saw he was awake and talking.

Rico aimed a brush at his hair and crept out of the flat. He'd get coffee downstairs in the bar.

Unsurprisingly, not many people were around in the hotel. Vague bangs were coming from the kitchen, so some of the guests must have booked an early breakfast. Rico switched on the coffee machine in the bar and waited for it to heat up. It was a beautiful morning, just like yesterday. Who'd have guessed a storm would come up so quickly? He pressed the buttons for a large black, and took it outside. The truth was, he should have checked, never mind guessed, but if he and Andi hadn't gone out, that family could all have been lost. It was a complicated one, wasn't it? And now he'd better see if *Lakeside Lady* really was okay, ahead of Dad's arrival today.

The flooding had retreated from the path down to the boathouse, and Rico strode along, testing his voice when he was out of earshot of the terrace. Better, if still a touch croaky. And great, the path was dry all the way in spite of the storm, though there was a lot more driftwood floating around on the lake this morning. Stuff could sit for years on riverbanks miles upstream, then there'd be a flood year, and down it would all come into the lake and – Rico stopped dead. What was that? Oh no…

A dirty white and soggy ball of fur was lying on a mass of driftwood bobbing up and down in the entrance to the boathouse. Rico grabbed a boathook and pulled the wood to the edge of the jetty. A cat. The same one they'd seen around the place a few times now? Was it even alive? He stared uncertainly – were you supposed to just grab hold of a potentially injured animal and haul it onto land? But he couldn't leave it there. Rico knelt as close to the bobbing driftwood as he could get, his ribs twinging. He grasped the cat as gently as possible and lifted it into his arms. It was warm; at least, it wasn't stiff and cold, and as far as he could see it wasn't bleeding, but then, it had been in the water. Rico hurried back to the bar and wrapped the cat in a towel. What should he–? But Stacy would know.

Upstairs, the flat was still shrouded in silence. 'Stace!

Patient for you!'

'What? Are you okay? Oh – poor thing. Where did you find it?'

Stacy tumbled out of bed and accepted the cat. She ran her hands over its body, then rubbed it with the towel while Rico explained. The animal gave a thin miaow and opened its eyes.

'Fetch a box, Rico, and we'll leave it in peace for a bit. Where's the nearest vet? We should get it checked over.'

Rico went down to the kitchens for a box, and they made a bed for the cat and left it in the corner of the living room. By this time, Janie and John were up too, and now Janie had three patients to worry about. Rico caught Stacy's eye and they grinned at each other.

By the time they'd had breakfast, the cat had its head up and was taking more notice of what was going on, but it wasn't venturing out of the box. Rico sat down to consult the phone book – the nearest vet was in Rorschach. He called, and was told to bring the cat in if he was worried.

'I think we should,' said Stacy. 'If it's a stray we might end up paying for treatment, but we can't leave it like this. And who knows, the vet might recognise it. Or it might be chipped.'

Rico lifted his car key, but Stacy promptly removed it from his hand. 'Oh no, you don't. You're still taking it easy after yesterday, remember? I'll drive. You can hold the box and make sure the cat doesn't escape. And Mum, can you and Dad stick around here in case Ralph arrives while we're gone? I wouldn't put it past him to be well on his way by now.'

At the vet's, Rico stood by with Stacy while the cat was given a swift examination.

'Nothing seems broken, but it's definitely a bit subdued.' The vet took the cat's temperature. 'Slightly elevated. She probably swallowed or inhaled too much water. We'll get an X-ray and take it from there.'

'Is she chipped?'

Stacy stroked the cat's head, and Rico bit his lip. Stace was looking broody… But a cat in a fourth-floor flat at the top of a wellness hotel wouldn't work. Or would it? They couldn't risk animals wandering in and out of the spa, and Stacy herself had sent the cat packing a few times. It just felt different when you'd rescued a poor creature who was screaming out for love and a home.

The vet held a scanner to the cat's neck. 'No chip. Have a seat in the waiting room, and we'll let you know what the X-ray shows.'

'We can't keep it,' said Stacy, when they were sitting watching a tank full of tropical fish in the waiting room.

'No. Shall we hang onto it until it's better, though, then take it to the cat home? I'm not sure your mum would forgive us if we went home without it.'

'Good plan.'

Was he imagining the look of relief on her face? They could *not* have a cat…

The X-ray was clear, and fifteen minutes later they were en route for Lakeside with a borrowed litter tray, a bag of expensive cat meds and the cat, who'd been given two injections and was sulking in its box. The vet was going to ask around about missing cats, but agreed the cat home would be an option in a day or two. Rico glanced across at Stacy. Her eyes were on the road, but there was a determined tilt to her chin. She was brewing something, wasn't she?

Zoe stowed her violin in its case and pulled the zip round before stepping across the room for a hug.

'Oh Alex. This has to go well. I can't mess it up.'

He stroked her hair. This was it. Time to head off for the audition that could change their lives. 'You won't.'

They were staying with Zoe's friend Susanna in her flat to the east of Zurich, and all he'd done that morning was make tea and listen to Zoe practising frantically, but she seemed to want his company. That was good, wasn't it? He'd been afraid he'd end up surplus to requirements again, but that hadn't happened.

No sooner had the thought entered his head than Zoe dashed any hopes he'd had for the rest of the day.

'Can you come into town with me now? I'll go in for the audition by myself, though. I need to concentrate completely on what I'm playing.'

Direct, as she always was about her music. Alex managed not to wince. Her music – her vocation – would always come before him. Even if this audition didn't go the way Zoe wanted it to, they would end up in this situation again. And again, and again. Was this how he wanted to live his life? It wasn't, but the alternative was no Zoe.

The audition was in a theatre near Lake Zurich. Zoe didn't speak much on the train journey into the centre, and Alex was silent too, holding her hand. The train was better than the car, as far as coming into the centre of Zurich was concerned. The charges in the multi-storey car parks made your eyes water, and anyway, the train journey from Susanna's place was quicker than the road. They arrived at the underground level of Zurich main station and were spewed onto the platform along with about a million others. Looked like Friday was a busy day in Zurich.

Up at ground level, Zoe stood on tiptoe to kiss him, then gave him a little push towards the side entrance. 'On you go and wander round the old town, have a beer or whatever. I'll see myself to the theatre.'

Alex caught her for a long hug. 'All the luck in the world, Zoe. But you won't need it.'

Her eyes were bright. 'I so will. I'll text you when I've finished.' She swivelled round and marched off in the direction of the Bahnhofstrasse, the most famous and arguably most expensive shopping street in Zurich. It led all the way down to the lake, and right at the bottom was the theatre. If Zoe had her way, it was a road she'd be travelling down every day soon.

Alex watched until she vanished into the crowds, but she didn't turn round. He trailed across the station hall and on outside. A short stroll later, he was sitting in a bar with outside tables on the banks of the Limmat, the beer Zoe recommended in front of him.

He sipped moodily. Zoe would be on a tram now, or maybe even arriving at the theatre. And all he could do was wait. He would finish his beer, then walk down to the lake and the theatre, ready to join Zoe the moment she texted.

It was an hour and a half before his pocket vibrated. Alex, now on a bench by Lake Zurich, a much smaller and thinner lake than Constance, grappled for his phone then sat staring at it. A message from Zoe, and this could change his life. Talk about mixed feelings… Deep breath, Alex. And tap.

I HAVE A JOB AS FIRST VIOLIN!!!!

And breathe. He tapped to connect. 'Brilliant news! Where are you?' And it was brilliant news, because it was what Zoe wanted. So why was he nearly in tears?

'Just about to leave the theatre.'

'I'm down at the lake, near the ferry landing.'

'Be with you in five!'

Alex walked up towards the crossing, soon spotting Zoe on the other side as she jogged along the road, violin case under her arm and dark hair flying, every cell in her body in jubilant motion. She could have been a dancer, too, couldn't she? Tears flashed into his eyes again. Now she had her place as first violin in one of the top three prestigious orchestras in Switzerland, with the world at her feet.

Zoe ran across the road and flew into his arms for a hug.

'Oh Alex, it was fabulous! They were so nice. Both set pieces went well, then they asked me to play something from *Fiddler on the Roof* and then part of a Bartok concerto, and Daniel Marino accompanied me on the piano for that – I wasn't great there but of course it was unseen and he said I had great promise, Alex! I can start on the eighteenth.'

Two more weeks. He had her for two more weeks. Alex tried hard to sound delighted – he *was* delighted, but he was gutted too. She'd belong to the city again, not to the lake. His lake.

'That's amazing – you're amazing. I'm so glad for you.'

She twisted away and peered up at him. 'That sounded as if you had a "but" to add on there. What's wrong?'

'Nothing. Just – life'll be different, won't it? You'll be in Zurich.'

'You could come too. Or we could meet at weekends, or…' Her face clouded.

'I work weekends, you work weekends – it's hard enough to find time together when our jobs are ten kilometres apart. With you here… Don't look like that – I'm truly delighted for you, but change is always difficult.' What a stupid, lame thing to say.

'So you don't want to come with me? I can't take this job and live in Rorschach, you must see that. Do you want me to stay the rest of my life with a tiny orchestra that will never go anywhere? Think, Alex. There are dozens and dozens of receptionist jobs to be had around here, but a violin job in this orchestra is a total rarity. I can't be flexible. You could.'

Alex said nothing. If he moved to Zurich, he'd be abandoning his mother and letting them down at Lakeside. And he'd still be playing second fiddle – oh, the irony – to Zoe's music.

He gripped her hand. 'Come on. I'll buy you a late lunch and we'll toast your new job. We can leave the hard decisions for another time.'

Chapter Twenty-Eight

Saturday, 2nd June

Stacy ran downstairs to reception. Her parents were heading for home tomorrow, and already Mum had gone into mourning for Switzerland. What with regrets about leaving Stacy, trying to make sure Rico was far enough along the road to recovery, and looking after the cat, which she'd named Snowy, Janie had plenty to keep her occupied. Stacy hadn't dared utter the words 'cat home'. Some things were better left to say on Skype, or better still on email. And meantime, it was the big changeover day and she was here to help Flavia with the guests checking out. Maria would be in this afternoon for new arrivals checking in.

For the first half hour she was busy, handing out minibar receipts and calling taxis, accepting compliments and 'see you next year' as guests checked out and left. Not many people were staying through the weekend this time, so the spa was mainly occupied by locals. Stacy glanced over to the glass cabinet that Peter, the restaurant manager, had brought from home and set up at the side of the hallway for their spa shop items. They still didn't know who had taken those bottles from the trolley, but at least they'd made it impossible for anyone to take more.

A familiar shriek and a giggle from the lift heralded the arrival of Mr and Mrs Paxton, the rather loud couple who'd spent the week organising pub quizzes – an idea Rico was going to steal – and generally being the life and soul of the hotel. Stacy handed over their minibar receipt.

Mrs Paxton stretched across the desk to shake hands. 'It's been a blast. Thank you for having us and – everything.'

Her husband sniggered, and a sudden waft of something familiar floated over the desk. Stacy swallowed. If that wasn't the same perfume as the lily of the valley shower gel they'd put into bottles for the shop, it was very similar – and they didn't have that kind anywhere else in the hotel, did they? Suspicion whirling around in her head, she watched as the pair left. Nothing to be done, was there?

'I'm not sorry to see the back of those two,' muttered Flavia, and Stacy had to agree. You didn't have to like all your guests, did you?

But here at least were some she did like. Old Mrs Rose arrived at the desk with her granddaughter, and Stacy checked them out with a genuine smile this time.

'I do hope the first hour of your visit won't put you off coming back,' she said, going round the desk to accompany the three to the door.

The granddaughter laughed. 'A strange man in her room! Gran'll be dining out on that story for the rest of her life, don't worry! We've had a fabulous time.'

Mrs Rose gave Stacy a lovely big smile. 'Yes, thank you, dear.'

A horrible feeling of déjà vue came over Stacy as Mrs Rose leaned close to pat her shoulder. *If that wasn't the same perfume as the lily of the valley shower gel they'd put into bottles for the shop, it was very similar…* As soon as the front door closed behind the family, Stacy charged into the spa.

'Margrit, tell me Mrs Rose or her family or one of the Paxtons bought some lily of the valley shower gel.'

Margrit stared, but she fished out the receipts list she was keeping. 'Nope. Why?'

Stacy leaned on a nearby chair. 'Nothing,' she said weakly. 'Or nothing that won't remain one of life's minor mysteries, anyway.'

She trailed back to reception, which was quiet now. Heaven only knew who had taken those bottles, but it was time to leave the hotel to carry on by itself for an hour or two while she concentrated on Mum and Dad.

Alex clutched his head and stumbled through to Susanna's bathroom to swallow another paracetamol. To say he had the hangover from hell was the understatement of the century. Feeling dire in someone else's flat was the pits, and to make matters a zillion times worse, Zoe and Susanna had got up at the crack of dawn to play duets. Zoe was still pretty sniffy with him, and while part of him understood this, another part was gutted that she wasn't gutted about leaving Rorschach and moving to Zurich. To this very flat, in fact. They still hadn't talked about what would happen to their relationship, and that wasn't a good sign, was it?

His phone rang while he was standing in the kitchen, trying to decide if he had enough energy to go for a walk in the fresh air. Why had he drunk all that wine last night? Because Zoe was celebrating, and he'd been trying to look as if he was too, for her, while all the time he was in deep, dark mourning inside. Alex fumbled his phone out and bloody hell, this was his mother. Had he told her he'd be in Zurich this weekend? For the life of him Alex couldn't remember.

'Hey, Ma.'

'Hey yourself. Fancy some spaghetti tonight, or are you busy? We could do it another night too.'

She sounded dull, and this was Ma-speak for 'I'm having a bad day'. Alex drummed his fingers on the worktop. It was one o'clock…

'Spag would be great. I'm still in Zurich, but I'll be home in an hour or two. Sometime after five? What sauce are you doing?'

'Carbonara?'

'Yum. You do carbonara like no one else. It'll just be me, I think – Zoe's practising with her friend.'

'Come when you're ready, then.'

And listen to that, the mere thought of Alex on his way to see her soon was enough to have Ma sounding better. No way could he move to Zurich. It wasn't her fault she had agoraphobia.

Alex put his head round the living room door, and the two girls stopped playing.

'Ma called, Zoe – she's not great. I'm going there. Are you staying?'

She nodded. 'I'll be back tomorrow or Monday. Drive carefully, huh?'

Alex went to pack his bag. She did care, she did.

Stacy grabbed her father the moment her mother vanished into the family bathroom to get ready for dinner.

'Let's head down to the terrace and have a pre-aperitif there. Rico's in the shower too and Ralph won't be home for half an hour, so we won't be undisturbed.'

'Is this where you give me some more daughterly advice?'

Her father gave her a pointed look, and Stacy smiled innocently. 'I do have a couple of ideas for you, though I wouldn't call them advice. Come and hear them.'

Downstairs, the terrace was still only half-full, and they found a table right at the end, close to the lake, which was retreating daily now.

John raised his wine glass. 'To you and Rico, and your plans for the future.'

Stacy clinked. 'And to you and Mum, and your plans.'

'What do you think we should do, then?'

'Are you up for big changes? Here's my suggestion: find yourselves a new home. I'm pretty sure Gareth and Jo would jump at the chance of living over the shop, for the next few years at least. If you had a place with a bit of garden, you could get a dog. You know you've a soft spot for dogs. But whatever you do, Dad, you have to accept change, even when it's tough. Look at how much this hotel has changed since Rico's mum died. It was a good place with her and Ralph in charge, before he let it go so much. Now it's a different good place, and Ralph is happy with it.'

John gave her an oddly crooked smile, then sipped his wine. 'Well, Stacy, I'll give all that some thought. Especially the dog idea.'

Stacy leaned back, satisfied. Dad needed time to think, and he had to persuade Mum, too. But Mum liked a challenge. First a wedding to plan, then a removal, a grandchild on the side plus a dog to fuss over... her mother would be in her element.

'You bad people, you – starting without us!'

Yikes, it was Mum already, clutching a glass of white

wine, with Rico following on.

'Come and make up for lost time, then. To a good trip home for you tomorrow!' Stacy lifted her wine glass, and everyone clinked.

Stacy caught Rico's eye, and thankfulness warmed through her. He had completely recovered from his near drowning, though she'd be keeping an eye on him for a bit, and Ralph would be doing the same. Everything was okay, now. The little girl was doing well too, though she was still in hospital. Surely this was the end of their run of bad luck?

'Stacy thinks we should get a dog, love.' John put his glass down.

'Mm. Or a cat. What a pity it would be too complicated to take Snowy home.' Janie's mouth drooped.

'A dog would be better, Mum. You can take it for walks and go to classes and have lots of fun with it. A nice spaniel or something.'

Janie put her head on one side. 'Or a Westie. I've always liked Westies. It's a pity we don't have a garden, though.'

'That could be changed, you know.' Stacy winked at her father as Janie stared dreamily into space. This might be easier than she'd thought. A garden would be great for the grandchildren, too.

Rico went pink, and Stacy ducked her head to hide a smile. He was trying not to laugh, wasn't he?

He stood up. 'Look, here's Dad. I'll get more drinks in, shall I?'

A young family sitting at the next table rose to leave, and Stacy looked on indulgently as their little boy whispered to an enormous soft toy – a sheep – on his knee. They didn't have many children as hotel guests, but this family was staying all week. And come to think of it, they didn't have a children's menu yet, so maybe this little boy could help her make one. The child passed her chair and gave her a tiny smile. He was a lovely kiddie – dark hair and big brown eyes, and the most gorgeous little face.

Stacy leaned towards him. 'What's your sheep's name, Noah?'

'Shaun. I got him for my birthday – I was four!' said the little boy in his north German accent.

'He's one of many animals we brought along,' said Noah's mother, and Stacy racked her brains to remember the woman's name. Sarah, yes, Sarah Mayer, and her husband was Greg. She watched as the family went inside, the parents holding hands and Noah with his head cuddled next to Shaun's. It was enough to make her feel quite broody… Stop it, Stacy. Like she'd told Rico, it wasn't time yet.

Chapter Twenty-Nine

Sunday, 3rd June

Rico straightened up and dusted his hands on plaster-covered denim shorts. He'd spent the morning removing as much as he could of the kitchen and bathroom in the bikers' flat, ready for the refurb. Tomorrow, the builders and plumbers would be here, putting up partition walls in the old living room, turning it into two bedrooms with en suites. There would be a fair bit of noise for a few days, but the guests had been warned, and as compensation they'd been given the choice of vouchers for spa treatments or boat trips on the passenger ferries that went up, down and across the lake. Most had opted for the boats, and Rico tucked this away in his mind to mull over later. When they'd made their first million, maybe they could buy their own little cruise ship and offer trips too? But for now, it was time to go home for lunch – the last meal with Stacy's parents for a while. She was taking them to the airport this afternoon.

Stacy was talking in the living room as he went into their flat – on the phone? Or no, there was Emily too, sounding pretty happy; they were Skyping, so Janie and John must still be having that nostalgic walk round the village they'd been talking about at breakfast. Rico swerved into the bathroom to check he didn't have dust all over his face. Emily would never let him hear the end of it if he went to say hello looking like Bob the Builder. The girls' conversation drifted along the hall, and Rico hesitated, towel in hand.

'We're moving in June. Alan's organising a house-clean party to get the place ready for us, and his dad's helping with the garden – we're going to grow all our own veg, Stace. Well, a lot of it, anyway. And it'll be great when we have a family. There's loads of room for swing sets and so on, and a lovely shady apple tree to play under. I can't wait to show you!'

'It sounds like the kind of place you can stay for years, Emmy – you're a lucky thing!'

Rico froze. There was a little edge to Stacy's voice. What did that mean?

Emily must have noticed too, for she continued more gently. 'I'll send you lots of pics as we redecorate, shall I – and of course you'll see it next time you're over.'

'Can't wait. I'm glad the purchase went through so quickly.'

Rico realised he was eavesdropping, and banged his way into the kitchen for a glass of water. A house. Would Stacy want a house with a garden too, when they were married? It wasn't an unreasonable wish… and then children. He'd seen her face last night, when she was chatting to little Noah. They'd need to talk about this, but it would have to wait until they were alone at home again. A lump rose in Rico's throat. The vision of his master's course was sliding further and further away.

Stacy joined him a few minutes later. 'Emmy said hello. How's things in the other flat?'

Rico put his arms round her and rested his chin on her head.

He should stick to practicalities for the moment. 'Dusty. But well on schedule. I had a look round in the cellar too, and it's drying out nicely so we should get the sauna running again in a week or two. They're saying this has been much less of a flood than in 1999, and it's because of the measures they took back then to improve drainage and so on.'

Stacy kissed his chin. 'See? All that worry, and now things are so much better than they might have been. Hey, Ralph's visiting your cousins tonight. How about booking the fish place in Arbon for dinner, seeing as we'll be home alone? If we don't go out we'll end up working in the bikers' flat all evening, won't we?'

He would have promised her anything. 'Sounds good. Give me half an hour.'

Rico strode into the bedroom. Stacy was right – everything was going to be fine. Everything, except his master's course. He stood under the shower and allowed hot water to rain down on his shoulders. Would the world come to an end, if he just stayed on as hotel manager, and found a nice little house for the two of them? Of course not. It wasn't his life's dream, but it would still be a good life, wouldn't it?

Stacy waved madly as her parents turned round on the other side of the boarding pass check at Zurich Airport. They waved back, but she could see Mum's tears from here and oh, help, she'd be in floods too in a minute. Janie and John vanished into security, and Stacy wiped her eyes. Mum had been very brave – not a tear or a wail all the way to Zurich and through the airport, though her shiny eyes and the droop of her shoulders when she thought no one was looking told Stacy what her mother was feeling about the coming separation. But in the end, they'd be fine, those two. Janie had taken a huge step towards accepting Stacy's life was here, and that the wedding plans – or the timing at least – were up to her daughter and Rico. And Dad was looking much better than he had a couple of weeks ago, and with the coming grandchild, not to mention the soon-to-be family dog and potential house-move, Mum and Dad would have plenty to keep them busy.

Stacy treated herself to a cup of expensive airport coffee, and set off for home again. It would feel odd tonight, with only her and Rico at home, though it would be a nice odd. The best odd ever, in fact. Stacy hummed as Lake Constance glittered into sight in the distance. Home.

Noah was perched on the leather sofa in the entrance hallway when she went into the hotel. He was a solitary little figure, tapping at an iPad on his lap, two soft toys propped up beside him.

Stacy stopped to chat. 'All alone today?'

He jerked his head in the direction of the spa. 'My mum's getting her nails done, and my dad's gone in there. But I'm not alone, Foxy and Timmy are here.' He indicated his fox and tiger, both obviously well-washed and well-loved. 'Do you have any animals?'

Stacy sat down beside him. 'We're looking after a cat just now, because she hasn't been well.'

Interest flared in Noah's face, and Stacy hurried to distract him before he asked to see Snowy. 'Where's Shaun today?'

'He's upstairs, playing with Hammy and the others. Can I have an apple?' He pointed to the fruit bowl at reception.

'Sure. Do you want it halved?' Stacy got to her feet.

'Could you cut it into pieces for me? Then we can share it better.' He picked up the tiger and cuddled it.

Oh, how gorgeous he was. Stacy went through to the kitchens, sliced an apple into eight wedges and took them in a sandwich bag to Noah, who ate one and 'fed' another to Foxy and Timmy before stuffing the rest into his rucksack.

His mother appeared and took him outside, and Stacy went on upstairs, trying hard not to feel broody again. It wasn't easy.

The sun was setting in a deep orange glow over the lake as they drove home later that evening. They'd had a lovely meal in Arbon, sitting on a restaurant terrace by the lake and eating their favourite Knusperli, small chunks of fried fish with different sauces to dip them in. You could see here too that the flooding was going down nicely, and the restaurant owner's relief when he was talking to Rico about it was clear. Stacy listened to their conversation – it still felt surreal that she could understand whole conversations in another language now, and even join in. The general feeling by the lake was upbeat, yet… She squinted up at Rico in the driving seat. He was strangely silent. And the shadow in his dark eyes was worrying. But they were home, and it was time to get a handle on whatever was troubling Rico.

'Let's have a walk before we go in,' she suggested.

They strolled along the lake bank, holding hands tightly. Parts of the path were still muddy, but none of it was underwater. Stacy gave Rico's arm a hug with her free hand.

'Out with it. We've done enough of worrying about stuff and saying nothing to last us for a lifetime,' she said bluntly.

He flushed. 'You'll call me a worrywart. But – will we get through the season without making too much of a loss? I don't want to let Dad – and you – down.'

'You won't do that,' said Stacy. 'We know hotel-keeping's seasonal and chancy, and we've had bad luck with the floods. But that's a once-in-twenty years thing, Rico, love. We'll get by, and we've got each other.'

His shoulders relaxed, and Stacy congratulated herself on finding the right tone. They were both worrywarts, that was the trouble.

Back at the hotel, they met the Mayer family in reception. Noah was clutching an enormous white seal this time, and Stacy stopped beside him.

'Who's this?'

'Selik. He's my favourite but he likes to stay in the hotel because he's so big,' said Noah, his eyes fixed solemnly on Stacy's.

Stacy exchanged a smile with his mother, who was looking pale.

Sarah took Noah's hand. 'Always tricky for these larger animals. They don't really enjoy bike tours. Noah and his dad cycled all the way to Romanshorn today, didn't you?'

The little boy jumped up and down in his hurry to tell Stacy all about it. 'Mama went in the train, and we all came back in the train. I like how you can take bikes on the train here.'

'Yes, it's very useful,' agreed Stacy. And one day, she'd like a little boy just like him, wouldn't she?

'You had an evening off, then?' said Greg Mayer. 'Must be pretty intensive, being in hotel management.'

'It is. Fun, though,' said Rico. 'What do you guys do?'

'Sarah's a librarian, and I'm in IT. I set up a company last year – one of our projects might interest you. It's an app for companies who need to make shift plans for their staff. We–'

Dismayed, Stacy saw that Rico's face had frozen in a

polite, interested expression. This was tough – Greg was living Rico's dream.

Stacy was ready to jump in when Greg stopped talking. 'That does sound like something we could use. Keeping everyone happy can be a nightmare.'

Greg expanded on his plans, enthusiasm shining from his eyes, and Stacy could feel the tension in Rico. She watched miserably as Noah went to take a pear from the fruit bowl, then plumped down on the floor at his father's feet. Greg picked him up.

'I'll let you know when it goes on the market,' he said. 'Meanwhile, we'd better get this cyclist to bed!' The family moved off to the lift, Selik dangling from Noah's hand as he leaned over Greg's shoulder.

Rico straightened up. 'I'll walk round and check it's all quiet,' he said abruptly. 'You go on up.'

He strode off into the restaurant without a word about plans or IT or... anything. Sick at heart, Stacy trailed upstairs. In the flat, Ralph was home already, flipping channels on the television, so she and Rico couldn't even discuss whatever was still worrying him. She should have known a few sentences wouldn't be enough.

Ralph switched the sound off and deposited Snowy the cat, who was looking thoroughly at home on his lap, on the floor. 'You look a bit down. Problems?'

'I was wishing Rico could go back to uni after summer,' said Stacy, sinking down beside him. 'Or even in February. Do you think the hotel will make enough this year to let him do that?'

Ralph grimaced. 'To be honest, I don't think so. Not for a while. I'm sorry, Stacy – I wish he could, too. He's had a lot to cope with over the past couple of years, what with his mum's death, and me letting the hotel go like I did – and then of course he fell in love with a lovely young lady who was engaged to someone else at the time.' He winked at her. 'Lucky that turned out well in the end! You're perfect for each other.'

'I know.' Stacy propped both elbows on her knees and leaned her chin in her hands. 'Just – I'm sure he'd love to go to uni this year, and you know how he frets about stuff.'

Ralph's eyes were wistful. 'Rico will be okay about waiting. Don't forget, managing the hotel for a year or two was his idea.'

Stacy stared at the TV, seeing nothing. Rico wasn't the only one who had to wait for dreams. Little Noah was reminding her every day how much she'd like a child of their own, someday. But it wouldn't be soon, would it? Another year for Rico as hotel manager, then up to two more years doing his course and setting up a business – it could be close to five years before they were in a position to start a family without counting every penny on the planet.

Suddenly, it felt like a very long wait.

Chapter Thirty

Monday, 4th June

Alex joined the queue of cars waiting at the level crossing outside Rorschach. To say he was pleased to be going back to work after his few days off would be an exaggeration, but at least he had a job to go back to. The car in front inched forwards as the level crossing gates jerked up, and Alex shifted into first gear. In a way, this job was the worst thing that could have happened to his relationship with Zoe. If he'd still been job-hunting, he'd have been more open to a move halfway across the country. Alex pushed a hand through his hair. It still wouldn't have worked, would it? There was his mother, too.

Zoe had arrived home last night, and today, she'd be packing. He'd tried to talk about their future, but all she could concentrate on was the idea of being first violin in such a prestigious orchestra. Tours to exotic places would be part of her life now; she'd play in Rome, Paris, New York. Nothing she'd said yesterday had told him she wanted to end things with him, but heavy certainty was growing in his gut every day. The relationship was doomed. The question was if it would be better for them both to draw a line right now, or let it fizzle out like a firework that was too damp to get going properly. But as there was nothing he could do while Zoe wasn't ready to discuss it, it would be love at long-distance for the pair of them for the foreseeable. Alex gripped the wheel. At least things were going better with his mother again. She'd been sympathetic about the predicament with Zoe, but he hadn't wanted to go into it too much in case she started blaming herself for anchoring him to this area, and oh, hell... what a stinking mess it all was.

Alex pulled into the car park at Lakeside, grabbed his rucksack from the passenger seat and slammed the door harder than was necessary. Chill, man. If you go inside feeling like this, you'll end up biting someone's head off or making stupid mistakes. Okay – he had five minutes. He would go and look at the lake.

He wandered along to the boat house – you could see how far the water had gone down now. He stood for a moment, drinking in the summer vibe, then turned back across the terrace and into the hotel through the bar. Two of the waiters and a couple of the guests out having an early breakfast greeted him with big smiles, and a warm little glow started in Alex's middle. This was his workplace, and he liked being here.

Stacy was at reception. 'Well-timed! I have to make tea for the builders up in the ex-bikers' flat in a moment.'

Ah, yes, they were renovating. Alex joined her to look through the guest list. 'So no biking beds for the foreseeable?'

'That's right. If we have spare rooms and bikers are prepared to pay the normal price, you can give them those, of course.'

She pointed out a couple of things in the guest list – a businessman checking out a day later than originally intended, and a guest who had a nut allergy, and Alex made a note. It looked like being a nice peaceful day. Good.

Stacy lifted her phone and moved away. 'I'll leave you to it. By the way, the Lakeside family's grown over the weekend.' Her eyes danced at him.

'Oh? You mean I'm not the newest member of staff any more?'

'Not quite. Your friend the white cat is in our flat recovering from a nasty accident with the lake on Friday, and what we're going to do with her is anyone's guess.'

Alex listened to the story, then Stacy's phone buzzed.

'I have to go. I'll come back and have coffee with you later, huh? I want to know about your mum.' She gave him a quick smile, and vanished round the corner.

Alex was kept busy for the next hour or two as guests came down for breakfast and stopped off to ask about whatever, and – yes. Conviction grew in Alex. This was a good job, with great people. He did *not* want to give it up.

A man appeared with a little boy who was clutching the most enormous soft toy, and Alex grinned at the pair as they passed.

'Selik's hungry!' The little boy held up his seal.

Alex winked. 'Tell him the muesli's very good this morning.'

The little boy giggled, then ran after his father. Alex clicked into the guest list. That would be Herr Mayer and Noah from Hamburg. Frau Mayer must be having a lie-in.

At half past nine, Stacy arrived with two large coffees and a packet of biscuits. 'Coffee time – we'll go into the office, then we can still keep an eye on the desk. Tell me how your mum's getting on – and how was your weekend?'

Alex slumped. Stacy and Rico knew nothing about Zoe's audition and his job dilemma, and it might be better to keep it like that. He didn't want them to think he'd taken the job only to leave again a month or two later.

'The weekend was good, the hangover less so.' Should he have said that to his boss? She was laughing, though, so it was all right. 'Ma's back to what passes as normal. I wish I could work out a way to help her get back among people. She must get lonely, but she doesn't talk to me about it.'

'How about we go together and visit sometime? I feel someone medical should be taking an interest in her, and maybe she'll accept me once I get my feet in the door.'

'You don't know my ma. That might be enough to make her disown me altogether. She's proud as they come.'

Stacy lifted her coffee cup. 'Right… we definitely don't want to endanger your relationship, because that's the most important thing to her. Keep thinking. Maybe if we found something your mum could help us with, she'd feel she was being useful and then she might be more likely to accept my help with her agoraphobia.'

The bell on reception pinged, and Alex jumped up. By the time he'd dealt with Mr Mayer's query about children's playgrounds in the area, Stacy had gone. Alex sighed. It was back to thinking for them both yet again, and so far, no one had come up with anything resembling an idea that Ma would accept.

Stacy was finishing spa duty that afternoon when inspiration stuck, and she nearly dropped the bottle of massage oil she was returning to the cupboard after recommending it to one of the guests. She glanced round the room. The tub occupants were looking relaxed, chatting quietly or leaning back with closed eyes, lucky people.

Fortunately, Margrit had arrived for the late afternoon and evening shift. A quick phone call, and Stacy left her to it and went to lean on the desk, where Alex was handing over to Maria.

'Alex, does your mother like cats?'

His eyebrows nearly hit the ceiling, and Stacy smothered a giggle. 'I've just called the vet, and he said there's no sign of any owner looking for the white cat. Thing is, it's getting quite lively now that it's recovering, and we're not at home for most of the day. I was wondering if your mum might like to cat-sit for a week or two? The alternative is taking it straight to the cat home, where it would end up anyway if no one claims it.'

Alex was nodding – not exactly enthusiastically, but enough to show he was open to the suggestion.

'Ma used to have a cat, but it died about three years ago and she didn't replace it. I'm sure she'd be up for a week as cat lady. But why…?'

Stacy gave him her best smile. 'If she agrees, you and I can take Snowy over to her together. You can't possibly transport a cat and all its things by yourself, can you?' She opened her eyes wide at him.

'No?' A slow grin spread over Alex's face. 'Brilliant. And once you're in, she'll see how nice you are.'

He immediately went pink, and now she was blushing too. Stacy pointed to his phone on the desk. 'Give her a call. Be as persuasive as you can. We can do it right away, if she agrees.'

Denise Berger did agree, and Stacy went to look for a box to transport the cat's litter tray and various other bits and pieces it had been using in the flat. Snowy's cushion, heck, was she getting teary because a cat she'd never wished for was moving into new quarters? That was one downside of their living arrangements here, they could never have a pet. Even a dog tramping through the front hall several times a day wouldn't give the squeaky-clean and healthy impression they wanted to give. This was much the best way, for Snowy, too, even though she'd be in another flat with no outside access.

'I hope this works,' said Alex, when they were driving into Rorschach. 'She'll see us coming, you know. She might not let you in.'

'I'll be holding the cat. You'll have your arms full with everything else.' Stacy spoke stoutly, but she was worried too. Her last visit here hadn't ended well.

This time, however, the door to Denise's flat opened a few seconds after Stacy pressed the bell, and Alex behind her all but shoved her inside and closed the door again while his mother stood to the side of her hallway, her eyes on the white cat in Stacy's arms.

'Oh my – what a love she is.' She reached out and stroked the cat's head. Snowy purred obligingly.

'Thank you so much for taking her,' said Stacy, smiling warmly. 'She needs somewhere she has company, and she was all alone in our flat for most of the day. The vet said he'd let us know if her owner turns up, but it seems reasonable to wait another week or two before we take her to the cat home.'

Denise sniffed. 'Not every cat can cope in that cat home. And the owners could be away on holiday, who knows?'

'That's what we thought too.' Stacy handed over her bundle of white fur. 'Alex has got her bits and pieces.'

She followed Alex into a generous living room with a balcony and a lovely view of the lake, and unpacked Snowy's things while Denise fussed over the cat.

'Alex, son, see if you can find the balcony netting for me. I think it's in my cellar compartment.'

Alex clattered downstairs, and Stacy explained about the medication Snowy was still taking.

Denise put the meds into a drawer. 'If Alex finds the netting we can make the balcony secure for her, that's what I did with my own cat. We had a cat ladder up to the kitchen window, too, but she might not be here long enough to need it.'

'No. Mrs Berger, about last time. It was just that Alex was worried and we wanted to help. I'm sorry if it came over as too familiar.'

'You can call me Denise. I'm absolutely fine as I am, but I see now you were only trying to help.' She filled a bowl with water and set it on the floor.

Alex returned with the netting, and he and Stacy attached it to various hooks still on the balcony and house wall. When they'd finished, the balcony looked like some kind of cage, but Snowy would be able to get out into the fresh air without escaping, and the litter tray could stay out here too. It wouldn't have been Stacy's choice of balcony decorations, but if Denise was happy with it, who was she to object?

She lifted Snowy to say goodbye. 'I'll miss you, sweetheart.' It was true. They hadn't got on the first time they'd met, her and Snowy, but they'd grown on each other.

'You can come and see her sometimes, if you like.' Denise spoke stiffly. 'Call before you come, though.'

'I'd love that. Thank you. We can talk hotels – you might have some tips for us from your time in hotel work.'

Denise smiled briefly and Stacy left with Alex, feeling as if they'd clocked up a double win. One for Snowy, and hopefully, one for her and Denise. In time, maybe she'd be able to help Alex's mum after all.

Chapter Thirty-One

Tuesday, 5th June

Tuesday morning, and all was well in the tubs room. Stacy finished her early tour of the spa area and went back to the front hall, where Alex was at the desk and Rico was working in the office. He was still pretty down, but hearing Ralph's depressing prognosis about their finances on Sunday afternoon had reinforced Stacy's decision to postpone any talk about their future until the two of them were home alone. She didn't like to think of Rico pining about the master's degree he hadn't started yet, but he'd never agree to going back to uni if it was going to stretch them too much.

'Time for morning coffee?' She put her head round the office door, and he looked up from the computer.

'Iced coffee for me. If you get them in, I'll join you on the terrace in five. I want to show this to Alex first.'

Stacy fetched iced coffees and sat down at the edge of the terrace. It was pretty full, nearly all the guests were opting for breakfast outside this week. The Mayer family were over at the other side, the parents with their heads together, deep in talk, and Noah with his seal on his lap, stroking its back while he whispered in its ear. What a love he was. Stacy watched them for a while, sipping her drink. Heavens, it was a good thing Noah had his animals – his parents didn't seem to give him much of their attention. She'd been here for over five minutes and the pair had yet to speak to their son. It didn't look like much of a family holiday for poor little Noah. And if Rico didn't hurry up his iced coffee was going to be warm as toast.

The Mayers departed as Rico came out, and they exchanged a few words before he joined her at the table.

'They're off to St Gallen today, to the Monet exhibition,' he said. 'We should do that sometime too. It's on until July.'

'Good plan,' said Stacy, and it was – for adults. Noah would be bored out of his skull.

'Dad's upstairs helping the builders and I said I'd join them. Alex is going to the dentist at half past – he swallowed a filling last night, poor sod. Can you cover the desk until he's back?'

Rico tipped back his coffee and went up to the bikers' flat, now to be called the attic floor, and Stacy settled down at the front desk. This was nice, a normal morning. The sun was shining, the guests were happy, and the drone of the pumps was thankfully gone from their lives. She clicked through the bookings for the next few weeks. They'd be almost full for the rest of the month, which was good news. Maybe–

'I can't find Hammy.' Noah was standing at the desk, his eyes tragic.

Stacy went round to his side and laid a hand on his shoulder. The little boy was alone, and it was clear that tears weren't far off.

'Oh dear. What kind of animal is he?' she said sympathetically. As if she couldn't guess.

'A hamster. A brown one.'

Logical. 'Where did you last see Hammy, Noah, love?'

'He was in my pocket when we went for breakfast,' said Noah, and two tears ran down his cheeks.

Stacy's heart sank. 'Ah. He's, um, a life-sized hamster, then?' Hm. That might make him more difficult to find – hamsters weren't huge. Pity he hadn't lost Selik the seal.

Noah nodded vigorously, blinking hard. Stacy grabbed a tissue and wiped his eyes. 'Come on – I'll help you look.'

She put the 'Ring for attention' sign beside the bell on the desk, and led Noah through to the restaurant, which was now half empty. They walked around and – in Noah's case – crawled under a few tables, but there was no small cuddly toy to be seen.

'Perhaps you lost him in your bedroom? Or in the bathroom?' suggested Stacy. 'Listen – your mum's calling inside, let's go and–'

'Don't tell her!' Noah pulled at her arm, his eyes wide. 'She'd be mad!'

Mad about a missing soft toy? Stacy stared. That didn't sound good, but what could she do? 'Okay. I'll carry on looking for him when you're away, how's that?'

Noah dashed off, leaving Stacy wondering anew.

A few moments later, he was back with a bag of apple slices. 'We're leaving in ten minutes,' he said. 'I brought this for Hammy – if he smells apple he might come out.'

He crawled under the table the family had used at breakfast, waving a piece of apple at the flower tubs at the side and whispering, 'Hammy! Come on! Breakfast!' More tears were running down his cheeks.

A horrible suspicion entered Stacy's head. This was getting macabre. She bent down to be on eye level with Noah under the table.

'Noah – this might be a silly question, but – is Hammy a real, live hamster?'

The little boy crawled out. 'Yes. I got him for my birthday and he's supposed to be with my Oma but I brought him in my rucksack and my Oma thinks he's at my friend's and now I can't find him!' More tears ran down his cheeks.

A wild desire to laugh swept over Stacy, and she pressed a hand to her mouth. This really wasn't funny – poor animal, and poor Noah, but…

'Sweetheart – I do think we have to tell your mum and dad. I'll help so they're not cross, don't worry. But we have to find poor Hammy.'

She took Noah's hand and led him inside, where Greg Mayer was alone in the hallway.

'Mummy's not feeling well, Noah – we'll just have a quiet day by the lake,' he said, his face taut, then gaped at Stacy. 'Anything wrong?'

Noah burst into noisy tears, still gripping Stacy's hand. Greg's lips twitched when Stacy filled him in on Hammy's unexpected holiday, then he crouched beside Noah.

'I'll go up and have a good look in the bedroom. You stay with Stacy and search down here, huh?'

'Is there anything I can do to help your wife?' asked Stacy. 'I could give her a quick check, or we have a doctor on call if she needs one.'

Greg inched her to one side while Noah crawled around the hallway sofa and coffee table, waving a slice of apple. 'It's her mother,' he said. 'She's waiting for the results of a breast lump biopsy. Her grandmother died of it and Sarah's worried sick, but Mum wouldn't hear of us postponing the holiday. It just gets on top of Sarah, sometimes.'

Hot shame coursed through Stacy. She had misjudged the

couple – and by the look of him, Greg was worried sick as well. 'I'm so sorry. We'll cross everything it's all okay, and please do let me know if you hear anything while you're here.'

Greg nodded. 'I'll do that. Thank you – it helps to know that people care.'

Stacy put a hand on his arm. 'If I can do anything at all – look after Noah, or have a chat with Sarah, just say the word, huh?'

Greg vanished upstairs, and Stacy went to help Noah.

'He's not here,' said the little boy, abandoning the sofa.

'Let's go back to the terrace. I think he's more likely to be there, if you're sure he was in your pocket earlier. We'll see if some of the bar staff can help, too.'

Rico was helping the plumber install the washbasin in one of the en suites in the new attic floor when his phone buzzed in his pocket. At last, he could have a breather without looking like a wimp. Plumbing was murder on your back, especially when you were as tall as he was. He took his phone out to the balcony to answer. 'Stace?'

'Rico, you have to come down here. We need reinforcements.'

She sounded half-hysterical and for a wild moment he wondered if she'd raided the wine cellar. did Margrit have something to celebrate? Stacy snorted, and he realised – she was trying not to laugh.

'What's up? If it's anything funny, I want to know – an injection of humour would do me the world of good.'

'Oh dear, it isn't in the least funny. Noah's lost his hamster. A live one.'

Rico's head reeled. 'He had a hamster here in the hotel? I'm on my way.'

He was running down the stairs when it struck him he had no idea where Stacy was or where the hamster was lost. Judging by the commotion on the terrace, though, the action was outside. Which may or may not be a good thing...

A chaotic scene met his eyes when he went out to the terrace. Noah was in floods of noisy tears, Greg was shifting plant pots around and two of the waiters were dismantling the bank of sandbags that had kept the lake at bay last week. Rico looked around for Stacy and spotted her behind the bar with the barman. They were removing the contents of the below-bar cupboards and putting everything up on top. Meanwhile, several guests were wandering around peering under tables too, while others were placidly having breakfast or enjoying cold drinks, ignoring what was going on around them.

'Any luck? Has anyone seen the hamster?' Nobody answered, so Rico went over to the bar and touched Stacy's shoulder. 'I'm here. How can I help?'

She stood up, and they exchanged grins.

'It's not funny, Rico, poor Noah's distraught and heaven only knows where Hammy is.'

'Do we know for sure he's here, and not swimming to Germany, or snoozing somewhere inside?'

'We're sure. One of the guests saw him just before I called you. He was running along the side where the flower tubs are, heading in this direction, but she lost sight of him before we could catch him.'

'Right. I'll take over here. You'd better go and console Noah.'

Rico spent an interesting ten minutes clearing out bottles

of liqueurs that people rarely asked for, and was about to remove the grid to see beneath the fridge when shouts came from the bottom of the terrace.

'Got him! He's here!' Robin the waiter was holding something high in the air and grinning from ear to ear.

Noah sped across the terrace while everyone cheered. Rico slapped Greg's shoulder. 'Did you know you had a hamster with you?'

'What do you think? It was our fault, though. Poor Noah's been feeling neglected. We'll make it up to him now – hey, Hammy! Great to see you safe, mate!'

Stacy came round the bar as Noah brought Hammy over to show her. 'He shouldn't stay in your pocket, Noah, love. There's not enough space for him to be comfy in there. Let's go inside and find him a nice box or something.'

'It'll need to be "or something",' said Greg. 'He snacks on cardboard.'

'We'll see what we can find in the medical supplies cupboard,' said Stacy. 'Come on, Noah.'

The two of them went inside, Noah cradling his precious hamster, and Rico turned back to the scene on the terrace. 'Okay, guys. Let's get this place back to what passes for normal here, and then it'll be coffee on the house all round. Thanks for helping, everyone.'

Greg slapped his shoulder. 'Add the coffees to our bill. It's the least we can do.'

Stacy and Noah joined them a moment later with Hammy in a sturdy carton.

'Kim – our manicurist – is going home to get an old bird cage you can have for him,' Stacy said to Greg.

He put a hand on the little boy's head. 'Noah, how are you going to thank all these lovely people?'

Noah blinked round uncertainly. 'I don't know.'

Stacy crouched beside him. 'I do. When you're back home, you can send us a lovely photo of Hammy back in his own cage,' she said. 'We'll put it up behind the bar, then we'll always remember him.'

Rico slung an arm around Stacy as Greg led Noah upstairs to show the returned hamster to his mother. 'A photo behind the bar, huh? Do you think there's any danger we'd forget the day a hamster went AWOL?'

'None at all,' said Stacy, and he kissed her head.

'Have I missed something?' Ralph was standing beside the desk, a bemused expression on his face.

Rico couldn't help laughing. 'The first Lakeside hamster hunt. Robin won. We'll tell you the details over dinner, shall we?'

Ralph stared. 'Hamster hunt… It could only happen at Lakeside. But you're on. And dinner's on me.'

Chapter Thirty-Two

Wednesday, 6th June

Alex's phone buzzed as a message came in. It was his afternoon break in five minutes; he would deal with it then. He finished checking out two men who'd been here for a conference in Arbon, then put the 'Ring for attention' notice up and went to fetch something to drink.

Back in the office, he pulled out his phone, and yes, as he'd suspected – it was Zoe. *Is this a good time to call?*

Alex's thumbs hovered. Did he really want to have what might turn into a complicated conversation when he might have to jump back to reception at short notice? No, but she wouldn't have sent this if it wasn't important. She was moving to Zurich on Friday, and still hadn't said if she was breaking up with him or not. She wouldn't do that on the phone, of course, so maybe… He tapped to call her number.

'Alex, are you on duty this weekend? Only I thought if you could come to Zurich, I can show you the places I'll be working when I start my job, and we didn't have time last weekend.'

And that was his fault, because he'd got drunk and swanned off home in a huff. 'I'm off on Sunday. Shall I come after work on Saturday?'

'That would be brilliant! I'll tell Susanna – she's having a party on Saturday night. See you soon!'

Alex was left listening to a dead connection. Was it even possible to have a relationship when you were living a hundred kilometres apart?

Stacy came in while he was still gawping at his phone.

'Heavens, you look blue. Want to talk about it?'

'Zoe's got a job in Zurich. A posh orchestra and a once-in-a-lifetime chance kind of job.'

Stacy sat down. 'Good for her! Alex – what does this mean for you?'

He shook his head. 'I'm not leaving, if that's what you're worried about. I love working here and there's Ma, too, I can't just up sticks. Zoe and I – well, we'll see how we get on.'

Stacy put a hand on his shoulder. 'Give me a shout if I can help, huh? It was actually your mum I wanted to talk to you about. The vet called at lunchtime.'

Alex's heart thudded all the way to Australia. If the vet had found Snowy's owner, Ma was going to be devastated. He'd visited her last night – she doted on the cat, and the feeling appeared to be mutual. He blinked silently at Stacy.

'He – the vet – has found Snowy's owner, but she's dead, I'm afraid. An old lady from Staad. Snowy's real name is Queenie and she must have run off at some point and lost her way.'

Alex's brain was whirring. 'Right. Does the family want her?'

'No, so Denise has to decide if we take her to the cat home, or not. Can you ask her?'

Alex grinned. 'Ma would disown me all over again if I as much as suggested the cat home for that animal. I'll ask her what she wants to do, but I know what her answer will be. Snowy's set up for life in Rorschach. Do we know how old she is?'

'The family think about four. Remind Denise I'm going over on Friday, huh? I'll pop round in the afternoon and take some cake.' Stacy got up to leave, then about-turned in the doorway, her face thoughtful. 'Alex – are you and Zoe doing anything tonight?'

'Don't think so – why?'

'Can you find out? I have a plan, but it needs Zoe to agree to it. Ask if I can call her. I'll mind the desk for you.'

She slid out and closed the office door behind her, grinning broadly. Alex lifted his phone again. Receptionist? He was the messenger here…

Rico sat back as the waiter at the Alpstein approached, expertly balancing three plates which he set before them. They had come to the hotel further along the lake bank for Ralph's last dinner, partly to support their fellow-sufferers in the flood, and partly because the Alpstein was famed for having the best fish dishes in the region. Stacy whipped out her phone and took a quick photo of her plate.

'Emily would love it here. She's a huge fish fan. I remember we had perch fillets on our first visit to Lakeside last year.' She sighed nostalgically.

Rico didn't reply. Now that Emily and Alan were saving every last penny for their house, who knew when they'd be making their next trip to Switzerland – not your least expensive tourist destination, even when you had friends with spare beds.

'Cheer up, Stacy love,' said Ralph, lifting his knife and

fork. 'I think we've got the worst of things behind us.'

'And how many times have we said that in the past few weeks?' said Rico, grimacing at his father. Dad's permanently positive attitude did grate sometimes, especially when you weren't sure of the road into your future. A little realism went a long way, sometimes. They had a tough year in front of them no matter what.

'Chill, son. You need to practise being laid back if you're going to be a hotel manager,' said Ralph, lifting his glass to clink with them both.

Rico's lips tightened, and he took a sip of wine to hide his irritation. *Going* to be a hotel manager? He was a hotel manager already. Stacy, bless her, patted his knee under the table as she lightened the mood, telling Ralph the full story of Hammy the stowaway hamster.

'I don't know what we'd do without you, Stacy,' said Ralph, wiping away tears of laughter with his napkin. 'You have a real talent for catching every awkward situation and solving the problem brilliantly before setting everything straight again. Edie was like that too, wasn't she, Rico?'

Now that was something they could agree on. Rico smiled reluctantly. Had Dad just accused him of basically marrying his mother?

'Yup. Same sense of humour. Vital in a hotel.'

Stacy was looking at her watch. 'Guys, another half hour, and then we have to go back to Lakeside – I have a surprise for Ralph's last evening. We can have dessert on the terrace there. Finish your grub!'

Rico turned to his father, but Dad's face looked like he felt – baffled. What was Stacy up to now?

Alex waited for Zoe to get her things from the back seat, then clicked the key to lock his car. He took a deep breath of night air, gazing up at the hotel. This was the first time he'd brought Zoe here – would it be the last time, too?

The low buzz of people laughing and talking on the terrace drifted through the night. They were heading towards midsummer so it wasn't quite dark yet, but it soon would be. The thought had barely passed through Alex's mind when the terrace lighting clicked on.

'Cool.' Zoe was gazing up at the hotel. 'Looks like a good place for you to work.'

What did that mean? It was horrible, the way he was always looking for hidden meanings in what Zoe said, but never dared to ask in case… in case she ended things with him. But maybe certainty would be better.

'Come and see inside. I'll give you a guided tour of my reception desk, then you can get your violin ready in the office while I check Stacy and the others are in the right place.'

He was still showing Zoe around when Stacy came through from the terrace.

'I sneaked Rico and Ralph in the back way – they're on the terrace, with large-sized question marks coming out of their ears. You must be Zoe. I hear you've bagged a fab new job.'

Zoe's eyes shone. 'It's the dream of – oh, more than a lifetime. Of forever.'

Alex touched her head, then spoke to Stacy. 'When do you want Zoe to start playing?'

'I thought you could come through in about five minutes and play your way down to our table? We're at the far edge on the right. Alex, you can join us, then you'll get the full benefit of Zoe's music too.'

Zoe's eyes were dreamy, and Alex pointed out the way through to the terrace before she was so lost in her music that she wouldn't hear him.

'End table, look. You can see Rico and Ralph sitting there.'

'Got it. You can leave me alone now – I'll start in two or three minutes.'

She started to tune her violin, and Alex followed Stacy into the bar, where she collected four coffees and four grappas then headed for the far end of the terrace. Serenading Ralph had been her idea, and Zoe had leapt at the chance of entertaining an entire terrace full of people.

Stacy motioned him into the chair beside Ralph. 'Ralph – Alex and his girlfriend Zoe and I have prepared something special for your last night here. Sit tight for a moment until it starts.'

Ralph and Rico looked at each other, then sat back. Alex's stomach couldn't have been churning more if he'd been the one about to perform. Oh, hopefully they'd like Zoe's music, and hopefully too she'd stick to the request for well-known tunes from musicals. Some of the stuff she played at home was – highbrow, or avant-garde, or whatever you called it. And here she was. Alex stared at his cup on the table, hardly breathing as a note rang across the terrace, then another, and the haunting opening melody from *Fiddler on the Roof* swelled into the night.

The buzz of talk on the terrace fell silent, and Alex lifted his eyes to see Zoe's slight figure weaving between the tables, her eyes fixed on nothing, her expression a curious mixture of dreamy and intent as it always was when she was playing. She moved into a medley from *Fiddler on the Roof*, stopping a few yards from their table.

Ralph's face was a picture, and Stacy was unashamedly mopping her eyes. Zoe started on to another medley, from *Cats* this time, and from there into *The Sound of Music*. It was as if everyone present was holding their breath as *The Lonely Goatherd* was followed by *Sixteen going on Seventeen*, and then *Edelweiss* was pouring over the terrace and down to the lake. Someone began to sing, and a moment later everyone was joining in. Alex couldn't take his eyes off Zoe. Even now, playing popular songs, there was an intensity in her, a single-mindedness he knew he didn't have – it was her gift, what made her music special.

The last notes hung in the air, then Zoe lowered her violin, and applause crashed down. Ralph got up to hug her, and Rico signalled for a chair.

Ralph's eyes were bright. 'That was – remarkable. Unforgettable. Thank you so much, Zoe most of all, but Stacy and Alex too for organising this, and helping Lakeside be the special place Edie wanted it to be.'

Alex listened as Ralph asked questions and Zoe talked about the new job and her ambitions, her eyes glowing. Rico ordered more drinks all round, though Alex stuck to coffee. He had to drive Zoe and her precious violin home.

They got up to go twenty minutes later, and it took another twenty minutes to cross the terrace, so many people wanted to congratulate and thank Zoe. Alex left her packing up her violin in the office, and went back into the hall to find Stacy coming from the bar.

She put a hand on his arm. 'Thank you. That was amazing. She's so gifted.'

'I know.' Oh shit, his voice was shaking. 'I won't keep her, will I?'

Stacy shook her head. 'Let her go, Alex. She'll come back in her own way.'

Zoe took Alex's hand as they walked back to the car, and bittersweet nostalgia flared in his chest. The day after tomorrow, he was helping her move to Zurich. She was leaving him for her music, but she would always be part of his life.

Stacy waved as Alex and Zoe moved off into the night, then turned to go back to her two men on the terrace. She was winding between the tables when Sarah Mayer caught her arm.

'It's good news,' she said. 'Nothing sinister for Mum.'

'That's brilliant,' said Stacy warmly. 'You can put it behind you, now.'

'What's sinister?' Noah was scribbling in a colouring book.

'Something unfortunate – like losing your hamster in a busy hotel,' his father told him, and Noah giggled.

Stacy left them to it. A nice happy ending for the Mayer family. Good.

To her surprise, Ralph had spread out a pile of paperwork on their table.

'Okay, *Kinder*. We've had the pleasure before the business, so let's talk business for five minutes. Believe me, when we're finished you'll agree this is every bit as wonderful as Zoe and her violin.'

Rico wrinkled his nose at Stacy. 'Are we his children?'

She giggled. 'You are. When we're married I will be too, so we'd better listen – sounds like it's serious.'

She leaned forward to see the papers Ralph was laying

out on the table top. He'd even put his hated reading glasses on, so it was definitely important. Hopefully he was right about this being wonderful – the season hadn't started well for Lakeside.

Ralph sat back and looked from Rico to Stacy. 'Stace, you asked me something about the hotel finances on Sunday, and I gave you a rather pessimistic reply. Then I decided to do some maths to see if my instincts were correct.'

Rico glared at Stacy. 'First I've heard of it. What did you–'

'Listen up first,' said Stacy, excitement growing in her middle. Was this going to be what she was hoping for?

Ralph pointed out a row of figures. 'Okay. Incomings and outgoings for the year up until end May.' He slid his finger across to a column on a different sheet. 'And these are my projected figures until the end of the summer season.'

Rico's eyes widened. 'And you based these on…?'

'On your bookings, and also on the spa takings that are unconnected with hotel guests. There are more of these than I'd thought. I've taken into account the bills we – I mean you – expect, including something for the garden, which will probably need replanting after the water goes down.'

Stacy was still catching up with the maths. She glanced at Ralph, and his eyes twinkled back at her.

'Ralph – if I asked you the same question now, would your reply be any different?'

He beamed at her, and Stacy beamed right back. Good, good…

'Okay, if nobody's going to fill me in, I'll just–' Rico made as if he was going to stand up, and Stacy gave him a little push.

'I asked your dad if the hotel was making enough for

you to start your master's in the foreseeable, and he thought it wasn't,' she said, enjoying the way Rico's eyes were widening. 'But apparently that was wrong.'

'September might be a bit of a stretch, son,' said Ralph. 'But February would definitely be possible. We could give Stacy more of the managerial duties, and Alex would be there to help with the German. And we'd need another few hours of spa nurse to compensate for Stacy, but that wouldn't be a problem. I'd be on call to help too, of course. I think you're sorted, you know.'

'I don't know what to say.' Rico's voice was gruff with emotion. 'I would love to go back to uni, but I don't want to jeopardise our profits, and I don't want to let the hotel down, either.'

'Nonsense.'

'*Quatsch*.'

Stacy and Ralph both spoke together, and they all laughed.

'Then it's settled, as far as I'm concerned,' said Stacy. 'Look on it as an investment for our future, Rico. We're going to do this.'

Rico's eyes were shining, and pride was spilling out of Ralph's eyes as he gazed at his son.

'Of course, all this comes with conditions,' said Ralph. 'You do not forget to check the weather forecast before you take *Lakeside Lady* out again.'

Stacy raised her grappa glass. 'Agreed. Let's drink to no more problems. And no more dodgy boat trips.' She leaned over to kiss Rico. 'And no more floods and bedraggled cats. And most especially–'

She paused, enjoying the moment while the other two looked at her with wide eyes. 'Most especially… no more stowaway hamsters!'

Ralph guffawed, and Stacy leaned over to kiss Rico. Problems? There were definitely no more problems.

Acknowledgements and Author's note

Melinda Huber is the pen name I use for my feel-good fiction. In a different life, I write dark psychological suspense novels as Linda Huber. These are all set in the UK, whereas Melinda's books are set in Switzerland, in my home area on the banks of lovely Lake Constance. Most of the towns, villages and tourist attractions in the Escape to Switzerland series exist, and are well worth a visit. The village of Grimsbach, however, and the Lakeside Hotel itself are entirely fictional – I wish they weren't! In real life, there's no space for Grimsbach "between Horn and Steinach", but the views enjoyed by Stacy and friends are the same views I see every day from my home a little further down Lake Constance.

I'm grateful to so many people for their help getting these books on the road. As always, love and thanks to my sons, Matthias and Pascal, for help and support in all kinds of ways, especially for their technical and IT know-how.

Thanks also to everyone who gave me help and advice about rewriting my original novellas, with special mentions for Helen Pryke and Mandy James for their editing and proofreading skills and generally for being great people with eagle eyes for mistakes!

More thanks to my writing buddies here in Switzerland,

Louise Mangos and Alison Baillie, for help, encouragement and all those glasses of fizz.

Another special mention for James at GoOnWrite for the beautiful cover images, and to Yvonne Betancourt for formatting the paperback.

And to all those writers, book bloggers, friends and others who are so supportive on social media – a huge and heartfelt 'THANK YOU. So often it's the online friends, people I may never have met in real life, who are first port of call when advice and encouragement are needed. I hope I can give back as much help as I get from you.

Biggest thanks of all, though, go to the readers – knowing that people are reading my books is a dream come true. If you've enjoyed this book, please do consider leaving a rating or short review on Amazon or Goodreads. One sentence is enough, and every rating and review counts towards making a book more visible in today's crowded marketplace. Thank you!

For all the latest information about my books, the characters, the writing life and life in general here in lovely Switzerland, see my website: lindahuber.net

(And to anyone who fancies a visit to Switzerland after reading this book – do it! You won't regret it.)

Linda x

Christmas at the Lakeside Hotel: a taster:

Chapter One

Friday, 30th November

Did she have everything? Carol Peterson squeezed a pair of tennis socks into the larger of her two suitcases and went back to the list on the chest of drawers. Her swimming gear would go in the Switzerland case, so the one she was taking to Australia was finished, and just as well, because you couldn't get another thing in there. Now for the smaller one, and blimey, packing for seven days in a Swiss spa hotel followed by four weeks in boiling hot sunshine in Perth meant she had to cram almost her entire wardrobe into these two cases. And that was before you even thought about Christmas presents for the grandchildren and the obligatory two tins of tomato soup, the kind the kids loved but was hard to get in Australia.

She slid her winter boots into a plastic bag and put them in the bottom of the small case – and now it was half full already. Maybe she should wear them on the flight? Oh, dear… Maureen's suggestion of the spa week first 'to make you even more beautiful for your family Christmas in Oz' was maybe a good idea, but the logistics were complicated. They were booked in for seven days of pre-Christmas indulgence in the Lakeside Hotel and Spa, which Maureen's sister had raved about last summer. Afterwards, Maureen would come home to London and Carol would continue her journey to Perth.

And how wonderful it would be to see Barry and Diane and the children again. Carol hugged herself, then sighed. It was such a long time since her last visit – Emma, her little granddaughter, would be four soon, and Carol had never seen baby Jonny in real life. He wasn't even a baby now; he was fifteen months old and she'd never cuddled him. It was tough when your family was so far away. Bursts of intensive visits plus Skype didn't make up for the lack of regular contact. Barry had wanted her to go with them when they emigrated five years ago, but it hadn't felt like the right time to Carol. Her life was here in London – or so she'd thought at the time. Now, with the reality of growing grandchildren she never got to hug, Carol wasn't so sure. If Barry asked her the same question again, and it was odds-on he would, what would she say this time? It was the million-dollar question, and really, there could only be one answer. She'd saved up six weeks' holidays and decimated her bank account for this trip, and when she came home at the end of it, she'd be confronted with another year and a half before she could afford to go again. Carol lifted the photo of Emma and Jonny, and pressed it to her heart. Eight more sleeps and she'd have them in her arms.

She wound a strap round the Australia case before organising the waiting piles of clothes into the Switzerland one, pressing her meds bag in at the top. Fingers crossed she wasn't going to need any of these. Had she packed the nasal spray? No, she hadn't – and oh, if only her ears behaved themselves this time. The six weeks after the last flight home from Australia had been filled with pain and antibiotics followed by more pain and more antibiotics. Talk about the ear infection from hell… Carol shivered. Imagine if she was sick for her whole lovely visit. Please, no, that mustn't happen.

'You'll be fine,' she said aloud, determinedly stamping down the insistent little whisper in her head. You haven't been on a plane since. Supposing you're not fine?

She zipped up the second case, thinking determinedly cheerful thoughts. She had saved every penny she could for this trip, and she was going to have a good time if it killed her. It would be fine. This time tomorrow, she'd be sitting in the dining room at the Lakeside Hotel, eating whatever they ate for dinner there. What did they eat in Switzerland? Schnitzel? Fondue? This was her first visit there and she was going to enjoy it.

A car horn tooted outside, and Carol grabbed the large case and bumped it downstairs.

Maureen was on the doorstep and the taxi was waiting by the gate. 'Ready? Good – I'll take your case, shall I? Make sure you lock up properly!'

Carol hid a smile. Typical Maureen. They'd known each other since their schooldays, when Mo's nickname had been Boss Cow. She hadn't mellowed much, either…

Grinning, Carol ran back up for the smaller case, grabbed her hand luggage, and carefully locked the house she wouldn't see again until next year. Heathrow and the evening flight to Zurich, here she came.

Standalone psychological suspense novels by Linda Huber:

The Paradise Trees
The Cold Cold Sea
The Attic Room
Chosen Child
Ward Zero
Baby Dear
Death Wish
Stolen Sister
The Runaway
Daria's Daughter
Pact of Silence
The Un-Family

Printed in Great Britain
by Amazon